SWEET-BRIAR SPRING

BRENDA
WILBEE

Guideposts®

CARMEL • NEW YORK 10512

Other Books by Brenda Wilbee:

Sweetbriar
The Sweetbriar Bride

This Guideposts edition is published by special
arrangement with Harvest House Publishers.

SWEETBRIAR SPRING

Copyright © 1989 by Harvest House Publishers
Eugene, Oregon 97402

Library of Congress Cataloging-in-Publication Data

Wilbee, Brenda.
    Sweetbriar Spring / Brenda Wilbee.
      ISBN 0-89081-661-1
      I. Title.
    PS3573.I3877S94   1989
    813'.54--dc20   89-31536
                                                  CIP

Printed in the United States of America.

*In this Centennial Year
of Washington State,
I lovingly dedicate this book
to the memory of*

<u>*LOUISA BOREN DENNY,*</u>
Seattle's Sweetbriar Bride.

Generous to a fault, hospitable and kind, in countless deeds of mercy and unrecorded words, she expressed good-will toward humanity, and the recipients, a goodly company, might well arise up and call her "Blessed."

—Emily Inez Denny
Louisa's daughter

Acknowledgements

I first of all thank Laura Kalpakian, my Fiction 502 professor who turned friend, and before it was done, editor. A single mom with kids in tow, she's taught me it can be done—all of it: teach, write, win awards, raise kids, live overseas, buy a house, laugh, tease, cry, and keep on thinking up great plots.

My special thanks also goes to the 11 other students who, with me, survived her 1989 winter quarter Fiction 502 at Western Washington University:

Betty Cribbs for her encouragement.
Sara Stamey for "gagging" when I got oversentimental.
Eric Bosell for ironing out my Chinook and English.
Doug Daniels for learning to keep his mouth shut about
    getting lost in my historical detail.
Richard Roy for telling me he knew why Louisa didn't want
    to go back to Illinois—there isn't a hill in 1000 miles.
Kevin Rexroat for telling me he was going to kill David
    Denny if I had him say "what" one more time.
Debra Maciaszek for reading my other two books and
    telling me where I was straying the third time around.
Mike Hardy for just making me laugh.
Marty Ennes for coming up with the "perfect" ending.
Jeff Weaver for making sure the meat got tied up right
    (page 51).
And always, always "Jimbob" Marvin for never finding
    fault.

I thank too my good friend Judy Slotemaker for all the summer Friday mornings we met for coffee—and trashed each other's books. Those were good days of slashing and correcting, endorsing and applauding. Such friends are hard to come by.

And I must thank my dear friend Shirley Doop for listening to hour after hour of the "crazy man," the "murder of McCormick," and all the other details of the plot without once shutting me up.

I always must thank my three kids: Heather, 14, Phillip, 10, and Blake, 8. They cooked the suppers and cleaned the bathroom. They mowed the lawn and pulled the weeds. They hollered at their friends and told them to "shut up—mum is writing a book!" How can you NOT write when you have such support?

I can't thank Bill Jensen, head honcho of sales at Harvest House, enough—so I won't.

And finally, I thank myself because I deserve it. Only fools try to write a "pioneer romance" for their Master's thesis in an academic institution.

THE BORENS AND DENNYS

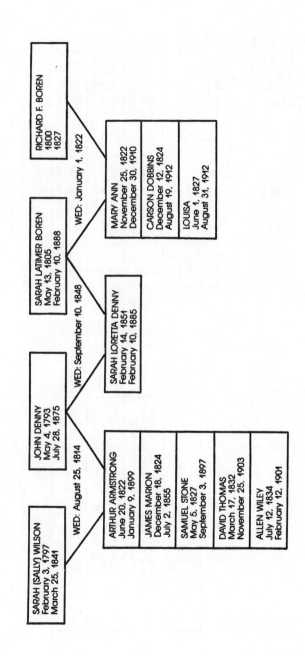

RICHARD F. BOREN
1800
1827

SARAH LATIMER BOREN
May 13, 1805
February 10, 1888

WED: January 1, 1822

JOHN DENNY
May 4, 1793
July 28, 1875

WED: September 10, 1848

SARAH (SALLY) WILSON
February 3, 1797
March 25, 1841

WED: August 25, 1814

MARY ANN
November 25, 1822
December 30, 1910

CARSON DOBBINS
December 12, 1824
August 19, 1912

LOUISA
June 1, 1827
August 31, 1912

SARAH LORETTA DENNY
February 14, 1851
February 10, 1885

ARTHUR ARMSTRONG
June 20, 1822
January 9, 1899

JAMES MARION
December 18, 1824
July 2, 1855

SAMUEL STONE
May 5, 1827
September 3, 1897

DAVID THOMAS
March 17, 1832
November 25, 1903

ALLEN WILEY
July 12, 1834
February 12, 1901

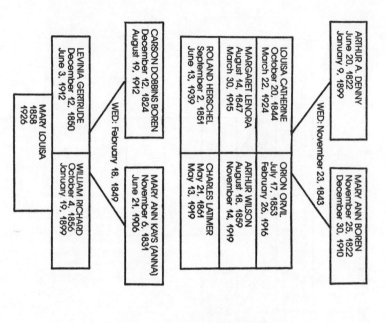

ARTHUR A. DENNY
June 20, 1822
January 9, 1899

MARY ANN BOREN
November 25, 1822
December 30, 1910

WED: November 23, 1843

LOUISA CATHERINE October 20, 1844 March 22, 1924	ORION ORVIL July 17, 1853 February 26, 1916
MARGARET LENORA August 14, 1847 March 30, 1915	ARTHUR WILSON August 18, 1859 November 14, 1916
ROLAND HERSCHEL September 2, 1851 June 13, 1939	CHARLES LATIMER May 21, 1861 May 13, 1919

CARSON DOBBINS BOREN
December 12, 1824
August 49, 1912

MARY ANN KAYS (ANNA)
November 6, 1831
June 24, 1906

WED: February 18, 1849

| LEVINIA GERTRUDE December 12, 1850 June 3, 1912 | WILLIAM RICHARD October 4, 1856 January 19, 1899 |

MARY LOUISA
1858
1926

DAVID THOMAS DENNY
March 17, 1832
November 25, 1903

LOUISA BOREN
June 4, 1827
August 31, 1912

WED: January 23, 1853

EMILY INEZ December 23, 1853 Unknown	ANNA L. November 26, 1864 May 5, 1888
MADGE DECATEUR March 16, 1856 January 17, 1889	DAVID THOMAS, JR. May 6, 1867 October 4, 1939
ABBIE LUCINDA August 25, 1858 June 25, 1913	JONATHON May 6, 1867 May 6, 1867
JOHN BUNYON January 30, 1862 Unknown	VICTOR W.S. August 9, 1869 August 15, 1924

SEATTLE 1854

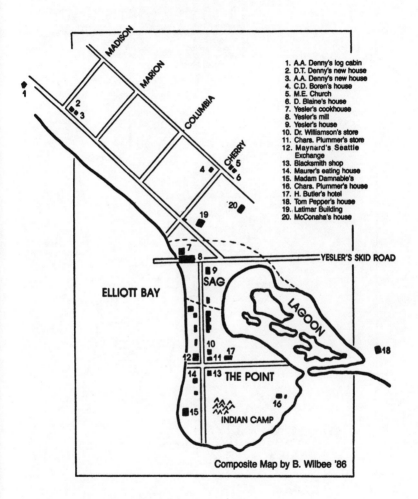

1. A.A. Denny's log cabin
2. D.T. Denny's new house
3. A.A. Denny's new house
4. C.D. Boren's house
5. M.E. Church
6. D. Blaine's house
7. Yesler's cookhouse
8. Yesler's mill
9. Yesler's house
10. Dr. Williamson's store
11. Chars. Plummer's store
12. Maynard's Seattle
    Exchange
13. Blacksmith shop
14. Maurer's eating house
15. Madam Damnable's
16. Chars. Plummer's house
17. H. Butler's hotel
18. Tom Pepper's house
19. Latimar Building
20. McConaha's house

MADISON
MARION
COLUMBIA
CHERRY

YESLER'S SKID ROAD

ELLIOTT BAY

SAG

LAGOON

THE POINT

INDIAN CAMP

Composite Map by B. Wilbee '86

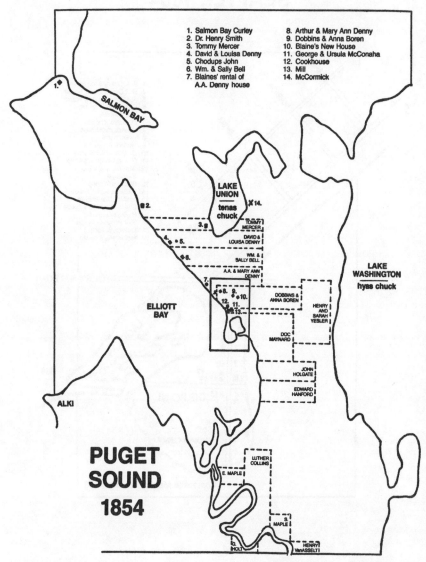

1. Salmon Bay Curley
2. Dr. Henry Smith
3. Tommy Mercer
4. David & Louisa Denny
5. Chodups John
6. Wm. & Sally Bell
7. Blaines' rental of
   A.A. Denny house
8. Arthur & Mary Ann Denny
9. Dobbins & Anna Boren
10. Blaine's New House
11. George & Ursula McConaha
12. Cookhouse
13. Mill
14. McCormick

SALMON BAY

LAKE UNION
tenas chuck

X 14.

TOMMY MERCER
DAVID & LOUISA DENNY
WM. & SALLY BELL
A.A. & MARY ANN DENNY

LAKE WASHINGTON
hyas chuck

ELLIOTT BAY

DOBBINS & ANNA BOREN

HENRY AND SARAH YESLER

DOC MAYNARD

ALKI

JOHN HOLGATE

EDWARD HANFORD

PUGET SOUND 1854

LUTHER COLLINS

E. MAPLE

S. MAPLE

Jo. HOLT

HENRY VanASSELT

Composite Map by B. Wilbee '89

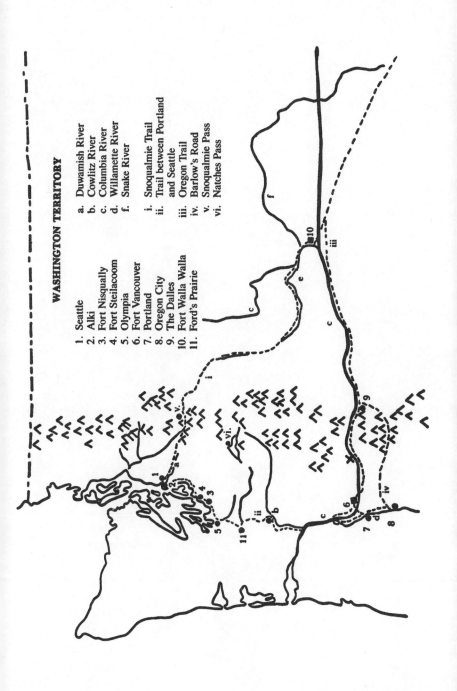

WASHINGTON TERRITORY

1. Seattle
2. Alki
3. Fort Nisqually
4. Fort Steilacoom
5. Olympia
6. Fort Vancouver
7. Portland
8. Oregon City
9. The Dalles
10. Fort Walla Walla
11. Ford's Prairie

a. Duwamish River
b. Cowlitz River
c. Columbia River
d. Willamette River
f. Snake River

i. Snoqualmie Trail
ii. Trail between Portland and Seattle
iii. Oregon Trail
iv. Barlow's Road
v. Snoqualmie Pass
vi. Natches Pass

Preface

The foundation of Seattle was laid in a mother's tears.

—Dr. Edmond S. Meany

One hundred thirty-eight years ago two young women kissed each other goodbye in a sweetbriar garden of Cherry Grove, Illinois, and they wept as if their hearts would break for they knew they'd never see each other again.

"The sweebriar!" Louisa cried. "It is God's promise of spring! Let me take some seeds to the Promised Land, and you keep some. That way we will never be parted! Not ever!"

"A tryst between us," said Pamelia, hugging her friend for the last time. "Spring will come, and we *will* meet again. If not in this world, in the one to come—and there we shall never be called upon to part. Remember God's promise, my dearest friend. *Spring will always come!*"

A tryst it was. Louisa Boren dried her eyes and pioneered west. In 1853 she married David Denny, Seattle's young founder, and all around the door of her cabin she planted her seeds, symbol of faith and victory.

In time the sweetbriar grew and scattered, and today the fragrant rose still grows along the beaches of Puget Sound amongst the natural growth of wild roses; and in June of each year the tender flowers open to the sea breeze, reminding us all of Louisa's struggle in those early days when faith faltered and tears were often wept.

So often we celebrate the realization of our fathers'

ambitions and courage of long ago days. Yet today we have Louisa's sweetbriar to remind us it came at a price. We would do well to celebrate this year, 1989, the year of Washington State's centennial, by commemorating Louisa Boren Denny for it was her tears that laid the foundation of Seattle. Her tears and her faith.

Sweetbriar Spring is the story of the long, dark winter of 1854—and of Louisa Boren Denny's victory of faith—in herself, in mankind, and in God.

—Brenda Wilbee

1854

The year of 1854 gave them plenty to talk about. No modern moving picture could be more crowded with exciting incidents.

—Roberta Frye Watt, Katy's daughter

Introduction

Sunday
New Year's Day, 1854

"WHAT A BOOK THE STORY OF MY LIFE WOULD MAKE!" Louisa Boren Denny exclaimed in a retrospective mood—yet, like the majority of the class she typifies, she has left the book unwritten, while hand and brain have been busy with the daily duties pressing on her.

—Emily Inez Denny, Louisa's daughter

Louisa Boren Denny walked north along Elliott Bay's rocky shoreline in the icy tranquillity, away from her log cabin and sleeping baby. A few stolen moments. David, her husband of less than a year, and Emily Inez, their baby, were both asleep—spread comfortably together on the pine-bough bed, fire crackling agreeably for a cold, Sunday afternoon.

She moved carefully, stepping onto the uneven ground with short, unsure steps. She was not strong yet, the baby being only nine days old. *Pease porridge hot, pease porridge cold, pease porridge in the pot, nine days old.* She stopped to inspect an odd rock at her feet.

A beautiful day today, although the sun was deceptive. Yellow and bright, it illuminated a clear blue sky that sang of summer. But it wasn't summer. It was winter and Louisa was dressed warmly in leggings, a thick scarf, and a heavy coat which fell below her knees. It was a day so clear and glorious a woman simply could not sit inside knitting another minute.

Louisa drew in a deep draught of the fresh, invigorating air, feeling its very freshness race out to the far reaches of her fingers and toes and mind. January 1, 1854: the very first day of a brand-new year. What would it bring?

The old year had been grim enough: so many dangers, so many mistakes, so many Indian troubles. Were their troubles behind them? she wondered. She thought of Masachie Jim and the lynching last summer, and knew they weren't. In a drunken rage the "bad" Indian had killed his *klootchman*, his woman. And then Luther Collins, one of King County's commissioners, had stupidly lynched the Indian—putting all the settlers into jeopardy. A mistake. A dreadful mistake.

The Indians' law of retaliation was as old as the hills: an eye for an eye. Only the Indians didn't care whose eye they exacted. Any would do, and for a long time they had been breathing their threats. Would these amount to anything, or would the danger blow over as Chief Seattle had commanded? But everyone knows it doesn't take a big wind to fan a spark! Louisa thought. All it takes is a breeze, a chance whiff, an angry word, someone's hurt feelings.

I will not think of the Indian troubles. Resolved, Louisa put the melancholy thoughts into a cupboard of her mind, shutting the door upon them as firmly as one bolts the lock against a thief.

She held the icy stone in her mitted hands and studied it carefully. Suddenly, impulsively, pulling back her arm and rising high on her toes, she threw her weight into a high, arched swing. The stone sailed over the water and fell with a plop into the sheltered bay of Puget Sound, a great body of water in the far northwest of the country. Quiet waves curled their lips over the frozen beach at her feet. Ah! She could feel her strength, sapped by childbirth less than a fortnight ago, return to her limbs. A seagull flew past, slicing the air with a ribbon of white. She watched it wing its way high into the sky, crossing the sun's rays and exploding into a dance of yellow sun shards, then emerge smaller, fainter, flying still onward.

She bent for another stone, a small flat one. This time she ducked sideways, squinted at the horizon where water met the snowcapped mountains of the Olympics across the Sound, then let it fly. Five skips!

Time to get back. She retraced her steps, passing the madrona trees with their red, peeling bark clinging tenaciously to the steep sand cliffs to her left. Scrub pines fought for root space at the top. Frozen stalks of beach grass spilled over the ragged edge. Beyond, the forest grew. Hemlock and Douglas fir, cedar and blue spruce—all towering into the sky. Everything so absolutely still.

Be still and know that I am God. A memory verse from childhood came to mind as she turned onto the trail that led up to her cabin. In the stillness of this place, God's whisper could be heard. It could be heard in the turn of a leaf waiting for rain. It could be heard in the turn of the tide, even in the wingtip of a seagull's flight.

Neither her sister nor her sister-in-law could understand Louisa's love for her cabin. "It's so far from Seattle," Mary Ann and Anna had said. It was—at least two miles north of the new sawmill town. But there was a glory here in this lonely, isolated clearing along the shore. Stones, collected from the beach, outlined the path ahead of her, guiding her home.

The cabin was as she'd left it, everything in order. In one glance she took in the simple furnishings: the giant, regulation shipstove all polished and gleaming; her wedding dishes sitting pretty on the corner hutch made of shipping crates and lined with pink cattice from Charles Terry's store across the bay in Alki; the stained newspapers glued and pasted to the log walls; her wall mirror; the pegs David had driven into the back of the door to hold their caps and coats; the wobbly, puncheon table shoved into the corner under the only window; dried peaches and shoulders of ham hung from the rafters with onion bunches and clusters of garlic; popcorn ears braided together; jerked venison; the plucked duck where she'd left it draining into a bucket by the stove; and bread, still wrapped in a towel, on the stove. The fire glowed yellow-orange around a stump of a log she'd thrown in just before leaving. "I'll build you a cabin as grand as King Solomon's palace," David had once told her. "I'll make it as described in the first chapter of the Song of Solomon, the seventeenth verse: *the beams will be of cedar, the rafters of fir.*" A tiny, crowded cabin, yes, but it testified of her husband's love for her, of her love for him, in every crowded beam and corner.

Be still and know that I am God. The stillness in the cabin wrapped her like a warm blanket and she slipped off her coat. For a long moment she stood shivering in the warmth, gazing down at her husband's kind and gentle face, the strong Denny profile, his cheeks slack in sleep. His left hand was thrown protectively around the baby, tucking her to his chest. Louisa kissed them, her heart overwhelmed with the love she felt for both. *Count your blessings, name them one by one, count your blessings, see what God has done....* She hummed the old hymn softly.

Her knitting was tucked into a basket on a shelf over the bed. She reached for it. Still cold, she pulled the rocker to the fire and picked up the woolen sock she was working on. A slipped stitch? How had that happened? She held the sock, ready to turn the heel, up to the light and frowned. She'd dropped it three inches up. There was nothing to do now, but to rip it out—a disheartening task, to see the sock unravel into a pile of loose ends.

She shivered. Some decisions were like that. Some mistakes set things to unraveling. The point of the knitting needle rested on her lips, and she leaned forward in the rocking chair. *Never mind,* she thought.

Part I

THE GOVERNOR ARRIVES
Wednesday, January 10

I have just seen Governor Stevens. He came to Seattle last night. He wears a red flannel shirt, no white one, coarse clothes and unshaven beard.

—Kate Blaine, the schoolteacher

-1-

The growth of Seattle in '53, '54, and '55 was steady and strong, and the atmosphere of those years happy. New people arrived. The mill hummed. Gardens of the pioneers' own planting were beginning to produce. White fences enclosed flower gardens, and kept the children in and the cows out. The Indians were friendly, some working in the mill, others peddling clams, salmon, and berries. To be sure, there were rumors of discontent among some of the tribes, but these were not alarming, for Governor Stevens, super-intendent of Indian affairs, would settle all of them.

—Roberta Frye Watt, Katy's daughter*

Not even the ten degrees registered on Arthur Denny's thermometer could stop the Seattle pioneers' excitement. They simply bundled up and headed for the cookhouse. Washington Territory's new governor had come to town!

Why, he looks just like a butterchurn dasher! Louisa Boren Denny thought, pressed against the logs of the back wall. Governor Stevens was short and scrawny, his large head topped by thick, straw-colored hair. Why, big Mr. Butler could turn the man upside down in a jiff and give him a good dashing! She smiled at her imagined picture of

---

*All references to Roberta Frye Watt come from her book *Four Wagons West* and are used by permission.

the governor oozing butter out his ears and upside-down pockets.

His clothes were coarse, like any backwoodsman. No white flannel shirt, but a red one. He had a nice face though, Louisa thought. Darting, small blue eyes. Blonde mustache, neatly trimmed. Unshaven beard. Thin lips. She was most surprised though when he spoke. There was a pomposity to his voice that made her uneasy. It raised questions, not answers. She slid her hand into David's and felt the gentle, reassuring pressure of her husband's fingers.

"In obedience to your call, I take pleasure in communicating information in relation to the condition and resources of this Territory," the governor began, "and in making suggestions in relation to its amelioration and development."

David leaned toward Louisa, not taking his eyes off the governor. "Stuffy," he whispered, grinning.

"Shh!" barked Mr. Butler beside them. David's fingers tightened and Louisa squeezed back. They both smiled.

The governor's three primary and immediate tasks, the Seattle pioneers had learned from the territory's only newspaper, were to secure the northern route for the transcontinental railroad still under survey by Congress and Jefferson Davis, Secretary of War; settle the Indian affairs and take a census; and put into motion the beginnings of government for the newly formed territory. David and Louisa, with their three-week-old baby strapped to David's back in an Indian pack and wrapped in blankets and a thick deerhide, had walked the two miles from their homestead into town to hear what Isaac Ingalls Stevens would have to say about all three issues.

The room was packed, the air stuffy. Both stove and fireplace crackled and popped. Lanterns flickered, spitting. Lumbermen stood hunched, collars undone, scruffy faces catching reflection in the dark windows. No Indians tonight, peeking through the darkened glass: the weather was simply too cold to be out and about. Louisa, satisfied that Emily, still asleep on her father's back, was comfortably warm and hadn't frozen on the way in, searched the crowd for her sister. Not many women out and about either: bedtime for the children.

But surely Mary Ann and Arthur had come to hear the governor! Louisa thought, standing on tiptoe to try and see through the massive shoulders of Seattle's pioneer lumbermen. Her husband may have been the Denny brother to find Elliott Bay and recognize it as a good place to build a city, but it was Arthur, the older Denny brother, who was, without a doubt, the man who was "building" the two-year-old town. "David?" she whispered, tugging on his hand and looking up at his gentle profile. "Do you see Arthur and Mary Ann anywhere?"

He shook his head. Disappointed, she settled back on her heels.

"The duty which has been assigned to me of exploring this Territory and the country eastward to the Mississippi to determine the question of the practicability of a railroad route has placed me in possession of its general character and condition. With the aid of the—"

"Enough of that poppycock, Governor!" shouted Lewis Wyckoff, the blacksmith. "Put your irons in the fire!"

"And speak English! This ain't Olympia, the capital!" hollered Luther Collins. He stood by the fireplace, one elbow perched on the mantel. "This here's Seattle! Just what *are* you going to do about the railroad?"

"And the mail service?" interrupted George McConaha, the town's only attorney.

Dr. Henry Smith rebutted with humor, "What mail service?" and snickers broke out.

"Begory!" the governor shouted, "if it's English you speak, well then, I'll speak English! Plain and simple!" He jumped onto the table and cheers went up. He stomped his foot to make sure the table was sound.

Louisa grinned. The men were clearly going to have a lot of fun. The women too—the few who were here. She caught sight of Kate Blaine and waved. Ursula McConaha, a few feet away, shifted her baby onto her other hip. When she saw Louisa she rolled her eyes in mock despair.

"I just got in from the backcountry," the governor hollered over the last of the whistles and foot stomping. "Ran across a couple of fellows at Mox La Push! They got a six-foot dam fed by the Cedar River and *two* circular saws! Could put you and your sawmill, Mr. Henry Yesler, right out to sea!"

Loud chortles ripened the festivity. Henry Yesler, owner of Seattle's sawmill, responded with a grin. "They got one problem though, Gov'ner," he said, dragging on his words. "Two saws ain't a whole lot of good when you got to belly your way out of mud and puddle diapers. Fanjoy and Eaton ain't got no boats to navigate the Duwamish. How they gonna haul that lumber out of mud and puddle once it's cut? The way I see it, the poor blokes are stuck up the crick without a paddle!"

Explosive laughter erupted. "Huzzah for Seattle!" bellowed Mr. Butler, and Louisa ducked to miss being clipped by his fist punching the air. She laughed along with everyone else. The idea that anyone could turn out more lumber than Seattle was just too funny to sit for.

Louisa saw Ursula poke George in the ribs. "What about the Pass?" Seattle's attorney asked.

"What pass?"

"Naches Pass, you idiot!" Luther Collins answered for George. He shoved a plug of tobacco into his cheek. "You just got in from the backcountry, didn't you? We're talking about the Citizens' Road! The one us and Olympia put through the Naches last fall! Scouted it for the railroad, we did—only that idiot McClellan you sent up there last fall declared it impassable!"

"That so-called road you built," said the governor, "is a bunch of stumps with a 800-foot drop this side of the Naches summit! As much as we need the railroad, we don't need it hurtling over that cliff!"

"BOO!" Dr. Henry Smith hissed, and the boos rose up like flies.

"How do you expect a railroad to go down such a grade?" swatted the governor.

"The Biles party did it! Didn't you run into some of them settling up the White River? If 148 people and 29 wagons can come through there, don't you think a train could? They could tell you straight enough!"

"A train!" declared the governor hotly, "hasn't got the time to lower each car by hand over the precipice the way the Biles party had to do it! That's the story they tell!"

David pulled Louisa in front of him and leaned around her, embracing her with both his arms. "That better?" he whispered. "Your back must be aching by now." She nodded and smiled, and leaned with relief against his chest and stomach. He propped his chin on top of her head and together they stood in the stuffy, hot room, listening to the arguments and debates fly. The air sizzled: the passes, the railroad, the need to get the settlers through the mountains so they wouldn't be diverted into Oregon, the discovery of coal up the Duwamish River, the upcoming elections to be held in 20 days, the petition into Congress for a steam-boat to run the mails. Louisa's head swam with the possibilities and developments.

"I'd like to change the order of business," said George McConaha, suddenly serious. He stood with feet spread, leaning back. His arms were crossed. Lantern light reflected off his clean-shaven face; a handsome face with a deep cleft in his chin, a finely chisled nose, and sharp, blue-green eyes that told of keen intelligence and common sense. "We got a missing man—a white man," he said. Feet shuffled. "There's been a few rumors of Indian unrest and we'd be advised, I think, to investigate—"

"Utter nonsense," interrupted Stevens, jumping in so quickly that it surprised Louisa. "The Indians appear placid enough and as soon as I get a head count, a census—"

"It would be better to get a head count of the white folks."

"—we can start negotiating treaties—"

"You're not listening, are you?" demanded George, voice hard and direct although his short, squat body still looked relaxed, resting comfortably. A formidable attorney if you put him in a courtroom, Louisa thought with an unwelcome constriction in her lungs, the fun gone out of the evening.

"What's there to listen to?" replied Stevens, annoyed with the cross-examination. Louisa turned her attention to the man on the table, the man who held their destiny in his hands.

"We have a missing man," George again declared. "The Indians find justice by retaliation. And we do have guilt on our hands." His were the only eyes that did not shift automatically to Luther Collins by the fire. The redheaded King County Commissioner stood stoically rigid, face burned red with anger at the direct jab in reference to his lynching of Masachie Jim, an Indian, last July.

"In this country you're bound to have a few missing men," said Stevens from the table, spitting the words over their heads impatiently. "It can't be helped. A wrong step over the trail, a tipped canoe. You know yourself, McConaha, how dangerous these canoes are that we paddle around in. We can't go around adding two plus two and insisting on five!"

Louisa could feel David tense. He and Arthur, along with George McConaha, were about the only ones in town who took the Indian rumors seriously. She herself didn't know what to think about the missing man. Until they found a body, what could any of them do? Even then, what could they do? she wondered.

"You're getting all worked up over nothing," said the governor. "If you're talking about Montgomery McCormick—" He spoke quickly, seeing that George was about to open his mouth. "No one's ever seen the man in these parts and yet every week the *Pioneer & Democrat* advertises for his whereabouts. I tell you, the man died of cholera the other side of Fort Hall and even now his body is decomposing in some hidden swale of the Oregon Trail!"

"That's not true!" cried George. "Two sailors tell me they saw a man fitting McCormick's description get off the *Franklin Adams* last summer right here in Seattle! And now that we're getting these notices every week in the paper—"

A buzz rose up around the room.

"David, let's go," said Louisa, wanting to hear no more. The governor, not George, had made her uneasy, and she didn't know why—because she agreed with him. Just because McCormick, or whatever his name was, was last seen in Seattle, didn't mean the Indians had killed him. George, as far as she was concerned hadn't proven anything. So why was the governor so disturbing? she wondered. "Please, David," she said again. "Let's go."

Reluctantly he nodded, and they worked their way to the door.

"Hello, Mrs. Yesler," she whispered, moving ahead of David. "Excuse us?"

"Let me see that baby before you scoot past. Yes, what a little duckling, just as big as a minute she is!"

Louisa's mind was hardly on her baby, anxious as she was to show her off. She only wanted to be out of the hot, stuffy room, away from the governor and all the fuss. Why did the man bother her so? "Excuse us, Ursula," she whispered, sliding past her friend. *His voice*, she suddenly realized. *It was so pompous, so cocky.* Moreover, she realized with a shiver, she did not believe him.

"Louisa, wait," said Ursula, putting out a hand to restrain her. "I just got to tell you—"

Louisa could just imagine: Ursula McConaha always had something to tell. "We have to go," Louisa whispered, glancing about the room, suddenly self-conscious and more anxious than ever to be gone.

"No, wait," Ursula whispered importantly. She tossed her thick auburn braid over her shoulder and shifted 18-month-old Eugenia to the other hip and leaned to whisper into Louisa's ear. George Jr., nine years old, and little Ursula, six years old, swatted at each other behind their mother's back.

"Pardon?" Louisa asked, bending over. She'd heard only Doc Maynard's name—that and something about someone eating mussels. It made no sense.

"Come on," said David, urging her forward.

The door flew open almost in their faces. Doc Maynard himself, winded and huffing, stood on the stoop and Louisa couldn't help but smile. No matter what, rascally Doc Maynard could be trusted to lighten the worst of worries. "He'll joke his way into the gates of hell," Arthur Denny had muttered under his breath more than once.

"Well, I'll be jiggered," Maynard complained happily, "you all started the meeting without me!" Only his merry sky-blue eyes were visible behind his glasses and between the wrappings of a scarf wound round and round his head, raccoon-tailed cap perched ridiculously high on top. He pulled down the scarf so his mouth appeared and barged on in, dragging behind him a stranger and making a lot of noise while he shuffled and stomped and peeled off scarf and hat. Heads turned. "Hello there, Governor!" he hollered. "Oops, can't see a blamed thing when these spectacles fog up like this." He jabbed the steel-rimmed glasses up onto his forehead and winked at Louisa, catching his hat as it fell. "Hey! Come on in, Eddie!" he bellowed, pulling on the elbow of a bulky man still in the shadows. At the same time he pulled a flask of whiskey from an inside pocket and took a quick swallow. "Ahh . . . that's better," he burped, winking again at Louisa so that she blushed. "Warm a fellow up, sure enough. Now in you come, Eddie. Or you'll be letting out all the hot air."

Eddie was bigger than even Mr. Butler—a giant, and Louisa could not help but stare. Her gaze lingered on his features, surprised and puzzled and curious. His face was large, yet soft and doughy. His cheeks were round like a baby's, youthful and rosy with cold. Yet liver spots riddled the wrinkled skin all about his ears and neck. A boy? A man? A giant. He lumbered in almost apologetically, limping, head ducked, rubbing his mouth and scratching about his ear with a wrist. Like an old confused hound dog, Louisa thought, feeling pity.

"Did I miss the show?" Maynard asked.

"No," said David. "We're just leaving early. Liza's not feeling real strong yet."

"Better get that baby covered then. A bit nippy out there."

The stranger suddenly raised his big head, eyes darting until he found Emily. Louisa gasped and stepped backward, away from the man's odd gaze. His eyes were glassy, liquid and clear and blue. Like those of a young child—or the very old, she realized with a shiver. He ducked quickly, as if frightened to be caught looking at the baby. He averted his eyes, but then nervously peeked again at the bundled-up Emily.

Louisa fumbled with the blankets in her arms and began tucking them quickly, the softest first and then the heaviest, around her baby, to shield her from the stranger. Who was he? she wondered, not knowing whether to be frightened, or sad.

"Whew!" David whistled when they were at last outside. "Odd sort of a brute, isn't he?" Fog swirled from his mouth as they walked down the path.

"Do you know who he is?" she asked, standing in the bitter, bitter cold. "It's like he's knocked his head and lost a bit of his stuffing."

They turned to look back. The strange man was silhouetted in the cookhouse door, filling the frame with his gigantic body. Loud voices roared behind him. Shadows leaped ahead, long legs and arms reaching monstrously across the lumpy ground in the path of light.

"I don't know," said David. "Montgomery McCormick maybe?"

"Hey, Eddie!" hollered Maynard. "Shut the door!"

"Guess not!" David laughed, bending his knees to bounce the backpack into place on his shoulders. "Too bad. If the man *was* McCormick, it would have at least solved one mystery around here."

Louisa hurried to lay the heavy deerskin, smelling of smoke and forest, across David's shoulders. Emily would stay nice and warm tucked down inside. "Let's go to Mary's house," she said.

• • •

The moon was full, and hung in a faintly starlit sky directly over the distant peaks of the Olympic Mountains across the Sound. David paused, struck by the surreal beauty. The moon's reflection lit the snow of the faraway mountain rims and entered the quiet water of Elliott Bay just 20 yards offshore, flecks and specks of gold dancing over the wet, inky blackness of the water's surface. Below, a round, white ball bobbed and rolled deeper down, radiance rippled. Waves lapped the beach a few feet away, slapping the hulls of Indian canoes, and he breathed deeply, sucking in the cold, rich scent of fresh-cut balsam wood. *Ah*, he thought in a rare moment of elation, *this is why I left Illinois!* Raw land and beauty. Challenge. Moments like this it all made sense. He stood breathing it all in, letting the governor's words slide, his troubled mind rest.

The mill, a constant whine 24 hours a day, had been shut down for the governor's talk, and the open platform which housed the giant, circular steam-fed saw stood bare, a silent skeleton in the backdrop of night. All around were stumps. What had Yesler said about Mox La Push? Mud and puddle diapers? Well, Seattle certainly was a mud-and-puddle town. Stumps everywhere you looked, poking from the ground all black and hollow in the early evening. From where he and Louisa stood, between cookhouse and mill, the stumps cluttered the triangle-shaped clearing of Seattle's center all the way to the woods. Two years before there had been nothing here except dusk and moon, he realized, rising to meet the unbroken forest.

Now almost a hundred settlers lived in and around the clearing, in log cabins tucked beneath the forest skirt. To the north, the cabins, nearly 30 in all, marked the trails his brother Arthur had platted to be streets one day: Front and Cherry and Second. The Latimer Building, a two-story hulk standing in the shadows of the cookhouse, sheltered most of the town's many bachelors. To the south and across a soggy spit of land was Doc Maynard's Point, a bluff rising out of tideflats and surrounded on three sides by water. Here were the stores and mercantiles, the carpentry and blacksmith shops, all bought cheap, ten dollars a lot, from Maynard. They were building their town all right.

True, the town wasn't much to boast of—yet. When the wind was right, a sulfur smell blew up from the lagoon where they were filling in the swamp with ballast and sawdust. And the smoke from the mill never let up. But they had big plans. Puget Sound was the shortest route to China, beating San Francisco by 200 miles. Elliott Bay was the deepest natural harbor on the Sound, able to accommodate ships from anywhere in the world. And Congress was ready to underwrite the transcontinental railroad to the first seaport that could most economically connect the States to the Orient. One plus one, and huzzah! It was only a matter of time before Seattle hit the map.

But they needed a governor to guide them carefully through the perilous transition from wilderness to civilization, thought David, and Stevens, he decided, staring glumly at the moon and feeling the exhilaration drain as quickly as it had surged, was not the man. "Liza," he said lightly, trying to banish his misgivings, "Chodups John tells me that's no man in the moon."

"It's a woman?"

"It's a frog."

She laughed quickly, and he looked down to see her smile. She was a pretty woman and tonight brought out all that was beautiful, making it easy for him to forget the governor and all his worries. Alabaster skin, with a deep rose flush in the full of her cheeks. Wide-spaced eyes, dark and sparkling. Hair the color of midnight—at its darkest hour, and as black as any Indian's. Tonight it fell in ringlets out the bottom of her bonnet and down her back. Five-foot-two and 26, and still so tiny she couldn't weigh much more, he guessed, than the hundred-pound potato sacks shipped up from California. Of course, he thought with a chuckle, she was daintier, and sweeter smelling.

She seemed to sense his tenderness. "Are we going to go over to Arthur and Mary Ann's?" she asked, lifting her face for a kiss.

"If you promise not to squabble with Arthur."

"Don't be silly," she said, and her laughter was music in the moonlight. "I never argue with Arthur."

He chuckled and took her hand.

Despite the cold, it was pleasant to be walking through the stumpy town over the snow-laced sawdust to the trail that led to Seattle's cabins in the still of evening, the dark setting around them like a fox laying her tail about her pups, the scent of cedar and fir in his stinging, cold nose, Louisa's hand in his own. He increased his pace, thinking of Emily on his back. They entered the woods, dark and deep. Now came the smoke of wood fires, the flicker of light from cabin windows.

It was a dark tunnel they entered, trees pressing in from all sides, black branches cutting off the darkened sky overhead. Bitter and cold and damp. They stepped carefully so as not to trip on a stump root or slap their faces with a far-reaching thicket switch.

"What was that?"

"I didn't hear anything."

"A twig snapped."

"A twig?" he laughed, surprised. "A twig snapping in the forest is not something to be alarmed about."

"No," she argued. "Someone is following us."

"You're letting Princess Angeline's talk about *stick siwash* spook you," he teased. Not so hard to do, he thought, when you were out in the woods on a cold, dark night. Indian legends told of dead spirits haunting the forests, sometimes chasing even grown men out of the dark in terror. He moved forward carefully, feeling in front of them for any unsuspected branch. Louisa pulled on his hand. He waited. *Was* there someone out there? he wondered, sensing that perhaps after all there was. But who?

"Someone is watching us from behind a tree," she whispered, a small voice in the shadows beside him.

Which tree?

They walked on, both listening. He heard the rustle of sword ferns behind them. Louisa heard it too. The scamper of a jackrabbit? They walked faster. *Stick siwash? Statalth?* Evil spirits? Why did he bother to listen to such stories?

A branch snapped. Unmistakably.

He stopped abruptly and turned around, planting his boots into the soft, spongy mulch of the forest floor, devoid of snow because of the density of the woods. "Hello? Anybody there?"

Only silence—the voice of ghosts—answered, and he did not like the feel of hair ridging up the back of his neck.

Somewhere a dog howled.

-2-

Opinion is divided on the efficiency of McClellan but the consensus of opinion is that he was sorely lacking in ability, and manifested many of those traits of indecision and delay that later characterized his work in the Civil War.

—Roberta Frye Watt, Katy's daughter

"Whoof! Whoof!"

"Moreover!" cried Louisa, dropping to her knees in relief to greet the black Labrador bounding out of the woods. The dog was a gift to Mary Ann from Captain Felker. "You had your puppies yet?"

David reached down to affectionately give the dog a pat on the head. "Disgusting name."

"I think it's rather clever. *And moreover the dogs came and licked Lazarus' sores...*"

"Must have been Moreover out here all this time," David said. "Sniffing down a raccoon or something."

Feeling foolish, and with Moreover leaping and bounding alongside them, they hurried down the last of the trail to Arthur and Mary Ann's cabin, laughing and giggling like children and making enough noise to raise the dead.

Inside they found Mary Ann sorting her flower seed packets at the table, rocking seven-month-old Orion on her knee.

"Hello, Mary! Planning our garden already?" Louisa asked, stomping off snow and mud and sawdust. The dog leaped past her and headed straight for the fire, leaving behind a splattered trail. "What are we planting? Skunk cabbages?"

"Auntie!" shrieked little voices from the loft.

"The children been put to bed?" Louisa asked, hugging her sister and little Orrie at the same time, pinching his cheek to make him smile.

Mary gave her a quick kiss. "Just. Arthur's tucking them in."

Louisa ducked out of her bonnet and draped it over a chair, relieved and happy to at last be in where it was warm and light, the ghosts locked outside with foolish, ungrounded fears.

"I was hoping and praying you'd bring this sweet baby by," Mary confessed. "I even made a pie." She put Orrie on a blanket on the floor, sitting him up and giving him a string of wooden spools to chew, then turned David to the fire and began pulling the deerhide and blankets off Emily. "You two seem to be in a merry, rare mood," she said, lifting Emily out of the pack and holding her up in the air. "What's so funny?"

"Oh, nothing," said Louisa, eyeing Emily carefully. Mary Ann kissed Emily's little red nose. "We just heard a *stick siwash* or two on the way up."

"*Auntie!*"

"Better get on up there," said Arthur, coming down the loft ladder.

Louisa kissed David quickly and, boots off and propped against the hearth to dry, she climbed up to the loft to whisper goodnight to Katy, 9, Nora, 5, and little Rollie, 2.

"Ooh! Your hands are so cold!" they giggled.

"The better to tickle you with!"

The Dennys had an odd family tree—two trunks persistently intertwined. Arthur Denny and Mary Ann Boren had married in 1843. Five years later Arthur's widowed father and Mary Ann's widowed mother had married, making Arthur and Mary Ann sister and brother as well as husband and wife. Three years later, in 1851, the combined Boren-Denny family had all gone west together. Half of them stayed in Oregon: Ma and Pa and six-month-old Loretta (the little sister they all shared), and three of the Denny brothers—James, Samuel, and Wiley. The other half of the family—Arthur and David Denny; Mary Ann, Louisa, and their brother Dobbins Boren, as well as his wife, Anna—had pushed north to Puget Sound where, to make the family tree more complicated yet, in 1853 Louisa, Mary Ann's younger sister, married David, Arthur's younger brother. Boren women, Doc Maynard had remarked at the time, seemed to like marrying Denny men.

"Tell us a story, Auntie!" the children begged. Louisa listened over the edge of the loft, and not hearing Emily fussing to be fed, snuggled down in the chilly comforters amongst a tangle of soft little arms and legs. My, how she'd missed the children in the three short weeks since moving back to the claim. Living in town, next door to Mary Ann, certainly had had its advantages, she thought, tousling their heads. But then it had its disadvantages too: Arthur.

"Once upon a time," she began, telling a familiar tale. Downstairs Arthur had brought in a load of wood and she could hear the tumble of logs rolling into a crate, the pleasant exchange of male voices.

"So you went to the meeting. The governor say anything new?" Arthur's voice.

"Bigelow's coal looks promising. His mine and Fanjoy's new sawmill at Mox La Push ought to bring in the settlers." David's voice.

"And so," whispered Louisa, coming to the end of her tale, "we'd each go to sleep under the stars, all shivery cold in our blankets, and watch Ma sing 'We Are Climbing Jacob's Ladder'—"

"—while she stirred maple sugar over the camp fire!" interrupted Katy.

"Can we sing it, Auntie?" Nora asked. "Just one verse?"

Louisa listened to their sweet voices singing off-key in her ear, and to the men's voices below, deep and easy, a pleasant mingling of sounds—soft and quiet and comforting.

"That governor is such a fool!" Arthur's voice boomed, shattering the quiet. Louisa sat up quickly to give kisses all around. "If McClellan can't find Naches Pass, how in the world is he supposed to find Snoqualmie?" Arthur demanded.

"The governor is sending someone else up from the other side."

"I'm telling you!" hollered Arthur, ignoring what David had just said. "Jefferson Davis doesn't need any help sabotaging the northern route for the transcontinental railroad—we got enough stupidity on our side to do the job quite nicely! But if Puget Sound can't get the railroad, we can't get the settlers! And there goes Seattle right off the map!"

"Who says McClellan *is* on our side? Maybe he'd like to see Seattle slide right off the map," Louisa offered, stepping from the ladder and looking back and forth between the two brothers, as different as night and day. Arthur, at 31, was tall and thin, with sandy hair and blue eyes; David, ten years younger, was a little broader through the chest and not quite so tall, with dark hair and brown eyes. "Maybe McClellan's a plant," she said, speaking to Arthur. "Like Ursula McConaha says. He is southern, you know, and the South doesn't want the railroad to go through anti-slavery country."

Arthur didn't blink. "For once I think Ursula McConaha might be right."

"Well, the governor is not southern," David said quietly. "I told you, Arthur, he's got someone else scouting the pass from the other side."

"Who?"

"I don't know. One of his civil engineers, I guess."

"You guess? Dave, you've got to *know* these things!"

"Arthur!" cried Louisa, exasperated. "If you want to know these things, *you* should have gone to the meeting!"

"Louisa," said Mary Ann kindly from the rocking chair where she held Emily, "sit down. Arthur's put on the kettle, and the pie is warming."

Sit down? she wondered, biting her tongue for Mary's sake. *All very well, but where?* David had the three-legged stool by the fire, Arthur the captain's chair squeezed in between the desk and table, Mary the only other chair. Boxes and barrels, labeled PORT OF SAN FRANCISCO, cluttered everything else. Arthur's commissary business with the various ship captains took up more space than his four children.

"Hey, Dave," said Arthur from his corner, scattered papers and open ledgers piled up on the desk behind his back. "What if we send Pat Kanim to scout that other crew through the Snoqualmie summit?"

"Arthur," sighed Mary Ann, "get up and give Louisa your chair."

"With Pat Kanim, the job is as good as done," he went on, ignoring them both, and Louisa figured it would be easier just to find a crate to sit on. "That man knows the mountains like the back of his hand. Naches Pass was good for getting the settlers into Olympia, but it really wasn't going to do Seattle a whole lot of good—not for years anyway. But, Dave, what if we can get the railroad through Snoqualmie Pass?"

David's eyebrows pushed up. "Settlers come right into Seattle—"

"That's right. They step off the train, blinking in astonishment at the beautiful, productive country they've come to live in!"

A splinter poking through Louisa's skirt reminded her sharply enough of Seattle's frontier realities. "Don't count your chickens," she cautioned, "before they hatch."

"Don't be such a spoilsport, Liza," Arthur said, frowning.

She leaned over to pick up Orrie and kissed his round, bald head. "Even if Pat Kanim succeeds," she persisted, "who says Jefferson Davis will agree to the northern route?"

"Nonsense! Puget Sound is the absolute shortest route to China—and Congress knows that! You know that! Come in!" he barked, answering the knock at the door, and rousing the sleeping dog into a low growl.

"Sorry to bother you." George McConaha stepped inside, apologizing with a hasty smile. "But the meeting's just broken up. Arthur, you've got to come down to the cookhouse and talk some sense into the governor. I've argued until I'm blue in the face. He still won't listen. Maybe if you tell him more about those fellows who saw Montgomery McCormick get off the boat not long after Collins lynched that Indian..."

Louisa felt her mouth go dry, and tears rise like flour and yeast. Her one night in town, her one night to visit with Mary, and they had to talk about this?

"The governor is a stupid man," said Arthur. "One of these days we're all going to wake up in the morning and find *ourselves* missing."

"That's not funny," said George from the door.

"Oh, George, come in and sit down," said David. "For a Democrat you sure are formal."

"You're not coming?"

"I'm not going anywhere," said Arthur. "If Stevens won't listen to you, he certainly won't listen to me. I'm an obnoxious Whig, remember? If I say jump, the man sits. If I say boo, the man yawns. No, the place to bring it up is in the legislature."

George swore softly. "I suppose you're right—if it's not too late," he added, shutting the door behind him and tossing his hat onto the table. He leaned up against a large whiskey barrel.

"Oh, for heaven's sake," said Louisa, biting back her tears. "What's there to talk about? The governor is right! The Indians are placid enough. They work in the mill, they buy and trade. We've made good friends with them. What about Chodups John?" she asked, daring David, daring any of them, to argue with her. "What about Yoke-Yakeman? Alki John? Salmon Bay Curley? Leschi? Pat Kanim? Shall I name more? Nelson. William. Princess Angeline. Jim and George Seattle. Chief Seattle himself."

"A man is missing," Arthur reminded her.

"Just because a man is missing *does not mean that an Indian killed him!*"

"Liza," said David. "The Indians have only one concept of justice—retaliation. An eye for an eye."

"But you don't even know if McCormick is dead!"

"You're right," George agreed, crossing his arms. "We don't. But justice, as far as the Indians are concerned, was not served last summer. And their unhappiness is festering like an infected wound."

"So what can they do?" she protested. "Chief Seattle himself told them no retaliation! And besides, it's not as if Mr. Collins hung an innocent man! Masachie Jim *killed* his *klootchman!* The Indians know that! Everyone knows that! George, you and Doc Maynard thought up those fancy words—what were they? Mal..."

"Malfeasance versus misfeasance?"

"Performance of a wrongful act versus improper performance of a lawful act," said Arthur, stroking his sandy beard with his fine, strong hand. "Words, Louisa. Just fancy words. They got Collins off on a technicality—but it doesn't alter anything for the Indians. One of ours killed one of theirs."

"Their justice demands an eye for an eye," said David wearily.

"And now we've got a missing man," said George, "last seen in Seattle."

"But Chief Seattle told the Indians to turn the other cheek!" she argued. "As allied chief of six tribes, he stood out there on the Point and *ordered* them to turn the other cheek! Chief Seattle—"

"You're sticking your head in the sand!" hollered Arthur. Tears rushed to her eyes.

"Here," said Mary Ann, getting up. "You can have my chair, Mr. McConaha."

"Where are you going?" Louisa asked.

"To change your baby's diapers. She's soaking wet."

"I'll help you." Orrie over her arm, Louisa gratefully followed Mary Ann into the bedroom, shutting the door behind them—the only way to silence the men. She bounced Orrie onto the bed so that he giggled. She breathed deeply and rubbed her temples.

"Emily looks like you," said Mary Ann, drawing off the soiled diaper and expertly lifting the newborn baby by the ankles to slide a dry cloth underneath.

"Mary, if they don't stop talking about Indian troubles, I'm going to scream."

"Louisa, they need to talk."

"Why can't they talk about the elections? Or something like the Maine Liquor Law? Or suffrage? Arthur is going to introduce that suffrage bill, isn't he?"

"If he gets elected."

"Well, he will. Everyone knows that." She watched her older sister straighten Emily's gown and tug playfully on her bootied feet. Emily blinked in the warm, cozy light.

"They're so sweet when they're this tiny," said Mary Ann. "I always forget. You'd think after having four—"

"I'll scream, Mary. I swear I will."

"Oh, Liza—"

"That's all they talk about! Indians and missing men! Listen to them out there!"

"Don't be angry. Someone needs to keep their ear to the ground."

"But I'm sick and tired of all the talk! There really is nothing we can do anyway. And talking about it all the time only makes us all crazy."

"Better crazy, than ignorant," Mary Ann said, rolling Emily into a clean blanket.

Suddenly Louisa remembered the governor's voice, so pompous and cocky, and she sat on the bed, weak, her stomach sick. She hadn't believed the governor. And here she was, sounding just like him. She felt goosebumps pop up along her arms. *What if Montgomery McCormick really was dead?* she wondered, going all hot and cold at once. What if Arthur and David were right? What if the Indians *had* killed him? "I think I'm scared, Mary."

Mary Ann smiled. "We're all a little scared, Liza, if we have the sense to admit it. But it's nothing we can't live with. We've been through worse. Come, I have a wonderful idea. I'm going to let you borrow Katy on the thirtieth."

"Why the thirtieth?" Louisa asked, puzzled.

"It's election day. David should be in town to vote for the legislature. And it being Monday, Mrs. Blaine won't be holding school—it's wash day. So Katy can have a bit of holiday. She can help you with Emily, and it'll give you something to look forward to. I worry about you, way out there," she said. "I have it all figured out. David can bring Katy back the next morning in time for the nine o'clock bell. I've already asked him. All that's left is for you to agree. Liza, do say yes."

Part II

ELECTION DAY
Monday, January 30

While the governor was touring Puget Sound, the Territory was preparing for the election on January 30th of members of the first territorial legislature and for a delegate to Congress.

—Roberta Frye Watt, Katy's daughter

-3-

It was not accidental that school was to open on Tuesday. Monday was washday, and Mrs. Blaine did not wish her weekly schedule upset; so all through that term, the children had their Saturday holiday on Monday.

—Roberta Frye Watt, Katy's daughter

"So tell me everyone in your class, and tell me all about your books," Louisa told Katy. "No, wait, before you begin..." She lifted her axe and let the sharp edge of the blade drop onto the ice that had formed in the rain barrel outside the front door of her cabin. The bitter cold had hung on, freezing everything in sight. The axe bounced off the ice. She laughed at herself, and at Katy—whose freckled nose poked out the door.

"Auntie," suggested nine-year-old Katy, "maybe you have to turn it the other way."

Louisa turned the handle in her freezing fingers and again lifted the axe. This time the blunt end smashed into the ice. Another swing and the ice broke into chunks and the slosh of water rattled the pieces. "Just like 'timber,' right Katy?" Louisa asked, laughing. She picked up the bucket and dipped in the lip, feeling the weight and rush of water.

Today was washday, and Katy's day to visit. Mrs. Blaine, the preacher's wife and the new school teacher, did not like to have her routine upset and so the children were given

45

their Saturday holidays on Monday, and David, after having gone into town early to cast his vote for the territory's very first legislature, had brought Katy on home with him. He'd stopped by the cabin just long enough to drop her off and grab his lunch. He and Tom Mercer, their neighbor to the north, were clearing some 20 aspens along the back of their adjoining claims.

Katy had brought a surprise: her mother's washboard. There were only four in all of Seattle, and Louisa was overjoyed to get it. The note tied to the leg of the washboard read: *Rollie is finally out of diapers!* But what of Orrie? Louisa wondered. Oh, well, she decided, she was *not* going to look a gift horse in the mouth.

Katy held the door open as Louisa hauled water back and forth between hearth and barrel. "Careful," Louisa said as she poured the last bucket of icy water into a cast-iron cauldron hung inside the large fireplace. "Don't pinch your fingers."

"Do you know everybody who goes to our new school, Auntie?"

"No, but I bet I could guess."

"Guess, Auntie!"

"I suppose you have the Mercer girls."

"Mary Jane only comes when Mr. Mercer makes her. Mary Jane likes to stay at home with little Alice. She says she doesn't like sums and memorizing countries' names she'll never see."

Louisa sighed and squatted on her haunches before the fire, thinking sadly of the four motherless girls, the oldest of whom was only 15, living half a mile away, through the woods and along the narrow trail that David and Tom had hacked through the forest shrubbery. Mrs. Mercer had died of Blue Mountain fever at The Dalles on the way west. The world west of the Mississippi, it seemed, was cruel and hard. Mothers died. Their babies died. Survivors were left to carry on the best they could. "Mary Jane needs to go to school," she told Katy. "Everybody needs to learn to read and write and study a little bit about the world." But she was thinking that it wasn't just the pioneers who died. People in Illinois died too. Almost a year had passed since word had come telling of Pamelia's death, her friend she'd left behind.

"Susie and Eliza Mercer, they come all the time," said Katy, as if that made up for their big sister's absence. "And Laura and Virginia and Olive Bell come too. Only Lavinia Bell is too little, you know. And there's little Ursula and George Jr. *"Georgie Peorgie,"* she singsonged, *"pudding and pie—"*

"I declare, Katy, why did Mr. and Mrs. McConaha name their children after themselves? Two Ursulas and two Georges! Why, you'd never know who you were talking to!" The fire smoked lazily around the wood. Louisa blew short, tight puffs, trying to tempt the flame to catch.

Katy giggled. "We don't let Georgie-Peorgie kiss us, Auntie."

"That's good. Now, tell me who else is in your class."

"There's Huldie Phillips. And Becky Horton. They're both my age. And there's me and Nora. We chase the boys."

Still the wood resisted. Louisa blew on the glowing embers until she thought her lungs would burst. "Can you hand me my sunbonnet, behind the door? Hanging on one of those hooks? That's a girl, thank you." She fanned the flame with the starched brim until smoke choked her and stung her eyes. Perspiration covered her cheeks and irritated her neck where her collar scratched. But Louisa did not quit until flames crackled.

When the water was at last boiling, she tipped in a can of lye, and when scum clouded the top, scooped it off with a long-handled wooden spoon. With a sharp butcher knife she sliced shavings off a bar of homemade soap into the lye water. She removed the linen tablecloth and set a large, galvanized bucket on the tabletop. She ladled boiling water out of the large cauldron into the bucket, then setting her new washboard into the soapy water, dipped in her hands.

Soap and lye. They stung her knuckles. Scalding water burnt her fingers. Ammonia tore at her eyes. *Sooner begun, sooner done,* she told herself, reluctantly reaching for the first of her baby's diapers.

Katy's chatter helped get her mind off wash day miseries—*and* filled in the paradoxical silence of the woods. In the unusual cold, sounds had magnified. In the icy, bitter weather of the past two weeks the forest silence had whispered a thousand sounds—exaggerating even the rattle of a leaf falling to the ground, the flutter of a bird's flight, the furry step of an animal. An Indian? she'd wondered too many times, running to the window. An ordinary tree bough snapping under the weight of heavy, wet snow could sound like gunfire, ricocheting through the forest, and each time it had happened she'd held her breath until her heart calmed. When it was truly silent, no sounds in all the forest, she'd creep to the door and peek out, sensing something, someone, watching and waiting, memory of the Indians' *stick siwash* preying uncomfortably on her mind. So Katy's busy words gratefully silenced these thousand sounds, bringing an unexpected and welcomed relief to Louisa's nerves.

"Tell me what books you study," Louisa said.

"McGuffey's reader, Mitchell's geography, and Davis' arithmetic. Want to hear my sums?"

Louisa smiled. "Of course." Louisa had once taught school—in Illinois. Another lifetime, she thought, listening to two plus two, and wondering at the separation of time between *now* and *then.* Between Illinois days and the forest cabin. *Up and down, in and out, twisting, up and down.* Her hands worked automatically. *In and out, up and down,* twisting in the *now* of the scalding water. Woolen drawers, muddy jeans, flannel shirts, the baby's red flannel diapers against the brass ripples of her new washboard. Her hands were here, but her mind rippled to *then,* memories and

Illinois. As children, she and Pamelia had both taken singing lessons from Mrs. Wessel, had skipped down the cow path every Saturday morning, eggs in a basket, to visit Mrs. Swan, an old lady who had two parrots in a cage on her kitchen table. Good days, with good memories; memories savored like lemon drops under the tongue. Did she want to go back? she wondered, staring at her reddened hands, feeling the dampness of the log walls and the harsh uncertainty of *now*.

After lunch Katy took a nap with Emily. Outside, snowflakes began to sift like flour from the sky and Louisa, standing before her washbucket, watched them float past the windowpane. She missed Pamelia, and over this past year had cried often over the double tragedy; Pamelia had died with her baby in childbirth. But, Louisa thought, dashing folds of her skirt briskly between her hands to rub out a milk stain, there was the sweetbriar was there not? Yes. *Yes.*

Pamelia had given her the seeds their last morning together in Illinois. A tryst between them. "Blossoms cover thorns," Pamelia had whispered when they'd hugged for the last time. "Just remember that, Louisa! Look for the beauty, the spring. Always!" A tryst between friends, a reminder. "We *will* meet again, Liza," Pamelia had promised. "If not in this world, on the other side."

And, on the other side of the wall of Louisa's cabin, just beneath the window and poking through the January snow, that same sweetbriar—their sweetbriar—grew, a warm comfort and more than a simple reminder of spring. The fragrant, five-petal rose, opening to the yellow seed center, was a reminder of hope. Of faith. Louisa grieved, yes, but not as those without faith. She and Pamelia would meet. She knew that. And in another and better world where they would not be called to part.

A sudden, raucous shrieking of a gull invited Louisa to dry her hands and crack the door. There it was, winging over the bank, its gray-tipped wings pumping, then soaring through the snowing sky. A wild sky, the beauty of gulls. Did she want to go back to Illinois? No, she thought, looking at the trees towering into heaven, brushing the very gates. Across the Sound mountains ridged the horizon, lost in mist. No, no, she smiled, shutting the door. Never.

In the wilderness the winter might be cold, the dampness biting, the rumors of Indian unrest unsettling, the forest sounds startling and unnerving. But in Illinois, where were the trees? The hills? This serene, comforting whisper of God in all that eye could see?

Once more she plunged her hands into the wash water. Winter would pass. Spring would come. Refreshed and sure, she tackled the very last of the laundry, wringing out corduroy jeans and pillowcases and bed sheets and hanging them one by one onto the lines David had strung from wall to wall, filling the room with the scent of fresh, clean clothes.

• • •

All done. Louisa held her fingers tenderly. A good day's work. She massaged her hands gently, wondering as always at how wicked the lye was. Her hands were not those of a young maiden anymore, and that made her strangely sad.

Katy, awake now and absorbed in the latest *Godey's Lady's Book* from the States, was sprawled onto the bed beside Emily, the two of them hidden by shirts and long underwear and rows of red diapers (the only flannel available at Dr. Williamson's store) dripping every now and then onto the mud floor and Indian mats. David would be home soon, tired and spent. Time to start the supper.

Louisa pulled aside a wall of diapers and smiled at her serious little double-chinned baby. "I'll be back," she said to her niece. "I'm going out to get some meat for supper." Katy nodded without looking up, chin in her fists. Emily though, searched out her mother's voice and Louisa bent into her narrow range of vision and kissed her, then tickled her chin.

The snow had stopped. But the sun was cold, lost in the deepening gray of the late afternoon sky. When would this bitter cold pass? Louisa wondered. When *would* spring come? You're too impatient, she chided herself, shivering. It's still only January.

She carried the butcher knife carefully, stepping through the fresh snow to the side of venison David had hung from a line between two trees overlooking the bluff and the gray water of Elliott Bay. She could see tracks in the new fall. Probably the Indians who used the trail to cut through the woods to Chodups John's shack out by the road. Salmon Bay Curley, she knew, was always using their trail for a short-cut. She looked again. No. They were animal tracks. A deer perhaps? Or a raccoon? She bent to decipher them. Too large. *A cougar.* A chill ran down her spine and she looked around apprehensively. Nothing. All was still. Too still, she thought, remembering the nine-foot cougar David had shot the spring before. Its weight alone, David had said, could have killed a man had it sprung from a tree. She searched the dark leafy boughs of the trees, looking for the glimmer of gold eyes in the dimness.

The venison hung ten feet off the ground, tied from a line of rope strung between two trees on the north side of the clearing. Louisa went over to the cedar where David had staked a wharf cleat and unwound the hemp in figure eights, lowering the line until the meat dropped down far enough for her to reach.

For almost 15 minutes, working steadily, Louisa sliced at a frozen slab from the shoulder, jabbing and sawing with the sharp end of her knife, twisting as the meat softened. A strange sound echoed in the woods and her fingers froze, her heart pounded; she whirled, but nothing moved in the fringes of the forest and nothing darkened the bleak sunlight in the clearing. It's a naked clearing, she thought, forcing herself to return to her task, but in the spring David would bring back her chickens and cows from her brother's pasture in town. In the spring . . . in the spring, she assured herself, breathing quickly. In the spring maybe Mary Ann would give her one of Moreover's pups. Louisa glanced at the comforting square of light that spilled from her cabin window as she worked the blade against the meat. One more savage thrust of the knife and the meat broke loose. Louisa felt the shadow overhead, but before she could run, the shadow snarled and fell from the sky, slamming her face into the icy embrace of the snow.

-4-

The pioneer women learned to face every sort of danger from riding rough water in an Indian canoe to hunting blackberries where bears, panthers and Indians roamed the deep forest.

—Emily Inez Denny, Louisa's daughter

Arms instinctively wrapped round her head, face stinging in the snow, Louisa heard a low, deep groan, a cry neither quite animal nor human, then snarls unmistakably animal, the swift crunch of snow and then quiet. Quiet. Quiet.

She couldn't trust the quiet. She lay as though dead for several minutes, disobeying every impulse that told her to flee. I must not panic...the cougar may yet be...I must not panic...it may still be lurking nearby.

Deliberately she counted to 50. The cold penetrated her heavy coat and she was shivering by the time she came to 33—the number of years Jesus had lived. She looked up. All was still. Why, it was the meat the cougar was after! she realized. Her breathing eased. She could see the knife a few feet away, flung somehow from her hand.

Slowly she rose to her knees and then to her feet, painfully aware of the ache in her shoulders, of the cruel, cruel cold. She stumbled forward toward the safety of the cabin, then stopped. She turned back to see the venison still hanging from the trees, the knife in the snow. "I can't," she whispered. "I can't." She lifted her eyes and took a deep breath and—at least momentarily—fought off fear as she staggered back through the snow to pick up the knife. Then, trembling, she walked back to the side of the venison and began once again to carve her family's supper.

• • •

"Where were you, Auntie?"

The cabin was cozy and warm and smelled of lye and clean things, and Louisa shut the door, grateful for the privacy afforded her by the walls of wet clothes. "The meat was frozen, Katy; it took awhile," she said, wondering that she could even speak.

She laid the meat and knife on the stove, between a pot of bubbling legumes and salt pork, then pulled off her coat.

She shuddered when she saw the long tears across the shoulders and back. It had been torn clean through to the lining. Stuffing hung in shreds. What if I hadn't been wearing a coat? What if— *I will lift up mine eyes unto the hills, from whence cometh my help.* The psalm had sustained her through all of the last difficult year, and she recited the words. *My help cometh from the Lord, which made heaven and earth. He will not suffer thy foot to be moved: he that keepeth thee will not slumber....*

Tears dripped down her cheeks. She wiped them away with the back of her arm, unable to take her eyes off the torn and shabby coat in her hand. What if I hadn't been wearing my coat? she wondered again, numb. And what if my coat hadn't been a good, strong one? No! No! She *had* been wearing her coat and the cougar had only wanted the meat—tied up out of its reach. No, she mustn't start asking all those "what if" questions. She mustn't. She had to trust Providence.

She hung the coat on the back of the door, hiding the ugly damage. Tomorrow she would do what she could to repair it. But what if— No, she thought, stopping herself. *The Lord shall preserve thy going out and thy coming in from this time forth, and even for evermore.*

Standing between two lines of clothes, Louisa salted and peppered the slab of meat, reciting the psalm over and over. She took the edge of a saucer and beat the venison until she felt the fibers break and her own strength return. Hadn't God sustained them before, bringing them safely out of danger? Hadn't He just done it again?

The meat sizzled on the hot skillet and she sliced onions in beside it. The potatoes, set near the fire, were plump to the touch. "Katy," she said, breathing evenly now, "it's about time to set the table. Your Uncle David will be along soon enough."

While Katy padded back and forth between the shipping-crate cupboard and the table, Louisa stood before her wall mirror. It was a large, beveled mirror, framed in mahogany and nailed firmly to the newspaper-covered logs beside the door. The mirror had belonged to her father, her real father, and she had always loved it for that reason. Both Ma and Arthur had forbidden her to take it on the Oregon Trail two years ago. "That thing is too heavy," they'd pronounced with finality.

But Louisa had stoutly refused to leave it behind. This mirror was all she had to remind her of a father who had died before she could walk. Leaning in close to inspect her frightened face and to wipe the dirt off her chin, she realized that only a year ago—one year and one week ago—she'd given the mirror to David for a wedding present. Had they really only been married a year? In some ways it seemed forever. In other ways, hardly at all.

The smudge wasn't dirt on her chin: it was blood. Dipping her skirt into the water on the stove, she cleansed the wound, wincing when it stung, conscious of a dreadful ache settling into her shoulders.

"Are you all right, Auntie?" Katy asked quietly.

"Yes. Yes, I am. I just fell while I was out. See my poor chin? But I'll be fine in a few minutes." Leaning in close to the mirror again, she pinched her cheeks and bit her lips to bring back the color that had been lost in her fright. She'd have to tell David as soon as he got home, she decided, brushing out her hair. He and Dobbins could go out and track the cougar in the morning. She heard Katy behind her and resolved to wait to tell David till after Katy left. The children lived in enough uncertainty as it was. *Where was David?*

She leaned over the table to glance anxiously out the window, the ache in her shoulders pressing down her spine as she stretched. After the baby had been born and they'd moved back to the homestead, David had quit his job at the mill. He and Tom Mercer found it more profitable to fell trees off their adjoining claims and, when a load was ready, to haul it into Henry Yesler's mill for cash. That way they accomplished two things at once. They earned money, and they cleared land. *What was keeping him?* she wondered again.

"Katy?" she asked, forcing a nonchalance to her voice, "Your pa say anything about cougars in Seattle?"

"Last week Pa and Uncle Dobbins went down to the Holgates and Hanfords to track one."

The news startled her. The Holgates lived on the south end of the bay. Were there two cougars? She cupped a hand to her eyes to see more clearly through the glass. *David, where are you?* She told herself cougars did not normally attack adults. But if they were hungry, which was probably true with this bitter cold, might a cougar attack a child walking through the woods to and from school? Louisa glanced again toward her niece before turning back to the window. A shadow emerged up the trail. Cougar? No. A man. David! David was home! No. David would have come from around the back. Louisa's stomach knotted. "Katy," she said deliberately, calmly, "I want you to go pick up the baby."

"But I'm not finished with the table, Auntie."

"Never mind that just now. Pick up the baby. Take her behind the bed and sit on the floor." Louisa spoke quickly, edging sideways, hand in front of her to separate the damp clothes in search of the loaded rifle hung over the stove. Her hair caught on a wet towel. She ducked and grabbed for the gun just as the latch jiggled.

The gun slid, crashing onto the stove, clattering pots and pans. She dove after it, then choked back a scream as the door creaked.

She bit her fist, blinking, the silence long. Then the door swung open and an Indian stuck in his head.

"*Skookum tillicum,*" he announced and stepped inside.

-5-

*The manner of life of my heroic mother ...
was such as to develop the noblest traits of character.
The patience, steadfastness, courage, hopefulness
and the consideration for the needs and trials of
others, wrought out in her during the pioneer days,
challenge the admiration of the world.*

—Emily Inez Denny, Louisa's daughter

"Skookum tillicum!"

Relief rushed through Louisa's arms and legs and knees and she sank weakly into the rocking chair, heart pounding in her ears. "Salmon Bay Curley, you scared me half to death!"

"David Denny?" the Indian asked, pulling his short body inside. Bewildered by all the rows of clothes, he stood on tip-toe to peer over a row of wet long johns and socks. His black eyes, framed by shocking curls, an oddity for an Indian, stared at her from between the hand-whittled clothes pegs.

"No, no, he's not home," said Louisa. But it was no use. Curley couldn't understand English well enough. "It's all right," she called out to Katy. "It's only Salmon Bay Curley. You remember Curley? He lives north of Dr. Smith. At *Shil-hole-ootseed*." Katy came around the bed and Louisa took the baby who had begun to wail.

"Curley, you really must knock before you come in! You scared me to death. I was thinking..." Katy's freckles were

58

popping off her nose. "Well, never mind. But from now on—you knock!"

Somehow she found her feet. She pushed aside a damp hanky that hung in her way and walked to the door, Emily screaming wildly in her arms. She tripped over a mat but caught herself by grabbing the back of a chair. Pain shot through her shoulder, then trickled down into her spine, spots of pinpricks that she could eventually see behind her eyes.

"You tell David Denny," said Curley watching her curiously, "you tell him . . . Pat Kanim and Tyee Tinkham *klat-a-wah Sno-qual-mie?*" He added, "Tinkham—Seattle," and smiled, revealing a wide gap between broken front teeth.

Louisa nodded numbly, promising to pass along the information and gratefully let Salmon Bay Curley out the door.

"Katy," she said, drawing a deep breath, "finish the table and I'll see if I can't quiet the baby." But Emily fought her mother's breast, wailing and thrashing, head thrown back, body arched. *My, my, this will never do*, Louisa thought, taking a firm grip on herself. The sudden memory of Mrs. Brogen came to mind, surprising her and making her laugh. She hadn't thought of the tightly corseted leader of their Bible class since leaving Illinois. "I declare, I don't know why those redskins weren't drowned in the flood," Mrs. Brogen had said a dozen times. Well, better cougars and redskins than Mrs. Brogen, Louisa reflected, holding Emily's rigid little body tightly to her chest and stroking, over and over, the baby's soft downy head. "Shh . . ." Louisa crooned, rocking and stroking. "Katy? What's a good song to sing to the baby?"

Katy's feet passed back and forth beneath the hanging clothes as she finished setting the table. "Mama always sings 'Silent Night' to Orrie when he has a tummy ache. Which side of the plates do the forks go on, Auntie?"

How like Mary, Louisa thought, to sing Christmas songs even in January. Katy lifted a diaper. "Which side?"

"Left."

"Auntie?"

"Yes, Katy? What is it?"

"A man just looked in the window."

"That fool Indian!" Louisa cried, furious, jumping to her feet, Emily still screaming in her arms. "What's he hanging around for? I told him David wasn't home! I swear..."

"Auntie, it wasn't an Indian. It was a white face."

"*A white face?*" She nearly laughed. But then she saw her niece's distress. "Come, come, Katy Denny," she teased gently, "that's just plain silly. You're seeing things. No white man is going to be poking his nose in our window." She chucked the child under the chin and patted the top of her head. "White men knock on the door and we say 'Come in.' That's the way it works." But Katy looked unconvinced. "It was Curley," Louisa assured her. "There's no reason to fret. Now, finish the table—and I'll see if I can't get Emily simmered down."

But Emily would have none of it. Not 'Silent Night'—or anything else.

"Maybe you can sing 'Holy, Holy, Holy'? Orrie likes that one, too," Katy offered. She climbed onto a chair, nose pressed to the windowpane. "Hey, Uncle David's home!" she shrieked, and before he could get past the doorstep she'd leaped into his arms, laughing and giggling to the tickle of his beard on her face. She snatched off his toque, an old worn cap Louisa had knit years and years ago.

"My, my," he declared. "It's not every day a man comes home to be greeted so enthusiastically. Hey, Liza!" he called out, raising his voice above Emily's wails. "I ran into Curley! He's full of all kinds of good news!" David pulled his head back to smile at his niece and then he kicked the door shut. Katy leaned to push the latch. They touched noses, laughing again.

"Liza?"

He put Katy down to move through the wet clothes. "Want me to take Emily?"

She felt tears puddle in her eyes; if she blinked they would spill.

David leaned over to kiss her. "You look like you're at your wits' end," he said gently.

"Oh, David," Louisa gulped, determined that he not see her cry. "You've simply got to get it through Curley's head he is to knock, not just barge in. Or gawk through the window."

But David just laughed. "He'll never knock, Liza. You know that. It's not the Indian way." He took Emily and Louisa sat amazed: the quiet was instant.

"Well, can you believe that?" She busied herself at the stove, among the spilled pots and pans. Her feelings were hurt. Along with everything else tonight, she felt like a failure as a mother. "So what's Curley's good news?" she asked, stifling tears.

"They crossed Snoqualmie! Pat Kanim got Lieutenant Tinkham, Stevens' civil engineer, through the pass! Middle of winter and they found the summit! But guess what?" he called out, "it's a real easy grade! Not even McClellan can argue it!"

"McClellan find the pass from this side then?" she asked, still staring at the beans on the stove and wondering what to do first.

"Nope. He didn't even try. He heard about the snow and turned around and came right back—didn't stop until he got to tidewater. He still swears the Cascades are totally impassable."

"So what about Lieutenant Tinkham and Pat Kanim? Katy? Can you reach the spoon over there for me?"

"They're in Seattle."

"*They're in Seattle?*" She turned and yanked aside the laundry. David lay on the bed, head on a pillow, Emily sprawled on his stomach, her skinny little arms and legs dangling over his rib cage. "Is *that* what Curley was trying to tell me? They really made it through the mountains?"

"Mm-m." A pleased grin on his face.

"So they've really crossed? David!" she exclaimed. "Arthur is right! We *can* put a road through Snoqualmie and the railroad—" She snatched the handkerchief off the line and sent it flying. The hanky landed on Emily's diapered bottom and Katy, peeking between two pillowcases, giggled.

It was news too good to be true! They would be a real town! With real houses, and stores that carried lace and pretty cloth and real candles and kerosene and maybe even penny candy for Emily when she grew up big enough to eat it! Louisa could hardly believe it. This meant ships, trade, more silks and tea from China—and mail.

"Guess we've proved that southern-fried McClellan a total idiot!" she cried. "Governor Stevens can take that McClellan report right back to Jefferson Davis in Washington, D.C. and the high and mighty Secretary of War can just put it in his hat!" Happily she returned to the stove, scooped the beans into a bowl and set it on the table, along with the biscuits, potatoes, the precious meat, and some of Tom Mercer's butter. "Come on, sit up," she called. "It's time for supper!"

"Papa win the election?" Katy asked, pulling out the chairs and striking a match to the smelly dogfish oil lamp in the center of the table. Louisa noticed that she'd glanced apprehensively out the window before sliding into her chair.

"Your papa never sets out to do anything unless he's going to win," said David.

"Did you vote for him, Uncle David?"

"Of course I voted for him."

"Did you vote for him, Auntie Louisa?"

"Ladies can't vote, Sugarplum."

"Why?"

They all crowded around the small table. Emily lay

tummy-down on David's lap and she fell asleep imme-diately. It's amazing how everything is safe and fine when David is home, Louisa thought, grateful for his presence, his nearness, the safety he offered. He said grace, then leaned across the corner to kiss her as he always did after the Amen.

"Bumped your chin?"

She nodded.

"Why, Auntie?"

"Why what, honey?"

"Why can't ladies vote?"

"Because they're ladies."

"Is that all?" the little girl asked, screwing up her nose at David. "That doesn't sound like a very good reason to me. I'm smarter than Georgie Peorgie, but he'll get to vote and I won't? Uncle David, who says only the boys get to vote?"

Louisa set her elbow on the table, fork in hand. "The preacher, I am sure," she told Katy, "will tell you that God did. Arthur win by much?" she asked, turning to David.

"Only 87 to 19." His grin stretched from ear to ear. "Now I can sleep at night, knowing Arthur will be sitting right under the governor's nose, keeping him straight on a few things."

"Did *you* win anything, Uncle David?" Katy asked.

"I've been appointed to the Grand Jury for the first term of District Court, if you can call that winning anything. Want me to skin your potato?"

Katy nodded and he proceeded to slice the potato in half, then scoop out the insides. Louisa watched, felt herself relax. The cougar and all that was dangerous melted in the warmth of David's gentle care.

"There you are," he said, smiling tenderly at Katy and slipping butter into each "skin." He set them on Katy's plate. "Can you cut your own meat?"

"I'm a big girl, Uncle David."

Louisa smiled. "So when does court convene? And what sort of things will you try?"

"Henry VanAsselt wants to apply for citizenship. And there's a couple of Indians who've broken into Dr. Williamson's store again. And there's the usual ballast charges against Captain Felker. Plenty to make it look official. Doc Maynard has been elected County Clerk. Thomas Russell will be sheriff for Alki. Your brother, Louisa, was elected sheriff for Seattle."

"I could have guessed."

"Uncle Dobbins won because he can shoot better than *anybody* else," said Katy, mouth full.

"That's right," said David. "Except me."

The little girl grinned.

"When is court being held?" Louisa asked.

"Two weeks."

"How long will it last?" She thought of the cougar and wondered if she wanted to be way out here all by herself while he was gone.

"I don't know. A few days maybe. Won't be as long as the legislature, that's sure. That could go on for weeks. Did I tell you George McConaha won the Democratic seat—for the Council?"

"This county would be foolish not to vote him in. He's the smartest man we've got. When do they convene?"

"Court's in two weeks—Monday the 13th. Legislature is two weeks after that—the 27th I think. Another month yet."

Emily burped loudly and David swung her up and held her sleepy face close to his, then pulled her in to touch noses, making Katy laugh. "She's an A-rab," he declared, looking down at Katy. "I hear tell that's what the A-rabs do. You learn that in school yet? They burp. And they don't say 'Excuse me, Sir.' Liza, pass the salt, please?"

"Here, I'll take her," Louisa offered. "You eat your supper."

"I've been thinking," he said. "How would you like to move further back, up towards the Mercer's? We've been clearing a lot of land back by *tenas chuck*, along the little lake. The soil is better for your spring garden," he added, seeing her tense.

"I like it here, David. Why are you always trying to move me?"

"I'm not. Did I say anything about moving into town? No, we'd still be on the claim, Liza. It's just closer to Tommy and the girls is all. And I think it's a better spot. Better soil. More sun. And," he said, poking a damp undershirt with his fork, "I could make the cabin a lot bigger. We wouldn't have to eat under the armpits of smelly long johns." He winked at Louisa and his laughter caught all them in a happy embrace.

● ● ●

David was washing the dishes when he noticed the coat. It hung funny off the hook, and without thinking he reached out to put it straight. Shreds met his wet hands. Horrified, he looked across the room to where Louisa was reading *Gulliver's Travels* to Katy.

" '...*bending my eyes downward as much as I could, I perceived it to be a human creature not six inches high*—' " Louisa looked up, saw the coat, and silenced him instantly with her eyes. Katy looked up too, puzzled. "It's nothing," said Louisa, smoothing back the child's bangs, then bent her head and began to read—quickly. " '*I felt above an hundred arrows discharged on my left hand, which pricked me like so many needles*—' "

David's stomach went weak and hot, knees wobbly. *A cougar. A cougar had done this.* He could not get his breath. His eye moved from the coat in his hand, to Louisa, to Katy and the baby. Oh, God, he thought. What have I done?

-6-

D.T. Denny was a man of much more than average ability. He thought much and deeply on questions which affected the welfare of man. Above all, he was a Christian and believed in a religion which he sought to live, not to exhibit.

—Rev. W.S. Harrington

What have I done? What am I doing here? Long after the others had gone to sleep, David lay awake, staring wide-eyed at the rafters overhead. The questions hammered with each beat of his heart.

The cougar had been a small one; he had that to be grateful for. Any bigger, it would have crushed her. He buried his nose in the coolness of Louisa's hair, afraid. It wasn't just the cougar. It was everything: the isolation of their cabin, the Indians, the dangers everywhere. What had he been thinking of when he'd set off from Illinois to seek his destiny in the wilderness? Was he to sacrifice his wife? His baby? And for what reason?

The night was quiet, the silence deafening. He longed to stretch, but with Louisa tucked into his arms he couldn't bring himself to let her go. Unbidden, last year's dangers rushed to mind. Seattle's hunger. The ships unable to get in. John Low lifting his hatchet against Old Alki. The thunderstorm toppling trees like twigs over their heads. Luther Collins lynching Masachie Jim. That was the worst. That

July. Hot. Sultry. Horrifying. An Indian dead by the hand of a white man. David feared—not the cougars and the everyday dangers they faced—but the Indians' retaliation.

For awhile Chief Seattle's words seemed to have been sufficient to stem the tide of centuries of primitive law. For the Chief, the ancient law of an eye for an eye had been replaced by Christ's command—turn the other cheek. But for the others? And what of the mysterious McCormick, missing since July? Had he been caught in the riptide, sacrificed—despite the Christian command of Chief Seattle? Had the Indians killed McCormick to satisfy their need for revenge?

Or was the governor right? David wondered. Perhaps McCormick *had* merely slipped off a trail. Or had fallen out of a canoe. Perhaps a cougar had jumped from a tree. David tightened his arms around Louisa. Stevens was right, he decided. There was nothing to fear. The lynching, after all, had been seven months ago, and the Indians had remained friendly enough. Neither Chodups John nor Salmon Bay Curley had had anything substantial to report in way of serious discontent. And months had passed since he'd heard anything from Chief Seattle and his sons.

He was fighting imaginary enemies, he decided, because he couldn't fight the concrete ones like cougars—and God knew what other tragedies that might lie ahead. Impulsively he bent to kiss Louisa's shoulder, thanking God for her safety, for the protection of her coat, the snow that had absorbed her fall, the fact that Katy hadn't gone out of the house. So many little things. He prayed out loud, whispering the words to himself. "Thank you, God, the father and mother of our souls," he prayed, imitating the Quaker's incorporation of the female into the godhead, "for these saving blessings."

"David?"

"Shh," he whispered, sorry he had wakened her.

"What's wrong?"

"I don't know what we're doing here, and I'm scared," he admitted, whispering quietly and reaching for her hand. He was grateful to feel her fingers closing around his own. "I keep thinking about that cougar, about the Indians and McCormick. I keep looking at Emily and I wonder what kind of country we're bringing her up in."

"Oh, David..." She turned in his arms and held both hands to his face. He grabbed her palm and kissed it, feeling the sting of tears in his eyes.

"Do you want to move back down to Oregon?" she asked quickly. "With Ma and Pa and James—"

"No!" he whispered fiercely, almost angry that she should bring up James, the Denny brother who wished *he* could have married Louisa. But her laughter, low in her throat, told him she only teased. He eased back into the pillows, grateful for her clear head, her quick humor.

"We could move back to Illinois," she offered. "And die of consumption—or boredom."

"Are you trying to tell me you're not afraid?"

She stroked his chin, running her finger along his jaw-line, then his lips, touching lightly. She eased up on the mattress to look down at him and smiled in the shadowed, flickering firelight. She slowly kissed his mouth and nose and eyes. "I am afraid," she said at last.

"Then what are we to do?" He lay quietly, accepting her gentle touch and ministration.

"We will trust God."

With her supple hand she touched his chest, his face, his arms, his thigh. A warm, comforting touch. "David," she whispered. "Do you think..."

He waited.

"Do you think maybe God has a job for you to do here in the wilderness?"

The question surprised him. "I don't know, Liza," he sighed, squeezing his eyes shut. "Sometimes I don't know why I'm here."

"You are a peacemaker, David—a man both the whites

and Indians trust. Perhaps you've been sent to lead everyone peacefully through a troubled time."

"But Arthur is the leader, not me."

"Arthur respects the Indians. He listens to them. He believes in them. But that isn't enough."

"What is enough then?"

"Love."

He lifted his head off the pillow.

"David, you have that love. You have it for the Indians and they have it for you. Who does Salmon Bay Curley come running to with news of the mountain crossing? And what of Jim and George Seattle? And Chief Seattle himself? Who brings you news of the southern tribes? Chodups John. He trusts you. They'll trust you to know what to do when there's trouble."

"Ah, Louisa," he sighed, pulling her down onto his chest and hugging her close, feeling the warmth and response of her body against his. "One thing I know is I love you."

"Together, and with God's help," she added, wrapping her arms around his neck and burying her nose against his shoulder, "we will go through whatever is ahead." She held her husband close. "I don't know how it works, but He does promise to be with us."

"But terrible things happen. I don't want to lose you—or Emily. I'm afraid—"

"In the end . . ." Her voice was dreamy and wise. "In the end," she said, kissing him, "I think we'll find we don't need to be afraid."

"But you *are* afraid."

"Yes." He could feel her guilty smile against his neck, and had to smile. "But when I have survived I will look back to these days and realize I was just a silly woman who wished for a board sidewalk outside her front door and someone delivering milk each morning."

She could always make him laugh.

•   •   •

Sunlight wakened him. Blinking, disoriented, it dawned on him slowly that Emily had slept through the entire night. He grinned and rubbed his beard into Louisa's chin. "You look so pretty lying there," he whispered. She smiled and let him bundle her into his arms, moaning when he squeezed her aching muscles too quickly. They lay like spoons in a drawer, quietly aware of each other in the icy chill of morning, waiting for the baby—or Katy, sound asleep beside them—to stir.

Part III

INDIAN TROUBLE
Tuesday, January 31

Although the real plotting that was going on among the Indians was not discovered by the settlers, there were hints of it and even warning....But the pioneers had grown used to this undercurrent of fear and that was one reason why they were not more alert to the imminent danger at this time. This sense of danger had become a part of the very life on the frontier—a nameless dread of something unseen and lurking in the shadows. Referring to the hardships of that period, the sweetbriar bride said in after years, "I wouldn't go through it again if you were to give me the whole state of Washington."

—Roberta Frye Watt, Katy's daughter

-7-

On those days when her husband was out felling timber for the San Francisco trade, the pioneer woman was alone many times from early morning until late at night....Fear of unseen foes was probably the hardest thing in her life, for what is more terrifying? The forest about her might at any time send forth a crouching beast or a stealthy Indian.

—Roberta Frye Watt, Katy's daughter

"It's no use," said Louisa once the fire was crackling, the bacon sizzling on the stove. She stood behind Katy in the icy chill of dawn, brush in hand and exasperated with herself beyond belief because the pain in her shoulders had set in something fierce. She couldn't even brush out the nest of Katy's tangled red hair, let alone keep her arms up long enough to do the French braids. "I'm as stiff as an old cow," she said, "and about as useless. What are we going to do with this mop, Katy? David, do you think you can brush out her hair, and maybe attempt the braids? Maybe just do pigtails this time."

"Pigtails!" Katy wailed, ducking her head and clapping her hands over her hair. "Pigtails! Nobody wears just plain old ugly *pigtails!* Auntie! Everyone will laugh at me!"

David squatted in front of Katy's chair at eye level. "Are you trying to tell me, Miss Denny, that *I'm* going to have to do your French braids this morning?"

"Do you know how?" Real tears threatened to spill.

In the dim light of early morning Louisa could see David's laughing eyes. She held out the brush, daring him.

"All right," he said, accepting. "But after I finish turning this ragamuffin into a real live princess, I'm going to do your hair, Mrs. Denny. And when I get home . . . I am going to undo it."

Katy looked up. "What do you want to do that for, Uncle David?"

• • •

It was hard to say goodbye. Louisa found herself envying David for his trip to Seattle. She was missing Mary Ann, and as much as she hated to admit it, she was lonely for the excitement—and yes, the safety—of town. But then, a cougar could leap from a tree in Seattle as well as it could two miles north. She kissed Katy on the nose and bundled her hat and scarf around tight. "Goodbye, David," she said, kissing him next. "Don't be late. The day will be long after Katy's visit."

From the stoop, her tattered coat thrown hastily about her shoulders, and scarf wound tightly about her head and mouth, Louisa watched them cross the clearing to the path leading to Tom Mercer's, David's stride long and easy, his rifle slung over his shoulder, Katy skipping alongside of him, kicking snow, holding his hand, her French braids loose and ready to come down, slapping in beat against her back. Her tin lunch pail was a flash of color in the dull gray of winter dawn. When they reached the forest proper, David turned to wave.

"Say hello to Tom and the girls!" Louisa hollered, pulling down on her scarf. She blew two kisses. "Oh! And Katy! Tell your mother hello! And tell her thanks very much for the washboard!"

Inside, the cabin was a mess. She glanced out the window. Shadows not yet wakened by the day looked like forest panthers. Clear the dishes, she told herself. Stoke the fire.

No time to be melancholy today—or lonely or fearful. Work was God's medicine for foolish anxiety. And there was much to be done. She stared at the laundry, still hanging from the lines and needing another day or two of a roaring fire to dry. The bread. David's blue flannel shirt to be mended. Her own coat. Did she have enough lard and ash to make more soap?

Emily woke, squalling and thrashing, throwing off her blankets in double thrusts of kicking feet. Louisa bent over the open trunk at the foot of the bed. "Hello, little girl."

Gently she cradled Emily in her arms. Had David brought in enough wood? she wondered, opening her dress to calm Emily's outrage over having slept all night and woken to an empty stomach.

• • •

"I forgot to get the wood," David said to Tom. "What with all that fuss over Katy's braids..." The two men rode high on the wagon seat of Tom Mercer's defrocked Conestoga, taking the sway as they bumped along the stumpy, two-mile road into Seattle. The older man held the reins.

"Louisa will manage," he said, then scratched his gray side-whiskers and rubbed the end of his large, flat nose.

"But she's got that lame shoulder."

"That wife of yours is made of whalebone. She may be all the size of a half-pint, but she's got the determination of a man twice her size. She'll figure a way. Now hush up back there!" he hollered happily over his shoulder at the children.

Katy and two of the four Mercer girls were balanced atop aspen trees in the wagon bed, giggling and shrieking whenever the wagon hit a stump root and sent them sprawling.

"Tell me your spelling words," Tom said, twisting to see the children and hoping to discourage them from their play. "Mr. Denny and I will take turns drilling you."

Eliza rattled them off, counting on her fingers. "Mississippi, Spain, interpretation, encyclopedia, oxen, miscellaneous—"

"Whoa! Whoa!" shouted Tom. "Not so fast!"

The horses pulled to a stop and they all laughed.

"Can you beat that, Dave?" Tom said, shaking his head and clicking his tongue at the horses. "Go on! Giddyap!"

"You got the best team in Seattle, Tommy."

"I got the *only* team in Seattle. Giddyap!" The horses strained and the wagon jerked forward.

"Father, father! Stop! Stop the wagon! *Eliza's fallen off!*"

"Whoa!" Tom hollered again. "I tell you, these horses are going to think I'm plumb crazy." He jumped down to help Eliza.

David waited, listening to the comforting, soothing voice of his neighbor as he brushed his little daughter off and set her back up onto the timber load. It had to be a lonely life Tommy led, he thought.

"Now you hang onto your diapers," Tom cautioned the girls. He clambered up beside David and took the reins.

"You hang onto your horses!" quipped Katy.

"Mind your manners, Katy," said David. "Come on Tommy, let's go. I'm going to feel a whole lot better when I get into town and find someone to help me hunt down that cougar."

"We'll all help you," said Tom.

• • •

After lunch, and Emily down for a nap, Louisa tossed the last stick of wood onto the fire and sat down to mend her coat. As the fire waned she realized she was going to have to venture out and somehow haul in more logs. Already the cabin was getting chilly. But how? Her shoulder could hardly support the weight of an armload. Well, she would have to think of something or the fire would die.

She eased into her coat, mended as best she could, and headed for the door. *Whoa!* she whistled, throwing open the door and nearly colliding with a tidy pile of wood stacked hip-high in front of her. What? How? Stunned, she stood blinking, unable to believe her eyes. *What was this?*

A fairy godmother? But it was no fairy tale. A stack of chopped fir and cedar sat neatly piled on the step. But who? Why had she heard nothing? Questions flitted through her mind unanswered.

She scanned the clearing. No one. David and Katy's tracks blazed a trail to the right and north. Footprints to the left made a path around to the back, tromping the snow in a narrow trail.

She tucked her chin into her coat and stepped out, walking around the wonderful pile of wood to follow the southerly prints to the back of the cabin where they scattered up and down in front of David's woodpile. Big footprints. But at least this wasn't the Indians' *stick siwash.* Nor an Englishman's fairy godmother. This was real. Human. She followed the tracks, imagining herself to be a mountain man on the hot scent of a desperado. A helpful desperado with boots.

But who?

The tracks continued to the trail that led past the privy and out to the Mercer Road. Chodups John? His shack wasn't too far down the trail. Had he seen she needed wood? Maybe David had run into him on the way to Mercer's and had asked him to bring some around. Probably, but she returned to her own cabin for the pistol; the memory of the cougar was too fresh. Holding the gun carefully by her side, Louisa slipped back around and followed the tracks, curious as a cat. But the footprints vanished at the edge of the woods and she stood staring, disappointed, at the clear forest floor. The boughs were so thick overhead, no snow had fallen on the trail and the tracks ended. "Yoohoo!" she called out. "Chodups John! Hello?"

No answer.

She trudged on toward the shack, pistol cocked, eyes checking the overhead boughs. No cougar. But no Chodups John either. She called his name as she approached the cedar shack. She knocked politely on the wall because there was no door to speak of, only a flap of canvas.

The smell struck her even before she'd touched the canvas flap. Phew. The stink nearly knocked her off her feet. She gagged, turned her head, took a deep breath, and looked into the shack. Gunny sacks littered the floor along with scattered boxes and crates, rusty tin buckets and fishnet. Moth-eaten Hudson Bay blankets lay piled on the floor in the corner. Well, one thing was for certain: Indians did not live the way white folks did. *But what was that smell? A dead skunk?* Sudden shivers rippled down her spine. "Chodups?" she whispered into the gloom.

Against all common sense she entered, blinking in the dim light, heart thumping against lungs that could not draw a full breath. Danger oozed from the walls. "Chodups?" she whispered again, wondering why she didn't flee. He came into focus slowly, her eyes taking time to adjust to the darkened room. He lay atop the musty blankets. "Chodups!" she breathed out, thinking him sick and dropping to her knees to touch him, to waken him. But the stench assaulted her again and her hand hovered in midair. His chest was exploded wide open and she stared down into a cavern of blood and flesh and exposed bone. He'd been shot point-blank. Blood, frozen and dried, streaked from his nostrils and she whimpered, unbelieving, when she saw that his eyes were rolled back in their sockets, staring blankly at the ceiling over their heads.

Somehow she found her feet and stumbled out into the light of day. She had to hurry. She had to get away. *What was that?* A noise crackled in the clearing. A sharp crack! Wildly, she swung, pistol out in front. But no one advanced.

Crack!

Gunfire?

The pistol went off in her hand, a second explosive ring in the woods. A jackrabbit dashed across the trail, ears back. It had only been a tree bough snapping! She'd fired at a breaking tree limb! She dropped the pistol, hot in her hand. She could have killed someone, she could have. . . . She felt the earth reach up to catch her— No! I can't faint. Not out here. Oh, God, she whimpered, fleeing back over the trail the way she'd come, two hands over her mouth to stuff back the fright.

At home, safe in her tidy, sweet-smelling cabin, she ignored the stabbing pain in her shoulder as she hauled in the wood quickly, two and three logs at a time. Sobbing, she threw the bolt at last and dragged the table in front of the door.

"Oh, dear God," she groaned. "This is no cougar. This is murder. Someone has killed Chodups John!" She bit her fist to stem the panic surging into her throat. She must not scream. She must get ahold of herself. But she wept, great shuddering sobs, and dropped her forehead against the wall and beat with her fists slowly upon the logs, her fear and aloneness too raw to stem. "Please...please bring David home," she pleaded, groaning, twisting her head against the splinters. "Oh, God, I can't get through the day. I can't. Please, dear God, send David home. Please..."

-8-

In my life here my acquaintance with the natives has been quite extensive. From that experience and after due thought, I have arrived at the conclusion that they, not having the law and yet doing by nature the things contained in the law, are a law unto themselves. In other words, there is redemption for them— they will be not judged for what they do not know.

—David Thomas Denny, April 30, 1896

When David arrived home late that night, the table had been moved from the door and he entered slowly, his face drawn with weariness. A scratch lacerated his face. "No cougar," he said, hanging up his coat. "The rain has melted all the snow and we lost the trail." He struggled with his muddy boot.

"David, Chodups is dead," Louisa said evenly.

He dropped his boot.

"Chodups John, he's dead. I found him. He was murdered." She gulped and continued with difficulty. "Someone shot him. While he slept. There's a big hole in his chest. I think he's been dead a few days."

David sat in a rush. He hunched over his knees, and Louisa heard him groan, a long, gutting groan and she dropped to her knees beside him as great sobs shook his body. He wiped his hand across his nose, weeping, fighting to control himself. The depth of his grief shocked her; she had not expected it.

80

"Would God condemn him?" he suddenly asked, pinching his eyes shut and speaking words of anguish that she had had no idea haunted him. "For not understanding Christ's redemption?"

"I don't know, David, oh, I don't know..."

"Would David Blaine condemn—"

She thought he might bite his lip in two. Was this the burden he carried? Despair over the natives' dark spiritual state? How had she not known? Is this what drove him to understand, to seek out their friendship? To learn the Duwamish language? To hear their stories, their legends, their beliefs?

"Would the preacher condemn...my friend?"

"I don't know...David, there *is* only one way of salvation."

"Is there?"

She looked into a torn and anguished face.

"If Chodups—" But he couldn't speak.

She had no answers, and could not help him. Not knowing what else to do, she went to stir the soup. "He needs to be buried," David said, coming to stand behind her, "and if it's been any time, it ought to be done right away." His voice was empty, full of sorrow and fatigue.

"It's too cold tonight. Wait until morning. Please, David. Please don't leave me."

"All right, Liza. But come sit with me."

They sat in the rocking chair together, and the minutes passed quietly while they listened to the clock tick, the soft sound of the soup simmering, Emily breathing quietly in her bed, the sleeting rain slashing against the logs outside. Neither of them said much, both too weary with their different griefs.

Finally David shook his head and sighed. "I just thought of something. Chodups warned us of the renegades last year, remember?"

She twisted in his lap to see his face, watching the

shadows play across his cheeks, reflect in his tired eyes. "I remember."

"Do you suppose he was going to warn us of something again?" He drew her back into his arms. "Tell me about the white face Katy saw in the window last night."

"She told you?"

"On the way to Tommy's house this morning. I thought it was nothing—her imagination. But now I'm not so sure. Do you know anything about it?"

"I thought it was Curley—but Katy was right. It *was* a white man—the same man who was outside when the cougar attacked me last night. David," she said, slowly, fearfully, "there was somebody outside our cabin last night—when the cougar attacked me. I heard a grunt, someone breathing, like a struggle of some kind, but then it was very quiet."

His voice was tight. "What are you telling me? Do you think this same man killed Chodups?"

"No," she explained, "I'm telling you that there were two sets of footprints out there. An Indian's, and a white man's. An Indian killed Chodups John. But it was a white man who was lurking around our house."

"How do you know?"

"After I calmed down, I went out to look."

"You what!" He bolted forward, nearly spilling her off his lap.

"Shh!" she protested. "You'll wake Emily!"

"You went back outside after discovering Chodups was dead—murdered? You went outside when you knew a murderer was on the loose? A murderer and a cougar!"

"Don't yell, please. I couldn't very well stay in here, locked up and going crazy, could I?" she said, slipping free and standing to her feet. "When the rain started I went outside before all the footprints could be ruined. I had to! I had to know! I had to look!"

He pulled back his hair with both hands and stared at her. "I need to think," he said.

She set the table and turned up the lamp. The blanket she'd hung over the window reminded her of the long, terrifying afternoon, alone and searching for answers, remembering every sound, every breath of sound she'd heard, and then, finally, creeping out before the afternoon rain could erase the snowy footprints.

"So what all did you find?" he finally asked, staring at the fire.

"Two sets of tracks."

"And?"

"One belongs to an Indian, another a white man. One was moccasins, the other boots."

"You amaze me, Liza."

"The Indian was Snoqualmie. One of Pat Kanim's men. I could tell because the footprints were made with *yachit.* You know the kind, made with dog fur and beads? There was enough snow around the shack to figure that much out."

He nodded.

"Those were the only footprints anywhere near Chodups' shack. That's why I know it wasn't the white man who killed him. It was an Indian, probably a squabble of some kind. Chodups was always fighting with his gambling friends over those bone games. If Pat Kanim is still in town, I think you better tell him. As chief, he'll need to know."

"I'll tell him. What about the other tracks—the white man's?"

"Boots. Great big boots. They were out by the venison where the cougar jumped me last night. They ran back and forth between our door and the woodpile. They were all under the window. They went down to the beach. They were much bigger than any Indian foot could ever be. And whoever he is, he limps, drags his right foot."

"Like how big?"

She looked at his feet. "Maybe three inches bigger than yours."

"Liza! No one has feet that big!"

"Mr. Butler does."

"Mr. Butler!"

"David, please. Emily..."

They ate their supper and she told him of the wood on her doorstep, everything as it had happened, all her suspicions, her conclusions. "So we have two different mysteries," she said, summing it up. "A murderer, and a guardian angel."

"I believe the first," David said grimly, "but not the second."

"He brought me wood," she defended. "And chased away the cougar. He must be very kind—and courageous," she added. "Whoever he is."

"And snoopy."

"I don't think he means harm."

"And you think this snoopy guardian angel is Mr. Butler?"

"I only said the footprints are his size. I don't know who he is. That's all I can patch together. I'm missing too many squares to make the quilt."

"What's the matter, Liza?"

She looked down at her lap. Was she to cry after all?

"What else?" he asked gently.

"David, I took the pistol... I was afraid of the cougar..."

He glanced over to the mantel. "Where is it?"

"After—after I saw Chodups, I was... well, a tree bough snapped and I thought it was someone shooting at me and I shot back, only... only it was just a tree and I got so scared I dropped the pistol and when I went back to get it—oh, David," she cried, looking up at him and seeing his face in fractured prisms of light through her tears, "when I went back to get it, it was gone. It's gone, David! And I don't know who has it!"

He got up to clear the dishes, and when Emily fussed to be fed, he changed her diapers. "Maybe we better move," he said softly, handing her Emily to nurse.

"No, don't start this again."

"No?" He set the water to boil. "Why not? Any other woman—"

"I am not any other woman!"

"But Liza! The worry, the fear—don't lie to me! I can see it in your eyes."

"It has been awful." She would not deny that. "But don't you remember what I said last night?"

"About the board sidewalk and someone to deliver milk? Oh, Liza, don't smile. Nothing's very funny right now."

"No. But God has brought us to this place. I know that." She clenched her fist. "Over and over He has spared our lives. Do you think we can give up now, just because of some stupid Indian dispute?"

"It's not just an Indian dispute. It's murder. And what about this crazy man with the big feet, lurking around our cabin? And what about the missing McCormick?" He swung around to face her.

"Yes, I'm afraid," she whispered, answering his unspoken question. "I am very afraid." She looked down at Emily, nursing at her breast. "This afternoon I thought I might go mad." She felt the warmth of tears flooding her eyes again. "Will you kiss my forehead, David?" she asked, weary and sick and wanting only to be held. "It hurts. I ground it into the logs and pierced my poor skin with slivers."

"Oh, Liza . . ." His kiss was light, gentle, and she looked up to smile. "You are a beautiful, brave woman," he whispered in a husky voice.

"No, I'm not. Pray for us. Deliver us into God's hands for safekeeping, and then, my dear David, I shall be brave."

Part IV

DISTRICT COURT CONVENES
Monday, February 13

On February 13th of '54, the first term of court convened in the cookhouse. With the coming of the new governor, the machinery of federal law had been set up.

—Roberta Frye Watt, Katy's daughter

-9-

The separation from dearly loved friends, left far behind, wrought upon the mind of the pioneer woman to make her sad to melancholy, but after a few years new ties were formed and new interests grasped to partially wear this away, but never entirely, it is my opinion.

—Emily Inez Denny, Louisa's daughter

Seattle! They were here! Louisa poked her face out the wet, round hole of the popping canvas of Tom Mercer's wagon as David let the horses careen on down the last of the hill into town. With fingers hooked between the overhead hickory bows and the wet, snapping tarpaulin, she clung for dear life, wrenching her still-painful shoulder but not caring a whit. All around her the wind blew wild, a belting northeaster punching the Sound with fury. She could hardly miss such excitement!

The wind hit with stinging needles of rain and sleet. It bit her cheeks and sucked her hair from beneath her collar and sent it slapping into her eyes like heavy, wet lace. She shivered in the sudden violence of the storm, but the violence only heightened her excitement. Today was District Court! *And Catherine Maynard's tea party!*

It had only been a fortnight since the cougar attack and Chodups John's murder, and yet to Louisa the two weeks had seemed endlessly long, every forest sound magnifying the unresolved mysteries that nagged and begged for answers that apparently would never come. When David brought news of the tea party, a celebration for the women while court convened, Louisa had surprised them both by bursting into tears.

The wagon hit a stump root and dropped hard. "Emily?" But the baby, nine weeks old now and wrapped snugly in Hudson Bay blankets and wedged between pine boughs and comforters, was oblivious to the roll and tip of the slamming, bouncing wagon. Louisa stuck her face back into the wind, glorying in the thrill of horses plunging headlong downhill in the driving rain. Behind were the long, frightful days. Ahead was the tea party and, best of all, a few days in town while court was in session—days of smiling faces, shared secrets, children's laughter, a wonderful, happy, carefree holiday! The Lord, she was discovering, was good in the midst of trouble.

They came out of the woods, and the wind moaned as it escaped the trees, a high-pitched wail that nearly erased the whine of the ever-swirling saw down at the mill. The wind muffled the men's voices, the drum of rain picking at the mill's corrugated tin roof, the crackle of sparks spitting from the incinerator out back, the crash of waves pounding the beach ten yards away. The wind muffled the brakes and harnesses as David plunged past the McConaha cabin and the Latimer Building, and then skirted around back of the mill and cookhouse and veered the horses across the sawdust and onto the Spit. Louisa, caught offguard in the back of the wagon, nearly lost her footing when the wagon caught on the corduroy puncheons before settling into a steady clickety-clack underfoot, iron-wrapped wheels rippling over the soggy logs of Commercial Street.

There was only one street in all of Seattle. The puncheon road stretched south from the mill, across the Sag, and up an incline to the spit of land the pioneers called Doc Maynard's "Point." Lined up on both sides were Seattle's four storefronts, Doc Maynard's bankrupt Seattle Exchange,

David Maurer's Eating House, the blacksmith shop, and Captain Felker's hotel—the only building in town boasting a coat of paint. The street itself ended abruptly at the Duwamish Indian camp, a sporadic collection of cedar-bough shelters and open fires along a 16-foot south bluff.

"Hee! Clk, clk! Whoa-o! WHOA-O!"

"We're here, Emily," whispered Louisa. She bent over the bed of blankets and her baby. Anticipation raced ahead of her. "Just *wait* until your Aunt Mary Ann sees how big you've grown since the governor was here!" she whispered.

"You ready, Liza?"

David stood in the rain, peering in. He reached after the overnight pack they'd brought along and tied it onto his shoulders, and then scooped them both up in his arms. Louisa laughed, ducking her head over Emily and trying to keep the rain out of her own eyes. "You don't have to carry me to the door," she reminded him happily. "It's my shoulder that's lame, not my legs."

He chuckled, and she could feel the wonderful vibration deep in his chest. But he didn't put her down until he'd mounted the two steps to the Maynards' storefront. "I'll hold the baby and you knock," he said, surprising her with a delightful, wet kiss.

But no one answered their knock. "Come on," he said, pushing open the door. "Much longer out here and we'll be soaked to the skin."

The weather followed after them, spitting on the splintered floorboards of the store and howling about their heels like dogs on a hunt. David put her down and when he slammed the door shut, the silence was instantaneous. Only gradually did the sound of the wind return, seeping through the cracks of the log walls. The sleet pelted against the logs in soft, hushed strokes, and oozed through the loose chinking to bleed in drips to the floor.

The store was dark, and smelled of emptiness and sawdust. Where was everyone? Was there no tea party? "Catherine?" Louisa called out in the eerie, dripping quiet.

"Maynard?" David echoed beside her.

A plume of light leaked from a far door, and Louisa hurried forward to knock. The door swung open, revealing the Maynards' home, a 12-by-16-foot space created out of little more than half of the closed-down store. The room was empty, but brightly lit with several lanterns and candles, a welcome contrast to the darkened store in front.

"There's no one here," Louisa said, dismayed. A fire crackled furiously in the hearth. Odd...she thought.

David stepped in and lifted the lid off a large pot simmering on the stove and sniffed. "Mm-m. Liza, smell this. Cider, the real stuff. Thought you said this was a tea party."

"*You* said it was a tea party," she said, taking the baby from him. Emily slept through the shuffling of blankets, the drawing off of her soiled diapers. "No sense standing around here waiting for the mystery to clear up, David," she told him, laying Emily on the bed so she could take off her own hat and coat. "You probably ought to get those horses up to the smithy."

"Come here."

"Why?"

"Because you look so pretty standing there."

Almost shyly, she allowed him to pull her into his arms. Anna, her brother's wife, had once told her that after the babies start coming your heart quits thumping at your husband's touch. Stuff and nonsense, she thought smiling, burying her nose into her husband's cold, wet neck, heart thumping very hard. He kissed the top of her head, then bent to kiss the tip of her nose. He lay a trail of kisses down her throat like drops of melting ice.

"The horses, David. And the Maynards, where can they be?" she whispered between the kisses. "David. The horses...and remember, there's the tea party and people will be arriving—David!" she cried suddenly, pulling away. "Are you *sure* there's a tea party?"

The horror of such a possibility took hold in her mind, and she felt the threat of foolish tears. All the way in she'd hardly been able to contain her excitement; she was on her way to a party. She looked forward even to pretty Ursula McConaha's gossip. In her mind she'd gone through dozens and dozens of conversations. *Oh, the cougar? Why, it was nothing. It only wanted the meat ... Chodups John? Well, I expect that was a little harder. No, I don't think we need to worry, though. It was an Indian squabble of some kind. You know how he was with those bone games.*

"You better go on," she said, drawing a deep breath. Such generous gestures were expected of women. "Doc Maynard must be over at the cookhouse already. And Catherine, I expect, will be back shortly. Go on," she urged properly when she saw that he hesitated. "Besides," she added, "Tom will take a dim view if he hears tell you've left the horses in the sleet to freeze."

David hesitated at the door. "I'll come back," he said, smiling at her, concerned. "After getting the horses squared away. On my way down to the cookhouse, all right?"

When he was gone she was suddenly conscious of the storm, the strangeness of being in someone else's house uninvited. The wind whistled down the chimney and rattled the glass pane. Above her in the attic, something seemed to rumble. She spun around and listened intently, but heard only the cider bubbling on the stove, the fire crackling. No. Wait. A scrape? Nothing. Nothing, she told herself. She chided herself for her nervousness.

Emily lay asleep on the bed, and Louisa tiptoed over and bent to hear the tiny, sweet breaths. She stroked the fuzz that had begun to grow on her infant daughter's head and suddenly she was crying, all the tension and fear of the last two weeks pouring out in hot tears coursing down her cheeks. A loud thump startled her and she leaped to her feet and before she could catch her breath, someone screamed.

•　•　•

David took a deep breath and pulling down on his toque, he leaped from the old Seattle Exchange and landed in muck and mud on the cedar slab boardwalk. The horses neighed a welcome. Charley, the glossy black gelding, snorted and pawed the ground impatiently. Tib accepted David's apologetic caress on her velvet, snow-white nose. "Better get you in out of this," he said, clambering up on the wagon seat and releasing the brake.

"Hello, Collins!" he hollered, catching sight of the rounded shoulders of the road supervisor coming down the street. Luther Collins waved halfheartedly and turned the corner to Maurer's Eating House. I don't know why I bother being friendly to the man, David thought. Only got him a polite rebuke for his trouble.

"Hee! Clk-clk!" One block down and across the street he turned the team into the smithy's stable. The wagon jounced in its frame when he jumped down. Sawdust and mud absorbed the worst of the jarring in his knees.

"Fine day to be out!"

"Hey there, Lewis!"

A tall, dark-haired, muscular man had opened a side door, loosing a spray of light from the smithy. "Tom Mercer let you have his horses again, I see! Boy, ain't they something?" The blacksmith let out a long, low whistle in open admiration. "Where's Tom? He not come in with you for the court meeting?"

"Didn't want to bring his little girls out in weather like this."

"Didn't stop you none."

"Tommy Mercer doesn't have a wife who begged to come to Catherine Maynard's tea party. Here, help me with this buckle, would you?"

"Sure. Hello, Louisa!" Lewis hollered through the canvas.

"I already dropped her off at Maynard's."

"Oh. Hey, you hear about the crazy man Maynard found? Well, he's come back."

David slid the bit out of Tib's mouth. "What crazy man? What are you talking about?"

"A guy named Eddie. You haven't heard about him? Way out where you are?"

"That same fellow Maynard brought to the cookhouse the night the governor was here?" David asked, suddenly remembering the odd man who'd stared out the door after he and Louisa had gone up to Arthur and Mary's.

"That's the one."

"Louisa said she thought he looked a bit like he'd bumped his head on something and lost his stuffing."

Lewis chuckled. "That's him all right. He's missing a few nuts and bolts."

"What's that supposed to mean?"

Lewis leaned over the back of Charley and crossed his arms, looking at David over the span of horses in the semi-dark. "What would you call a man who doesn't know any better than to bite the hand of them that feeds him?"

David slid the bridle off Tib's head, wondering at the trembling in his fingers. "So, who is this man?"

"We call him the crazy man," said Lewis, scratching his head for a minute. "A bona fide idiot. Doc Maynard found him out on the beach New Years. He and Catherine were out for a walk, even if it was near freezing, and they came across him down by the Indian camp—a white man without so much as a coat or hat. Rags around his feet, and so hungry he was eating mussels raw, right off the rocks. And crazy? Crazy as a loony bird, a harmless, overgrown idiot— well, you saw him. Maynard took him on home and amputated a toe before the gangrene got him. The night the governor was here was the first time, I think, Maynard had the man up and around. But the guy run off without so much as a how-do-you-do."

"That very night?" David asked, unwanted connections falling clumsily together in his mind.

"Yup." Lewis pulled up and began unhooking the harness. "Oh, he shows up now and then. Maynard quit worrying about him a long time ago—he runs off, but then keeps turning up like a bad penny. This last storm brought him stumbling back in pretty bad shape, though. Maynard says he may have to cut off a few more of his toes."

They guided the horses out of the harness, then into the back of the stable where it was dark, but dry. Together they rubbed Tib and Charley down. David's fingers throbbed from the cold. His heart raced with the news. Was this the crazy man, he wondered, who'd followed him and Louisa out to Arthur and Mary Ann's that night? And what about the tracks around their cabin? The large bootprints? The man, if he remembered right, was as big as Butler, if not bigger. Were those *his* prints Louisa had seen? But why? he wondered, running the curry comb over Tib's neck and flank.

"What do you make of a man who disappears like that?" said Lewis. "No one knows where he goes, or what he does, or how he manages at all."

It had to be, David thought, returning to the wagon to get the feed Tommy had thrown into the back. This crazy man had to be the face Katy had seen in the window, and the fellow who had brought Louisa the wood and chased off the cougar. Yet none of it made any sense.

"Here, let me get that," said Lewis, swinging the sack up over his broad shoulders. "You're too cold and wet to fool with this. Go on inside and get warm. I'll be along shortly."

David didn't argue. Shivering, he stumbled over the high threshold into the bright, hot room that was the smithy. The log walls were cluttered with tongs and shovels and saws and crowbars and shears. He beelined for the forge and ripped off his gloves. February. The flowers ought to be in bloom.

"You don't suppose he's the missing McCormick, do you?" he asked when the blacksmith entered.

"Nah." Lewis pulled up a stool and settled before the forge where the light played over his rugged young face, the heavy beard and black, sparkling eyes, and quick, flashing smile and straight, even white teeth. "Says his name is Eddie Moore."

David shrugged. "But can he be trusted to give the right name? If he's as crazy as you say he is . . ."

"You're pulling at straws," said Lewis.

"I suppose." David prepared to go. "Thanks for taking the horses. They be all right here for a few days?"

"Sure. But do you think Tom would mind if I took Tib out to Nagle's come morning? Got to take him an order of ten-penny nails. And you know me—never was one to resist showing off when I could."

"If showing off is your business, it's going to be all circus and no crowd way out there."

"Darned if you ain't right." Lewis pumped the bellows, eyeing carefully the burst of flame. He poked an iron into the fire. "Nagle and nothing else in that neck of the woods. 'Cepting maybe skunks and cougars. Never did find that one that jumped your wife, did you?"

"No. If you see it on your way out, do us a favor and shoot it."

"Will do. You staying with your brother tonight then?"

"McConahas'. Not much room with Arthur and Mary Ann anymore."

"Ah-h. No room in the inn. Don't know though," said Lewis, grinning slyly, "if putting up with that Ursula McConaha is going to be much better!"

David laughed.

Outside the rain had turned to snow. So much for flowers, he thought grimly.

-10-

Dr. Smith's arrival must have inspired the pioneers in their dreams of city building, for he came enthusiastic over the rumors of Congressional appropriations for the exploration of railroad routes across the continent. If one route terminated at Puget Sound, as it seemed reasonable that it would, Dr. Smith felt, after considering all of the little settlements, that Seattle was the logical terminus for such a road. He even went so far as to choose what is now Smith's Cove as the point where the railroad would touch the Sound, and took up his claim accordingly, away out from the other settlers.

—Roberta Frye Watt, Katy's daughter

Dr. Henry Smith looked up from his soup to see Luther Collins shuffle through the door of Maurer's Eating House and plant himself on the bar stool. David Maurer, the German proprietor, polished the insides of a dozen whiskey cups with the end of a badly stained tea towel. "Goot eefning, Collins!"

"When you getting pictures for this place?" Collins barked. "How about a bawdy lady—like the one they got in the eating house down in Olympia!"

Maurer did not respond, just smiled. He stood behind his bar, a long shelf of split cedar propped on top of oak whiskey barrels. Collins draped his long, booted legs around the bar stool post and leaned in. "Gimme a beer before I go over to the cookhouse. What do you think?" he asked, hitting the backs of his fingers against a newspaper on Maurer's splintery counter. "Think Omar is going to cross the Danube?"

"I hope dot he vil not," said Maurer. "It vill be var in Europe."

"No it won't," said Collins, rubbing beer foam from his red mustache. "The Russians know better than to—"

"Don't be so sure," said Henry, speaking up, his youthful, clean-shaven face suddenly serious. "England and France are both committed to the Ottoman Empire and the Russian czar is getting downright nasty. Bad news is just around the corner."

"Rubbish," said Collins, not turning around.

Henry laughed; he could always count on Luther to be churlish.

Two sailors in a far corner mumbled, one upping his ante. "Bet my dime the czar wishes he could back out and be done with it," said one, "but his pride won't let him now that the Turks have posted their notice."

"Who the deuce? Plummer? That you?" Henry asked, squinting in the half-light.

The captain of the *John Davis* tossed his cards onto the table. "Well, boys, looks like I'm done for the day." A slow chuckle came from his barrel chest. "Well now . . . if I wasn't drunk I'd say I was seeing Henry Smith across the room. That been you this whole time slurping your soup and ruining a man's concentration? You owe me a week's wages, Smith."

Henry grabbed his coffee and ambled over to the card game, feet gone stiff with the chill. "I don't believe it," he said, easing down into the chair a sailor had vacated. "What in tarnation are you doing, Plummer, way up here in the dead of winter?"

"No coal in San Francisco."

"So you're here to talk with Bigelow?"

"And Fanjoy and Tobin and Eaton. "I'm to pick up $24,000 worth of export."

Henry whistled. Then he laughed, green eyes dancing behind his glasses. "You're still looking at the wrong end of Elliott Bay, my friend. In Mox La Push you may find coal, but it's my end that's going to see the terminus of the transcontinental. And when that happens, then we're talking money." He eased his long legs out in front of him and rubbed a boot heel into the sawdust. "You heard, didn't you, that Tinkham's crossed Snoqualmie Pass?"

"That don't mean a hill of beans. Jeff Davis is not about to let the railroad go through country north of Dixie."

"It's not a matter of territory," said Henry firmly. "It's a matter of feasibility. Not only do the mountains at our back pose no problem, but the entire route from Lake Superior to the Pacific is described as fertile and well-adapted for settlement. The case is not so encouraging for either of the other proposed lines. The Central line zigzags through barren stretches of land where fuel and water are scarce. The Texas route lies right along the Gila, and that craggy gorge certainly can't be used for a railroad bed—unless it crosses the border into Mexico and makes a long stretch through a canyon not our own. When you look at the whole," said Henry, nursing his coffee and ignoring the amused expression in Plummer's face, "none of these inconveniences attach themselves to the northern route. Stevens has tracked it all the way through. It runs right through a highly productive territory, well-wooded, and well-watered, to say nothing of it being the shortest in length—and has at its western terminus, as we all know, the noblest harbor in all the world. The only objection that can be raised is the accumulation of snow in winter. Yet the railroads in the East encounter much worse snow all the time. They make it, don't they?"

"You're going off half-cocked because you got yourself a worthless piece of land, Henry, all full of rocks and stumps.

You don't know how else to redeem yourself," said Plummer, laughing easily.

But Henry only smiled, slender fingers thumping patiently against his mug. "You going to have time to come see all those rocks and stumps? And my mother before you head back?"

"Might if you tell me your sister is still living with you."

"She is."

A gentle smile appeared on the captain's face. "Going to have to give up sailing someday and settle down," he said, shoving his empty shot glass to the end of the table. "Maurer!"

"You might as well," said Henry, watching David Maurer measure two fingers. "John Chase does an admirable job of running that mercantile of yours, but it'd be a lot more fun to have you around to rib. He hasn't got your sense of humor, Plummer. And Ellender, you know, can't hold off all these bachelors around town forever, waiting for you."

"Hey, what's going on?" asked the captain.

David Maurer began shooing everyone out the door as he slid into his jacket.

"District Court. Guess it's time to go."

"District *what*?" Plummer crowed, choking quickly on his freshly filled Jack Daniels.

"Don't be such a snob. We're a real territory now. We're holding our first District Court—down at the cookhouse." Henry headed for the door and his coat. "Want to tag along?"

Captain Charles Plummer followed, still coughing. "Maynard still Court Clerk?" he asked. "Where is the scoundrel anyway?"

"Nursing a crazy man, I hear."

Plummer let that one slide by. Could be another of Henry Smith's practical jokes and he wasn't going to fall for it. "So what's the bad news?" he asked seriously.

"What bad news? Oh, would you look at that," Henry

said with disgust, standing on the stoop, hands in his pockets. "It's snowing."

The two men tromped into the weather, grabbing their coattails and sucking in their breath when the wind smacked them in the face.

"Oh! You mean my comment to Collins!" shouted Henry, chin down. "About the Eastern Question?"

Plummer nodded.

"Omar did cross the Danube!"

"So it's come down to war, has it?"

"Omar's 18,000 up against Parlot's 9,000! A three-hour combat with bayonets, the *New York Times* says! But the Turks maintained their own apparently! The Russians lost several officers...about 130 privates, I think, and about 500 wounded! Looks like Prussia and Austria are going to jump into the fray, along with England and France. It's going to be all of Europe at war before we know it!"

Plummer didn't catch all of it, but enough. "Does it ever strike you," he said sadly, tromping alongside the very tall pioneer, "that all we ever do in this world is wage war?"

"Not the ladies, Charles! Do remember the ladies!"

The captain nodded. "Why do you suppose that is, Henry?"

•　•　•

Across the street Louisa lunged for the rifle hung over the mantel and pointed it to the door. Nothing happened. The clock ticked in the silence. One o'clock. *Hickory dickory dock, the mouse ran up the clock.* She dared to take a breath in the quiet, and then broke open the chamber. The loud click frightened her. But the gun was loaded and ready to go. She edged toward the door, sliding her feet, knees trembling. Another shout broke the heavy silence. Not the door! The attic!

She skirted the bed, heart pushing against her lungs. She struck her shin against a stool in her rush to get to the ladder that climbed the log wall to the large hole in the corner of the ceiling. "Catherine!" she gasped, stunned to see Catherine Maynard's pretty face peering down at her over the edge.

"Goodness gracious! Do put that gun down!"

"Catherine—what in the world are you doing up there?"

"Louisa Denny! It's my house," replied Catherine. "What are you doing down there?"

-11-

For a long time the Pioneer & Democrat *of Olympia, Washington, one of the earliest newspapers of
the northwest, published an advertisement in its col-
umns inquiring for [Wm.] Montgomery McCormick,
sent to it from Pennsylvania.*

—Emily Inez Denny, Louisa's daughter

Skirts bunched, Catherine swung out a boot in search of a
hold. "We must have scared you half to death, Liza!"

Yes, thought Louisa, standing aside to let the doctor's
wife back down the ladder and step onto the floor, *you did.*
She gawked hesitantly up through the hole. "Doc Maynard
up there?"

"Yes, with our crazy man," Catherine explained. "Stumbled back home yesterday. No, don't be alarmed. He's
harmless. I'll tell you all about him in a minute, but right
now, give me that gun before one of us blows the other's
head off. Where's David?" she asked, replacing the rifle
over the mantel.

"He took the horses up to the smithy. You don't mind that
we let ourselves in? The sleet—"

"Of course not. You could have been out there all night
and we'd never have heard you. Goodness, can you believe
it's February? You don't suppose someone played a big joke
on us, do you, and turned back the calendar? Come, what
am I thinking? You look plumb worn out, and you must be

104

frozen clean through. Sit down and let me get you a cup of hot cider before all the other ladies arrive."

So there was to be a tea party after all, Louisa thought, gratefully sinking into the chair by the fire and accepting the hot cup Catherine put into her hands. "You're not having any?" she asked, amazed as always at how pretty Catherine Maynard was, and how calm.

"No. I want to hold this dear, sweet little thing," she said, leaning over the bed to pick Emily up and give her a kiss. "And I must catch you up on all that's been happening."

Catherine filled her in, beginning with New Year's Day and the discovery of the crazy man, Eddie Moore. "If you could just see him," Catherine said, "it would break your heart. He keeps running off, but it's gotten so he figures this is home. Last night when he came in, his feet were so frozen he could hardly hobble. The pain is unbearable, and Doc says we're going to have to amputate three more toes—just as soon as we can get more laudanum from Henry Smith. Mr. Butler lent him some boots, but Eddie took them off this last time out and lost them somewhere. Said they hurt his feet, and now the frostbite is worse than ever. Poor soul doesn't know what's good for him."

It didn't take Louisa long to put the missing pieces together. "Does he limp—drag his right foot?"

"Why, I guess he does. He was having a hard time getting used to having no little toe. Come in," she called when someone knocked on the door. David slid in.

"You *are* home, Catherine," he said, smiling, relief written all over his face.

"She was out at the privy," said Louisa, teasing.

"I was not!" Catherine laughed, and leaned over to smack Louisa's knee. Doc Maynard clumped on down the ladder.

"Well, well, if it isn't David and Louisa," declared the jovial pioneer. "Oops, did I wake the baby?"

"No, no," said Louisa, reaching for Emily. "She's probably hungry. It's past her feeding time. Shh, shh..." she whispered.

"Then I guess we better make ourselves scarce, huh, Dave, my boy? You ready to go over to the meeting?"

"Whenever you are."

"But Doc Maynard," Louisa protested. "What about—" she almost said "the crazy man." "What about Eddie Moore?"

"If you ladies keep your voices down he ought to sleep right through your little party. He's got enough opium and bourbon in him to sleep 'til judgment day."

"Is this the crazy man Lewis was telling me about just now?" asked David.

"Must be," said Maynard, winding his scarf about his neck and knotting it in the back. "Unless we got two idiots running around these parts. Snowing out there yet?"

"He's not Montgomery McCormick?"

"Nope. Should he be?"

"Would be nice."

"Well, he isn't. And I don't want you to worry your pretty little head about him, Louisa," Doc said. "We'll take him down to Fort Steilacoom just as soon as we can. The army— what there is of it—can worry about him down there. But for now he's sleeping like a baby. Who's that?" he muttered, jamming on his raccoon-tailed cap. "Why, Sally Bell! Come in! And what is this?" he asked, greeting the tiny, frail woman who stood at the door with her four little girls lined up behind her skirts.

"A pot of beans," said Sally, smiling shyly at the doctor.

"No, no. I meant this lovely new ribbon in your hat!"

•　　•　　•

"So where'd Collins go?" Henry Smith asked, poking his head into the cookhouse door. "Plummer, did we, or did we not, see him and Maurer headed this way?"

"They'll be along shortly, I'm sure. Hurry up, man," said Captain Plummer, "it's no picnic out here!" The wind whined about their ears, and when Henry pushed the door open, the wind blew them inside. Henry took off his fogged-up glasses and stood squinting. Several clusters of out-of-focus men were lounging about the hearth and stove, boots tossed off, frozen toes curled painfully to the heat. They seemed to be in various stages of finishing the last of their stew and cornmeal biscuits and pie. Fresh sawdust had been scattered over the floor, and a table and chairs had been set up at one end of the room, including a roped-off section of 12 chairs for the grand jury. Pretty fancy, Henry thought.

"Shut the door!" one of four strangers by the fire hollered.

"Sorry," Henry apologized, leaning his back against the door and sliding his glasses back on. "So who might you be?" he asked.

The one who had spoken stood and stretched out his hand. "Edward Lander."

"Ah! The Chief Justice!" Henry exclaimed, pumping the hand of the man who'd been appointed to his position the year before by President Pierce. "So you're here for the District Court! Glad to make your acquaintance, and welcome to Seattle! Looks like we might be a bit early?" he asked, putting out his hand to the other gentleman.

"A bit, but the fire is warm." Edward Lander introduced both Henry and Plummer to the prosecuting attorney, J.S. Clendenin, and then the other three attorneys brought in from around the territory to preside over the first session of court. "Elwood Evans, Frank Clark, and William Wallace," said Lander.

"Begory, but you ain't never *seen* the West till you seen Elliott Bay!" exclaimed one of the pioneers by the stove. Henry glanced over to where five or six settlers had congregated about a newcomer, toasting their toes and the newcomer's health. "Why, if'n it's yer health you're after," Frank Matthias offered, "Seattle's the right place to settle. The Indians around here don't never die."

"And you can take that as gospel truth from a squirrel-eating alligator," said Henry, laughing hard and going over to shake the man's hand.

"Name is Cherry." The newcomer held out a big fist. "Dr. Cherry. Same story go for the white folks around here?"

"They almost don't never kick out," said Frank without skipping a beat, "except from lead poisoning in the back or an arrow in the neck."

"Is this God's truth?" asked Dr. Cherry.

"God's truth," swore Henry.

"And it's a good thing, too," said Doc Maynard blowing through the door with David and tugging off his snow-covered scarf. "Why, this country is so healthy we don't dare put a white man in the ground for fear he'll come to, breathing again, and fight his way out of the grave!"

Judge Lander chuckled, and ripples of laughter passed around the room. "Say, what's going on today?" Dr. Cherry asked. "Things looked pretty polished."

"District Court, our first session," said Henry, fishing in his pocket and picking out a two-bit piece. "Hey, Yesler!" he hollered, grin on his face and heading toward the kitchen.

"You don't have to yell," grumbled the 40-year-old man, coming out to lean in the doorway. He wore a bloodied apron and carried a butcher knife. He rubbed the back of his hand under his nose. The blade flashed. "You boys are going to have to clean your plates," he complained. "Court's in half an hour and I want it spiffy in here. You want something, Henry?"

The young doctor held the two-bit up to the light and made some ado of looking through a hole that had been pierced through the middle.

"Hey, you smell a rat, Dave?" Doc Maynard asked, amused and eyeing Henry carefully.

Henry ignored him and blew through the hole while every man in the room watched, curiosity ripe. "You got a hammer and nail, Yesler?"

"Who's the poor chap this time, Henry?" David asked him.

"Don't know what you're talking about." But then Henry chuckled and winked. "Collins, if I can catch him."

"If that's the case," said Yesler, "hammer's on the shelf by the door."

The cookhouse was comfortably full by the time Luther Collins and David Maurer finally arrived, oblivious to the careful pauses in conversation and the cursory glances as they made their way to a spot by the hearth. Men smiled, waiting for Collins to spot the two-bit piece nailed to the floor in a prominent place in front of the fire. Would he try to snatch it up? Waiting for the duck to take to the water, Judge Lander opened the first session of court with the resounding snap of his gavel, smiling.

-12-

Even in those days of privation, the feminine love of the beautiful and personal adornment could not be entirely quenched. One among them, Mrs. Bell, always managed the dainty touch that is so dear to the feminine heart.... One day, she appeared in a lace cap trimmed with new blue ribbon. Where did she get the blue ribbon? They all knew only too well the limited stock of her refinery. She did not bring it with her and there were no shops to buy from. Where did she get it?

—Roberta Frye Watt, Katy's daughter

"I say, Sally Bell, just where did you get that blue velvet ribbon for your old lace cap?"

"Ahh, Louisa, she's such a fine baby," said Sally Bell, ignoring Ursula McConaha. "Does she cry much?"

"No," said Louisa, staring at the blue ribbon in Sally's hat. Where *had* Sally gotten such a pretty ribbon? she wondered.

"My, my!" laughed Ursula. "Sally is not going to tell *any* of us her secrets!"

Catherine Maynard's tea party was clearly a success, and Louisa wandered the room holding Emily, greeting old friends, her face flushed with excitement, proud to be showing off her baby and happy to see everyone—Mrs. Phillips, Mrs. Horton, Mrs. Yesler, Mrs. Butler, Elizabeth

Livingston Brannon, Mrs. Matthias, Kate Blaine, Mrs. Collins and Lucinda, Mrs. Smith and her daughter Ellender, Mrs. Holgate, Abbie Jane Hanford. One by one they had arrived in bundles of old feathered hats and out-of-style dresses made over with bits of lace to make them "new," traipsing in the sleeting snow and mud, bidding goodbye to husbands and fathers and brothers. The old store quickly filled with greetings and chatter and laughter—and smoke because the wind, worse than ever, rattled down the chimney of the cranky, potbellied stove.

"Don't worry about the mud—or snow," Catherine Maynard assured time and time again as the ladies lifted skirts and apologized, not sure where to wipe their feet. "There's no need to wash the likes of this floor. Can you believe it's February? Come in, come in! You'd think this was Ohio!"

Little girls hung about their mothers' aprons while a little boy got in the way, ogling the food as it was brought in and unwrapped and set on the old store shelves pushed out of the way, against the walls. Catherine Maynard had not planned just a tea party, but a wedding feast. "Elizabeth Livingston was married to Bill Brannon last month," Mrs. Butler explained to Louisa, fanning her face with a dusty, wrinkled fan, "and we haven't had a chance to do a proper shivaree. After court the men are all coming up to supper. Later on in the evening, we'll have a dance."

"But I didn't bring anything," Louisa protested, looking around for Elizabeth. "David didn't tell me!"

"It doesn't matter," Catherine assured her.

"You got that ribbon at Plummer & Chase!"

"Looks like she's at poor Sally again, Mary Ann," said Louisa, helping her sister off with her coat and greeting the children as they came romping through the door.

"Who?"

"Ursula McConaha. She's been badgering poor Sally Bell unmercifully about that blue ribbon in her hat." Louisa patted Emily's small back, amused and pleased to see Mary

Ann staring with curiosity, like the rest of them, at the blue ribbon.

"Doc Williamson's then?" guessed Ursula. "No, no. He sells only hardware and calico bolts."

"Where *did* she get it?" asked Mary Ann.

Mrs. Phillips, beside them, chuckled and tickled Orrie's chin. "May I hold him?"

"Thank you," said Mary Ann, smiling in relief. "But let me know if he gets too heavy."

"Now I know I've seen that same color somewhere before," said Ursula, her own baby on one hip, braid hanging down her back, her two other children chasing each other in circles around her skirt, shrieking and laughing and tugging Ursula almost off her feet whenever they grabbed for her dress to reverse the direction of their chase.

"I don't think she's going to leave Sally alone," said Mrs. Phillips, kissing Orrie's little neck. Orrie giggled and lurched backward, trusting Mrs. Phillips to hold on to him.

"I think you're right," Mary Ann agreed.

"Elizabeth!" Louisa called, catching sight of the young, pretty Englishwoman from Alki and drawing her into their conversation. "When do you and Bill leave for the White River?"

"As soon as this dreadful weather lets up," Elizabeth answered, her Yorkshire accent a quick polka in Louisa's ears. "I'm anxious to go. We've been staying in Latimer's boarding-house." She grimaced, wrinkling her nose so that she made Louisa and the others laugh. "Bachelors!" she whispered, rolling her eyes. "They are nothing more than pigs!"

"Mary Ann Denny!" exclaimed Ursula, joining their circle. "Your husband must be hiding blue velvet ribbons in that commissary of his—and not letting on to anyone but the Whigs!"

"Blue velvet *and* Blue Ruin!" snapped Mrs. Butler, overhearing, fanning away at her face. "I hear tell Arthur Denny has put away ten barrels of Blue Ruin for Captain Felker Saturday last."

"Two," corrected Mary Ann with a smile. "And he happens to be *storing* it, not selling it. He's an ardent tee-totaler—as you all know."

"Arthur Denny and my husband—and yours, Louisa," Ursula said, including Louisa with a quick tap on her arm, "are men of highest principle. Although in the case of my husband," she said suddenly, dropping her voice to a confiding whisper, "it has not always been so. In case you ladies didn't know it, he used to drink absolutely outrageously." She glanced around for any sign of Catherine. "Like Doc Maynard," she whispered, voice low.

"No!" came the chorus of stunned and shocked voices.

"Yes, can you believe it? But now he's been elected to the Council!"

"Hello, Liza."

"Anna!" cried Louisa, turning around to greet her sister-in-law. "Did you just come in?"

"No, we've been here awhile."

"How are you? Is Gerty here? Has she been doing any more drawing?" Emily squirmed in her arms and Louisa kissed her.

"I don't think so. Oh, she must be around here somewhere," sighed Anna heavily, jabbing a hairpin back into her blonde hair, caught tonight in braids wrapped around each ear. "Probably snitching those bonbons. She misses you. *I* miss you, Liza. It gets awful lonesome with you gone back to the homestead. Mary Ann doesn't have the time you did to come by for tea, or to help me with the darning. And you know Dobbins isn't one for talking."

"Now wherever did you get such a notion, Mrs. Blaine?" It was Mrs. Butler, and she sounded testy.

"Please. Call me Sister Kate," said the preacher's wife. Kate Blaine was holding her china cup and saucer with gloved hands, the only woman at the tea party with gloves. She was like a rose among weeds—with her mauve delane gown and gloves, and genuine morocco boots. Only Sally Bell came close to such finery with her worn-out lace hat decorated by the new blue ribbon.

"I don't even call my sister 'sister.' Now tell me, Mrs. Blaine, have you never read First Timothy chapter two? *Let a woman learn in silence with all submissiveness—*"

"*I permit no woman to teach or to have authority over men; she is to keep silent....* Yes, Sister Butler, I've read First Timothy chapter two. What has that to do with suffrage?"

"Anna," said Louisa, catching her sister-in-law's thin wrist. "Do we have another suffragist in Seattle? Or am I only hearing strange and glorious things?"

Anna's eyes brightened and for a moment Louisa caught a flash of the old Anna as she edged toward Mrs. Blaine, the happy Anna they had somehow left behind in Illinois. Together the two edged in on the discussion.

"It's quite clear to me," said Mrs. Butler, fanning her flushed face and speaking so rapidly that the little curls on either side of her cheeks bounced, "that the woman's place is in the home, not politics. If she is to be silently submissive to her husband, what need is there for her to vote? Instead of one vote, now there's two. Each side is simply doubled. Doesn't change a thing—the way I see it."

"But if she disagrees with her husband?" Kate Blaine persisted.

"And what wife doesn't? But that's the very point. A woman's got to back her husband—right or wrong. The vote would only tempt a woman to rub the pile the wrong way. Why, it would be sin to vote *against* her husband, stirring up trouble like that, breaking up the family over politics of all things! Surely you, a minister's wife, can see the sense of that!"

"One only has to read the Gospels," said Kate Blaine carefully, "to realize that Jesus would have disagreed strongly with the Apostle Paul—"

"But the Apostle Paul put it quite clearly. *I permit no woman—*"

"Precisely. He said *I*," interrupted the minister's wife. "Jesus did not say that. It was Paul's own personal opinion. And whose example are we going to follow? Jesus Christ's— or Paul's? Too, I suspect Paul meant something quite different than what it's been made out to mean. After all, Priscilla was the leader of one of Paul's churches—Ephesus, I think it was. No, perhaps I'm wrong on that."

"Wasn't it the Apostle Paul," blurted out Anna, "who wrote there is neither Jew nor Greek, slave nor freeman, male nor female, for we are all one in Christ Jesus?"

"Anna Boren," said Mrs. Butler hotly, "he was talking about *salvation* there, not political rights. You must not take verses out of context to prove your point."

Anna stiffened. The spunk in Anna had long since been buried by bitterness. If and when it came out, it came on the blade of a sharp tongue. Louisa hoped her sister-in-law would say no more.

She needn't have worried. Kate Blaine spoke sharply enough. "The Bible has been used out of context in order to *subject* women," she said. "Anna is quite right. Elizabeth Cady Stanton pointed out in her address to the Women's Rights convention in Syracuse eight years ago that when men can find no other argument, their last resort is the Bible. It has been interpreted—out of context, I might add—to favor the sale of liquor, endorse slavery, perpetuate capital punishment—*and* oppress women. But there is much in the Bible to support our equality. It's only been misinterpreted and made into 'God's truth' by men so that they may more comfortably continue their subjugation."

"Well," said Mrs. Butler in a proper huff. "And this is the woman we have teaching our dear little children? I suppose you disagree, Mrs. Blaine, with Martin Luther—the great founder of Protestantism? When he says that God made men broad in the shoulders and narrow in the hips so that they may rule over the woman, and that He made women narrow in the shoulders and broad in the hips so that they might better tend the needs of their husbands?"

"He said no such thing!" snapped Anna, green eyes flashing in her peaked face. "That's perfectly ridiculous!"

"He did too!" declared Mrs. Butler. "I read it in the paper just last week."

"Oh, those idiots," said Louisa, holding Emily tighter and laughing. "They've also quoted Martin Luther as saying God made Adam ruler over all creation and then Eve came along and spoiled everything. You're not going to take *that* lying down, are you, Mrs. Butler?" Louisa teased.

"Did he *really* say that?" asked Ursula, smacking George Jr. for yanking Katy's braid and making her howl. George pranced away screaming, and Emily woke with a startled cry.

"Now look what you've done!" scolded Ursula, swinging around to smack him again but he danced beyond her reach and she got little Ursula instead. "If Martin Luther really did say that, then I'm going to ask Bishop Demurs to convert me to the Catholic church, and right quick. Now you hush up your crying, little Ursula! Mama never meant to hurt you. Georgie!"

"Georgie Peorgie, pudding and pie—"

"Katy! That's enough!"

"But, Ma—he made me cry!"

Louisa turned and hurried through the crowded storefront to Catherine's "inner sanctum" where it would be quiet. Poor Emily, she thought, excusing herself from the clucks of sympathy and quick passing pats. *Poor thing is frightened out of her wits by all this noise!*

She must have screamed, but there was no reason. . . . She recognized him at once. His glassy eyes, pale blue and all liquid and glassy like a child's—like an old man's. His large, bulbous head, the round cheeks, the great liver spots all about his jowls and ears. Every head turned, the hush settling over the room like a snuffer on a candle. Only Emily wailed and Louisa stood clutching her baby, hardly daring to breathe. Right in front of them, just inside the door, stood the man from the cookhouse, the crazy man—her "guardian angel." Bandages covered both feet. Another wrapped his big head. Six-and-a-half feet tall, and he was as naked as the day he was born.

-13-

Edward M. Lander, who had been appointed Chief Justice of the new Territory by President Pierce, presided over this first district court....A wood fire in the stove made the place hot and stuffy. The room was crowded, for pioneers from all up and down the river settlements had come in, many with their clothes muddy and steaming in the heat. Indians hung around the outside staring curiously.

—Roberta Frye Watt, Katy's daughter

Quiet gradually settled in the cookhouse where the men had gathered for court. Doc Maynard, at the table with Lander and the other attorneys, shuffled through papers. Heads together, they conferred in whispers. David, on the end seat of the dozen chairs that had been arranged in the corner, watched Collins out of the corner of his eye.

The Chief Justice was a handsome man, with a clean-shaven face and a distinguished bearing. Despite the cookhouse's informal setting for a court of law, it seemed to David that the man commanded an atmosphere that spoke of a more ornate judge's chambers—not easily done considering that everyone was waiting for Collins, by the fire, to spot the coin.

"Please rise. The Honorable Chief Justice Edward M. Lander presides," said Maynard, Court Clerk.

"We already are," said Henry, and everyone snickered. "Since there's no place to sit down!"

"Well *we* aren't." Maynard glared, silencing the snickers. Those at the table and in the jury chairs stood. David stood.

Settlers, he realized, had come in all the way from Mox La Push to Salmon Bay, and their muddy, wet clothes were steaming in the heat of the stuffy room. He spotted Arthur, and was glad to see him. There was George McConaha. And Hillory Butler. Dobbins, too, was there. And the Indians, curious as always, were hanging about outside, looking through the windows, bundled and wrapped against the still-blowing storm.

David nodded at Curley in the open door and felt a sudden pang over Chodups John's absence. Maynard, ever the Indians' friend, caught a glimpse of someone he knew and waved. With steel-rimmed glasses now on, now pushed up on his forehead, now back down on his nose, he settled into his official position, fumbling through the last of the papers Lander slid his way.

The first item on the agenda was the swearing in of the impaneled grand jury. They sat in two rows of six, waiting in handmade chairs that creaked. Charles Terry was the foreman, and he sat in front and to the right, stroking his unruly black beard. An original settler, he was one of the few who had retained his claim at Alki, six miles across Elliott Bay. Just a year older than David, he owned what was left of the rival town. "A fellow by the name of Cherry," he whispered, leaning close to David, "standing next to Henry over there is thinking to buy in with me."

"Heard he was settling in Seattle," David whispered back.

"Nope. He's going to buy in with me."

The 12 jurors were William Bell, another original settler who had staked his claim on the Seattle side of Elliott Bay; Lewis Wyckoff, the blacksmith; E.A. Clark, a new settler—with a camera; S.B. Simmons, who had just opened a rooming house for the influx of bachelors and sailors; Frank Matthias, the carpenter; Charles Walker, another new man who lived near Luther Collins along the mouth of the

Duwamish; John Buckly and George Holt, bachelors from farther up the river; Timothy Grow, who worked for the Holgate and Hanford boys; H.H. Tobin and Dr. Bigelow from the Duwamish Coal Mine; and David.

Dr. Bigelow, a balding man with a bump in the middle of his forehead, had his chair propped back on two legs. David, sitting next to him, thought of Bigelow's coal mine, of the settlers it would draw. The room being uncomfortably stuffy, he loosened his shirt at the waist and neck and kept an eye on the open door where the cold air occasionally blustered its way through the crowd. After the initial minutes of being impressed, he was bored.

First there were the ballast charges against Captain Felker, then the swearing in of citizenship to Henry VanAsselt. They spent an hour debating what to do with the Indians who'd broken into Dr. Williamson's store. The two culprits, having already pleaded guilty, sat beside each other on the far end of the table, blinking and nodding as Maynard translated. David could hardly keep up, English legal terms incompatible with Duwamish simplicity. He wondered if the Indians could understand. Elwood Evans, the attorney from Olympia, defended them hotly, using legal jargon so successfully that he managed to muddy the issue until Clendenin, as prosecuting attorney, cleared it with more mumbo jumbo. Finally they reached a consensus. Maynard bent over the table to take the Chief Justice's dictation:

> We the undersigned are in favor of whipping the two Indians, cropping their heads and making them leave the place; forthwith, the said Indians having acknowledged breaking into and stealing money and goods from Dr. Williamson's store.

The official parchment was sent around for signatures and David added his "Hancock," wondering as he wrote how Louisa was doing. She had been through a lot the past few weeks and he was worried about leaving her at the Maynard's—with that crazy man upstairs. But he had to laugh. Here he'd been thinking to take Louisa away from her worries and somehow he'd managed to drop her right into the lap of the source!

• • •

"Baby?"

Louisa froze.

"Baby?" the giant man asked again.

He reached out one huge paw toward Louisa and Emily, and Louisa pulled the infant closer to her, the baby pressed against her thumping heart. She wanted to run, but couldn't find her feet and very nearly fainted when his hand lightly touched the child's head.

"Sad," he said, drawing the word out. "Sad baby..."

His voice, she realized, was like that of a child. Sudden pity filled Louisa's heart, and with it came courage. "The baby's not sad," she explained and behind her she could hear the other women shuffle, startled. "She's only just woken up. She's not sad."

In one fluid movement, Catherine moved swiftly past her, drawing the man back through the inner door, out of the storefront and into the Maynard's home. Louisa followed and closed the door behind her.

"Oh, what are we going to do!" cried Catherine. "The ladies..."

"He needs a blanket, for one thing," said Louisa, wits recovered. "How is it that he doesn't have any clothes?"

"He tore the last pair Mr. Butler lent him." Catherine pulled the comforter from her bed and draped it about the man. "I haven't had time to mend them yet. There," she said, laughing nervously. "Now he looks like Chief Seattle himself."

"His feet," said Louisa, looking down. Blood and puss stained the bandages. "Catherine, can we sit him by the fire?"

With Emily still crying in her arms, Louisa pulled the rocker close to the hearth while Catherine helped him into it. Someone knocked and Mary Ann's face appeared, peeking in.

"Liza? Catherine? Shall I send Katy for one of the men?"

"No, it's fine," said Louisa. "All the noise must have woken him up. He'll be all right in a minute. Catherine, get me that footstool and let's get his feet up. I don't like the looks of all this blood."

"Here, I'll do it," said Catherine. "You've got to get that baby hushed."

"Baby? Sad?"

Louisa paused to take a good look at the man who had stalked her cabin, intruding only when danger and hardship had lurked. "No, she's just frightened. Do you like babies, Mr. Moore?"

A sudden smile broke the man's round face, and he nodded eagerly, bobbing his great big head.

"Would you like to touch her?"

"Louisa!"

"Mary, it's all right," she said. "He won't hurt her. See?" She took the man's hand and showed him how to stroke Emily's cheek with the back of his finger. His sudden tears surprised her. He didn't even seem to know that he cried.

"She likes me," Eddie whispered, crying, staring down into Emily's squalling face while he softly stroked her smooth skin. "The baby likes me. Baby."

"Yes, she does," said Catherine kindly, standing behind him and gently rubbing his giant shoulders. "Mary," she said, "tell the ladies it's all right. He's just given us a scare. He means no harm. Oh, my," she sighed, looking at Louisa. "Whatever is to become of him? Didn't I tell you he'd break your heart?"

•   •   •

For another hour the jury debated who was going to do the whipping. Did such things always require all this painstaking discussion? David wondered, shifting uncomfortably on his chair and wishing they'd get on with it. He was anxious to get back to the Maynard's, to Louisa. He couldn't get his mind off the crazy man upstairs. Finally Maynard recorded:

> One Indian to receive 25 lashes by Hillory Butler.
>
> One Indian to receive 25 lashes by Dobbins Boren.

"Eh! It's my lucky day!" Collins crowed suddenly, stooping hastily and airily, and David looked up, grinning. "Two bits!" cried Collins, gloating. "Why, it ain't any fool who can pick up two bits so easily!" He bent to retrieve the coin, tugged, pulled, frowned, tugged again.

Howls greeted his failure to pocket the coin. The men hooted and hollered, and Luther's own words echoed around the room with guffaws. *It ain't any fool who can pick up two bits so easily!* Judge Lander sat back in his chair, demeanor lost, and laughter resounded around the room while Luther colored.

They dismissed court. There wasn't much point to it after that.

-14-

Now Mr. McConaha was a man of superior parts, and one I always held in the highest esteem. He had been previously addicted to the liquor habit, and I never saw a man make a more heroic effort than he did to overcome the habit.

—Arthur Denny, Father of Seattle

Pleasant, throaty laughter and tired voices called out to each other as the party at the Maynard's finally broke up well past midnight, couples and families each going their separate ways, bachelors lumbering off to the three boarding houses in town. Dogs barked. Somewhere a cat snarled and raced up a tree.

"It's just the Yesler's tomcat," said Ursula, seeing Louisa tense.

The sky was night-white, snow blowing hard. David and Louisa, along with Arthur and Mary Ann and the children, Dobbins and Anna and little Gerty, and the McConahas— little Ursula and George Jr. still at each other incessantly— stumbled through the driving snow.

"We're going to have to get that crazy man down to Fort Steilacoom, to the army," said Arthur. "We can take him with us, George, when we head down to Olympia for the legislature in a couple of weeks."

"What will the army do with him?" Mary Ann asked.

"I don't know. But left here, the man is only going to cause trouble."

The pioneer men, arriving en masse at the Maynard's after the court's adjournment, had been surprised, even alarmed to find the crazy man downstairs, rocking before the fire with Emily Denny in his gigantic arms. Louisa had defended him, but her story of his earlier kindness toward her had done nothing to relieve their concern. He was crazy, they said, who knew what he would do? And then during supper and the dance afterward the other women confessed to strange noises and odd footprints circling their cabins.

"But, Arthur," said Louisa, head bent into the snow, "he seems to only have hung around the cabins where there were small children—and babies."

"That's right!" said Anna. "Mrs. Yesler didn't complain of anything unusual, or Mrs. Holgate—or Abbie Jane!"

Arthur, carrying Orrie, pulled a blanket in tight around the baby's face for he had begun to cry. "All the more reason to worry."

"I don't think so," Louisa protested. "The man seems to love children!"

David took Louisa's hand to hold her back, letting the others go on. "What?" she asked, searching his face.

"I just want you to know," he said, his eyes dark and serious, "that no matter what the others say about all this, I think you've shown more Christian kindness than the whole lot put together, and I love you for that. You scare me sometimes," he added, "but I love you and I wouldn't have you any other way."

She smiled, grateful that he understood, and he kissed her. Louisa thought she might like to go on like this all night long, her husband's mouth gentle against hers, their baby between them in her arms, snow falling all around, wind snapping their scarves. But he took her hand again and together they hurried to catch the others. At the trail everyone said goodnight.

"Be careful," whispered Mary Ann, giving Louisa a kiss. "I'll see you in the morning."

"Yes, we'll all have tea, like the old days," she promised, kissing Anna, and then little Gerty. "You bring me your storybook tomorrow and I'll read to you. I promise," she called to the little girl.

"Hey! Collins!" George shouted, seeing Luther heading into the Latimer Building not too far away. *"Ain't any fool who can pick up two bits so easily!"* Louisa and Ursula, holding their babies, got the giggles.

The McConahas' house was dark and cold when they arrived, and once inside Louisa realized how exhausted she was. It seemed forever they stood in the dampness, not daring to move lest they stumble over the clutter that was apparently everywhere. George muttered oaths under his breath, tripping and skidding over toys and books sprawled between door and mantel. He swore when he collided with the laundry hanging from the ceiling.

"David?" Louisa whispered. She was so tired. Her shoulder throbbed, and it seemed too much to hear a man like George McConaha swearing, and over what? A little mess? She leaned backward into David's chest. His arms came around her and the baby, cold and wet, but strong.

"What is it?" he whispered.

She shook her head. It was enough just to feel his breath against her cheek, the quick brush of his wet beard, the strength of his hands on her shoulders, rubbing the one that hurt.

George's profile loomed out of the dark, match burning at his fingers. "Where's a lamp?"

"On the table," said Ursula. She still held Eugenia, asleep over her shoulder. George Jr. and little Ursula were told to run out to the privy.

"But, Ma!" they chorused.

"Now!" ordered Ursula sternly.

"But the *stick siwash* will get us!"

"That's why you go together!" hollered Ursula. "George, do something to make them mind!"

George only had to look once. They both scuttled fast, tripping over each other, more afraid of their father than an Indian legend.

"Ursula, you didn't bank the fire," said George quietly. "It's gone completely out."

"George! I didn't have time, and the baby—"

"Never mind, never mind."

"George! Put down that Bible!"

Was she seeing things? Louisa wondered in a panic. Ursula rushed to drop Eugenia on the bed and snatched the Bible from George's hands.

"God is going to punish you! And I'm as like to get a frying from the same bolt of lightning, you fool!"

"It's the only way to get the fire going fast." He grabbed her arm and snatched the Bible from her tight fingers.

"*George!*"

But he ripped out page after page and added them to the sputtering flame.

"Let me do it," David said quickly. "I can start a fire out of nothing."

In no time the fire was crackling and spitting and the children were back, Ursula nattering at them to get up to the loft.

"But it's cold, Ma!"

Louisa, numb through and through, both body and mind, automatically began the process of dressing Emily for bed. Ursula did the same with Eugenia. David, unasked, began to pick up the toys and put them into a crate. "Where does it go?" he asked when he was done.

"Under the bed. And thanks, Dave," said George.

"You'll sleep here with me," Ursula told Louisa, pulling down the sheets. She tucked Eugenia into a trundle. "The men can sleep on the floor."

"What about Emily?"

"I'll take care of her," said David.

Ursula said," Don't you worry a wink, Louisa. Right now you only need to think about getting into bed. You look all done in. Where's your things? I'll help you get undressed."

Louisa was too tired to resist and obediently let Ursula help her into her nightgown. It was a forced custom of the pioneers to dress and undress in mixed company, and George politely turned his back. She shivered when the nightie came down over her head, and waved Ursula away. The ties weren't important. She only wanted to lie down, to sleep, to rest. The day had been long, with unexpected surprises. A good day, but hard.

Ursula pulled the covers up. "It'll warm up soon enough," she said. David came to kiss her goodnight and he brushed her hair back with his fingers the way she loved. "Goodnight," he whispered, smiling tenderly.

"David?"

"Yes?"

"I love you."

He bent low to kiss her again. "And I love you. You go to sleep. I'll take care of Emily."

The sheets were ice-cold. But long after warmth worked its way into her bones, Louisa shivered. That poor crazy man, she thought while listening to the shuffle of feet, the quiet exchange of sleepy voices around her.

"Louisa, you awake?" Ursula crawled in beside her.

"Yes."

"What do you make of Elizabeth Livingston marrying the likes of Bill Brannon? And wanting to settle way up the White River? She told me tonight Captain Plummer thinks he can take them as far as Mox La Push next week. Why, you got to be out of your mind to be doing something like that, when you could be marrying the likes of Lewis Wyckoff— and staying in town." Ursula rolled to her side, shifting the mattress. "You ever figure out where Sally Bell got that delicious blue velvet ribbon for her ratty old hat? She says she didn't get it from Plummer &o Chase. Or Dr. Williamson's store. And your sister says it couldn't have come from Arthur's commissary, although I wonder."

"Quiet, Ursula!" hollered George from the floor.

The fire crackled in the dark stillness of the crowded cabin. Why, Louisa wondered, still shivering, had George burned pages out of the Bible? Did he think so little of the Word of God that he would burn it? And did he really used to drink as much as Ursula had led them to believe? She thought of Pa, homesteading in Oregon. "The wrong woman will lead a man to drink faster than a bad apple can spoil the barrel." But that wasn't fair. Ursula, despite her faults, was a good, kind woman.

The wind died down, but her ears had become accustomed to the continual howl and, as tired as she was, she couldn't sleep in the strange quiet. She wondered if it was still snowing.

"Hey! I just figured it out!" Ursula popped up suddenly, breaking the night. "That was no blue velvet ribbon Sally Bell wore in her hat! Why, she just cut a strip of the blue lining from the sugar barrels! That's what she did! I *knew* I saw that color blue somewhere before. *I declare!*"

Everyone but Louisa was asleep when Ursula padded over to the window in her bare feet.

"What is it?" she asked.

"If that crazy man isn't Montgomery McCormick, then who do you suppose Montgomery McCormick is?"

•   •   •

Clomp, clomp.

What was that? Louisa lifted her head off the pillow. Next to her Ursula sat up.

Clomp, clomp, clomp.

"And just where do you think you're going?" Ursula asked.

"I gotta go out to the privy, Ma."

"Not at this time of night, you don't."

"But Ma!" said little Ursula, stamping her foot with a loud clomp. "I gotta go!"

Louisa could see the child, boots on and unlaced, bare legs poking out, standing by the door and looking for all the world like a little waif shivering in her white nightie.

"I'll go out with her," said Louisa. "I can't sleep anyway."

"No, no, you stay put. I'll put on my shoes. Just a minute, darling."

"But, Ma! I gotta go! I can't wait!"

"*Ursula!*"

But the little girl was gone.

They heard the snarl just seconds before the long, anguished scream.

"URSULA!" both women cried, lunging for the door.

David was off the floor and out the door before he knew it, somehow grabbing a rifle on the way. The cougar raced through the moonlight for the woods, powerful legs flying over the snow. Little Ursula hung from his mighty jaws, caught between his teeth, her little arms and legs flailing backward, bouncing off stumps and snow. Her mother raced screaming after them, barefoot.

"Get her out of the way!" David yelled, throwing the gun to his shoulder. Oh, God, he prayed, sight pointed on the base of the cougar's skull, moving up as the panther raced. He didn't know that he pulled the trigger. The cougar somersaulted, landing in a heap ten feet further away. Little Ursula flew headlong into the ground and was still.

By the time they got to her, blood pooled the snow. David fought the others off and lifted the child in his arms and raced back for the cabin. "George! Get Maynard! NO! Henry! He's down at the Latimer Building! It's closer!" he cried, wind searing his lungs. "Louisa, get a lamp lit—and the fire hot," he commanded once he was inside, conscious that his own baby was crying from the floor, that little Eugenia had tumbled from her trundle bed and was wailing in a corner, that George Jr. hung off the ladder in his long johns gaping, and that his own long johns were hot and wet with blood. He lay little Ursula on the bed. Her throat had been torn open, blood spurted from the jugular. He set his fingers over the wound, feeling for the vein. "Oh God in heaven," he moaned. There, the base of her jaw. He could feel the feeble hammering; he pressed and prayed and kept on pressing and praying. "Liza, get a blanket. Quick." He saw the pathetic little feet, one boot still on and unlaced, a bony ankle poking out the top, the other foot all bare and blue. "Ursula, rub her feet and hands. Oh, God," he groaned, praying, when the child's eyes flew open.

"Ma!" she gurgled.

"Baby! Darling! Mama's here!"

Then Henry Smith was there, leaning over the bed, feeling for her pulse. Gently he probed around David's hand where his fingers still pressed the jugular. "No," David said when Henry reached up and folded the child's eyes shut.

"She's gone, Dave."

Ursula fell over her child, weeping, sobbing.

David could not let go. Louisa was there beside him, pulling him away. Dazed, he looked up into George's blanched face on the other side of the bed. He could no longer feel hammering under his fingers. Blood continued to drain from the small, torn throat, but not in spurts anymore. Slowly he released his pressure and the blood flowed only a little faster. She was dead.

He let Louisa lead him out of the cabin where he stood retching into the snow, dripping the little girl's blood from his fingers. George pushed past.

"George?" But his friend ran on, pistol in one hand, rifle in the other, snow flying behind his heels. "GEORGE!"

George did not stop until he came to the heap at the forest edge, then firing, he emptied both guns into the dead animal. "GOD!" he cried, face to the snowing sky, empty guns hanging from his hands. "GOD! MY LIFE! NOT MY CHILD'S! *MINE!*"

David did not know that he had any strength left, but somehow he reached George and pulled the anguished man into his arms. Louisa brought them blankets and then left them alone as George wept in the wet, silent snow.

Part V

WILLIAM YOUNG IS MISSING
Early March

In March the pioneers had their first un-happy experience with the Indians. William Young, the engineer in the new Terry-Renton sawmill at Alki, went to Whidbey Island accompanied by Indians and failed to return.

—Roberta Frye Watt, Katy's daughter

-15-

Saturday, March 4

Shortly after court was adjourned, George McConaha and Arthur Denny set out in a canoe—always in a canoe—to attend the first session of the legislature. Both Democrats and Whigs watched the slim canoe, manned by Indians, disappear around Duwamish Head bearing Seattle's first representatives to Olympia.

—Roberta Frye Watt, Katy's daughter

After little Ursula's death the court met for another two days, soberly going through the routine and then adjourning until October. Nothing much was accomplished, but the law of the federal government had been set into motion.

A week later Arthur and George left for the legislature, a cold, drizzly, Thursday morning, the rain long since melting the last of the snow and turning everything to mud. They took with them the crazy man, dressed in mended, borrowed clothes, feet bound against further infection. His toes, Doc Maynard and Henry Smith had decided, did not need further amputation, although he still hobbled painfully on Doc Maynard's arm to the waiting canoe.

The canoe, long and slim, with a notched bow, was used for open water. Two Indians knelt in the bow and stern. The three white men sat in the middle, Arthur and George taking their places without much comment, Eddie simply looking confused.

It was a somber departure, excitement dulling the tragedy that shadowed George's face—and Ursula's on the beach, George Jr. at her elbow, 18-month-old Eugenia in her arms.

David and Louisa had stayed in town the entire week, staying on for the simple funeral and burial, helping Ursula with chores that seemed too much for her to bear. And although Louisa had longed to go home, needing to be alone with David and to find her own solace, she could not find it in her heart to leave her bereft friend. Neither could David leave George.

"I'm right sorry about your girl," said Lewis Wyckoff, the blacksmith. He came up to stand beside Ursula, a big and powerful man next to her slight build.

Louisa saw tears, always on the rim of Ursula's eyes, drip as she stared out to the gray water and disappearing back of her husband. Lewis saw them too. Compassionately he put a hand on her shoulder. "If'n there's anything I can do for you, Ma'am, while your husband's gone, send the boy down to the smithy. I'll come on the double."

At home, another week past and the month of March begun, Louisa thought of all these things, how good everyone was in Seattle, how they came together in times of trouble and stood by for one another. She thought of David, her own dear husband, helping George each evening last week split wood for Ursula—two cords, enough to last until May and the projected adjournment of the legislature—and how he'd talked with George late into the night, of God and His unknown ways. She thought, too, of how conscientious Lewis was of Ursula now that George was gone, helping her out with various chores and walking her to church on Sundays.

"Emily," she singsonged, happy to be home where she belonged, and ready to give Emily her weekly Saturday bath, "it's time to get clean!" She poured the warmed water into a shallow basin before the hearth and set out the soap.

It was dreadful soap, and she hated it. Made from winter fats, bacon rinds, lard and tallow and bone drippings, mixed with wood ash and lye, it was not only smelly, but slippery—muck at the bottom of a tin can, and she undressed Emily reluctantly, hesitant as always to rub her down with the slimy goo. The comforts of Illinois and civilization were so far distant it was hard to even remember the creamy smoothness of real bar soap.

She sat on the floor before the fire, cross-legged with a towel in her lap, Emily turned over her arm in the shallow tub. She ran her fingers—and the sliding, scummy soap—between the folds and rolls of Emily's satin-soft skin. Emily slapped the water and cooed. Her little feet kicked. Water splashed everything within five feet and Louisa, comforted, laughed gently.

"All done!" she announced, pulling Emily into her lap and leaning low to make her baby smile. On the bed, Emily all diapered and dressed, Louisa jiggled her up and down to make her smile again.

"Princess Angeline!" she gasped when the door flew open. "You have *got to knock*—"

But how could she scold? Chief Seattle's daughter stood on the stoop, shivering and smiling, the wind popping the red handkerchief on her head, one that Louisa had given her two years before. She held her ten-month-old grandchild in her arms, a smile expanding and lighting up her wizened face, a face much too lined and wrinkled for a woman only 45 years old.

"Oh, never mind," said Louisa, delighted to see her now that the shock had passed, and knowing that it didn't matter a lick what she said anyway; Princess Angeline would never knock. There wasn't even a word for it in the Duwamish tongue. "Come in, come in!" she said, draping Emily over her arm and pulling her friend into the warmth of the cabin.

"You don't have to work for Sally today?" she asked. "No, no, of course not—it's Saturday," she answered for herself, chattering nonstop in her pleasure to see the Indian woman. "Here, put Joey on the floor. I'll get him something to play with, and then put on some tea for us. My, but it's been a long time since I've seen you. Here, Joey," she said, handing him a skein of yarn.

Little Joey's mother, Angeline's daughter, had hanged herself just before Christmas and the responsibility for Joey had fallen onto Angeline's shoulders. Joe Foster, one of the millhands, had not once bothered himself to look into the welfare of his half-breed son, and to make ends meet, Angeline had gone to work for Sally Bell on the homestead just to the south of Louisa, helping with heavier chores and tending Sally's four little girls when Sally, suffering from chronic lung fever, needed to nap.

"You want some flour? Or some sugar? Goodness," Louisa exclaimed, holding Emily out from her dress. "I just changed this child and look! She's soaking wet already!"

"Why you think when I come, I always want something?"

"Because you do," said Louisa, pulling a diaper off the shelf and laying Emily back down on the bed.

"Tsk, tsk," clucked Princess Angeline, "always washy didees." She picked up her grandson and held out his dress for Louisa to inspect. Dry moss wrapped his bottom.

"Which is easier?" Louisa sighed. "To wash diapers, or find dry moss in this weather?"

"I show you place to go look for."

"Louisa?"

Startled, Louisa turned from the bed to find David in the doorway. He was home early, the heavy fog of all week draped about his shoulders. He nodded to Angeline, greeting her in Duwamish, then he sagged against the threshold and Louisa's heart rose in her throat, but she kept her voice steady and asked him to close the door so the babies would not freeze.

He stumbled, caught himself, then clumsily pulled up a chair at the table. "William Young is missing. He went up to Whidbey Island a whole week ago and he hasn't come back."

"*Missing?*" Louisa squeaked out, the hair on the back of her neck standing up. She remembered William Young; he was Charles Terry's sawmill partner in Alki. The mysterious, missing Montgomery McCormick was one thing, but this? *Missing* now had a name, a face—a man they knew. "Maybe he got lost. Or maybe he—"

"No, Liza." David's fearful gaze met that of Louisa—and Angeline. "The Indians he'd hired to paddle him came back last night—with his money and hat and some crazy story that doesn't make sense. And one of the Indians was shot."

Louisa sat down on the bed, not wanting to hear any more. Angeline sat beside her. It seemed strange to sit with the Indian woman while David told the story. "Charles Terry paddled over this morning from Alki and now Thomas Russell, their new sheriff, wants to put together a posse to go after them. He needs Dobbins—and as many of the rest of us as can come." David paused and grimaced. "He needs me to translate. Doc Maynard can't do it, not now anyway. He's had a bit too much to drink." He crossed his arms over the tabletop and bent his face into them, and suddenly Louisa understood. Everything.

"Retaliation?" she asked, forcing the word from her mind to her tongue.

He didn't answer.

So it had come at last, she thought. Just as Arthur and David and George had known it would, though they had all hoped and prayed... Cold took over her limbs. "Is William Young dead?" she asked.

"I don't know—they don't know." David looked up, desperation in his eyes.

"I go now." Angeline wrapped Joey in a smelly old blanket.

"My heart," she said, "it break in two piece to hear of trouble between your people and my people."

"Do you need anything?" David asked. "Flour? A ham end?"

Angeline started to cry. "God damn you, David Denny!"

"Don't you mean 'God bless' me, Angeline?"

She nodded, wiping her face. "Yes, yes. God *bless*. I get your words all mixed up," she said, allowing him to put the ham and flour—and a pound of butter—into her grass bag.

When she was gone, David sat back down and put his head between his hands. "Oh, Liza, what am I going to do?"

"Do you have to do anything?"

"Chief Seattle has apparently sent Jim and George down to Alki, to meet me in Charles' store. And they'll only talk with me; they don't trust anyone else."

Of course not, she thought. David was the only one, besides Doc Maynard and Henry Smith who had bothered to learn the Duwamish language, and they knew how deeply David cared, how fair and just he was in his dealings with them. *Not like Luther Collins*, she thought with an unwelcome shiver. "When must you leave?" she asked, remembering too that it was she who had called him a peacemaker.

"I'll take you into Seattle as soon as we can leave. The posse gathers in the morning."

She set Emily down and went to him. He leaned into her touch, nearly making her cry. She didn't know which was worse: to go after the Indians, or to sit back and wait. Eternally wait. Who had the harder job, men or women?

"I'll pack you some dried salmon and some hardtack," she said, trying to be brave and strong and efficient, but finally giving in to the ancient, sacrificial voice of her sex, she said, "You will come back to me?"

He caught her tightly in his arms. And like all women before her, Louisa cried in her helplessness—and his.

"Men," muttered Anna later on that same evening after Dobbins and David had gulped down their supper in order to get to the posse meeting in the cookhouse. "Another white man is missing and what do they do? Run off and leave us—alone, undefended." She dropped her embroidery to scold three-year-old Gertrude.

"Come here, Gerty," said Louisa, searching for any sort of distraction. "Bring me a storybook and I'll read to you, darling." It was useless to answer Anna; her sister-in-law would never listen to anyone's troubles but her own. How could she possibly understand the necessity of bringing law and order to a wild country, when she only wanted to leave this God-forsaken wilderness and return to civilization? But it wasn't Anna's fault she was so miserable, Louisa thought more kindly. Anna wasn't the sort to withstand the rigors of pioneering. But it wasn't Dobbins' fault either, Louisa knew, thinking of her patient brother.

"I declare, Louisa, you have the patience of Job," Anna said while Gerty scrambled up the ladder to find her storybook.

"It's not patience," said Louisa, studying Anna's angry face. Soft wrinkles had cut two lines over her nose. Saucy eyes had dulled. "It's submission to destiny—assurance that God is with us."

Anna snorted and bit a thread.

Louisa felt Gertrude at her knee and reached out to lift the child onto her lap. "*Once upon a time,*" she began, "*there were three bears* . . ." and as she read, Anna bent over her cross-stitch, jabbing the needle in and out of the muslin.

Louisa could feel Anna's bundled rage. It sprang from her eyes like a defensive porcupine, daggers waiting to punish; she held her embroidery hoop tightly, powerfully, turning it in her reddened hands every minute to see the knots on the back.

"What makes you so unhappy?" Louisa asked suddenly, startled to hear her own voice. Embarrassed, but unable to snatch back the words, she fussed with Gertrude's hair, drawing her fingers through the thick, black ringlets, hair very much like her own. The two women dared not look at each other. "I'm sorry, Anna," she finally whispered. "It was truly thoughtless of me. I know how hard it is for you way out here, with no family of your own, with no parties or pretty things, and then what with all—" She stopped herself, unwilling to frighten Gerty.

They said nothing more of it, had a cup of tea, and somehow managed to get through the rest of the evening. Then, as Anna was about to wash the dishes, her hands plunged deep into scalding water, the sound of the men's voices rang from outside and little Gerty sprang to the door. Anna turned to Louisa with a stifled sob. "Shall I tell you why I'm so unhappy? Shall I?"

"Oh, Anna—"

"I'm with child again and I hate your brother!" She turned back to the dishpan, the steam mingling with the tears on her cheeks.

-16-

*One day last week a man started from Alki to go
down the Sound with three Indians in a canoe. The
Indians returned with his canoe, clothing, watch,
money, etc. and were quite badly wounded, so that one
of them died. Suspicions were raised that all was not
right.*

—Kate Blaine, the schoolteacher

The posse paddled out of Seattle early Sunday afternoon,
arriving in Alki in the gray darkness of the dinner hour.
There was a flurry of repressed greetings, the citizens of
Alki grateful, but burdened, to see their Seattle com-
patriots. And in a rare display of affection, David received
the embrace of his loyal friends, the two regal sons of Chief
Seattle.

Jim and George were of average height, well-muscled,
their bare chests slick with dogfish oil. Just recently, within
the last winter, they'd taken to wearing corduroy pants,
buckled with twine and shells. But like their father—the
proud, allied chief of six tribes encompassing some 4,000
warriors—they still refused to wear any sort of shirt. And
like their father, they wore the traditional Hudson Bay
blanket crossed from one shoulder to the other in such a
way as to completely and effectively cover themselves.

143

The meeting, held late that night in the back room of Charles Terry's Markook Trading Post, proved to be difficult. Memories of early days on the Sound kept getting in David's way; memories of help from the Indians, of hunting trips, of legend 'sharing around camp fires. The simple days, he realized sadly, were gone now, and he had to set aside the past to concentrate on the present. Worry for the future cautioned each word.

"Tell me again what happened," he said to the two braves, speaking in Duwamish, conscious that his voice was dull and dry. He sounded old and beaten. "I've heard it from Tom Russell. But I want it from you."

Jim told the story sorrowfully, going slowly so that David could understand the Duwamish. William Young had hired three Indian youths to take him up to Whidbey Island, to the custom's house. Young had wanted to negotiate a contract with the Hudson Bay Company, who had a farm on the north end of San Juan Island, and who could help him establish timber trade between Victoria—the English capital directly across the Sound on Vancouver Island—and Charles Terry's mill in Alki.

But the Indian youths had returned to Alki a few days later—without Young, and with a story of an ambush that didn't hold water. All three of the Indians had been injured, one badly.

"He'd taken a bullet in the abdomen," Dr. Cherry explained and David recognized at once the newcomer who'd been over at the cookhouse during District Court. "But I wasn't able to do much for him. He died a few hours later. And when I went to tell his two friends, I discovered them counting money. On closer inspection, I discovered it was Young's purse. I went straight to Russell."

"But by the time we got there," said Tom Russell, rubbing his chin, worry heavy in his eyes, "they'd fled."

"It was robbery then," said David, immensely relieved. "Not retaliation." But Jim Seattle shook his head, snuffing out David's relief. "Many hear about your court. You do not punish Luther Collins."

"Luther Collins!" David exploded. "Were we *supposed* to? Your father, Chief Seattle—" He stopped, choking back his anger, struggling to understand, his mind running a thousand directions for answers. Had Seattle *ordered* this retaliation? He stared at the floor between his boots. Retaliation—everything he'd feared. An eye for an eye and William Young dead, and Chief Seattle behind it. It was worse than he could possibly have imagined. He tried to pray, but couldn't. Was this too big even for God? Why was he here? he wondered. Why was he not home with his family? Why should he be negotiating this crisis, struggling to hear past the hard Duwamish words and to decipher the body language of men who said more with stance than tongue? He looked about the Markook Trading House to the dozen or so white men in the room with him: Tom Russell, Dobbins, Lewis Wyckoff, Frank Matthias, Tim Grow, Hillory Butler, Charles Terry . . . With the exception of George Frye, they were all older than himself. Much older. Why had this fallen to him? Why not Dobbins, or Tom Russell? They were the sheriffs. *Why not Arthur?*

But the weight was on his shoulders. The responsibility was his, and he would not shrug it off. "Let me get this straight," he said, taking a deep breath and beginning again. "This would not have happened *if* the court had put Luther Collins on trial?"

"Young men with hearts painted black do not listen to the wise words of the mighty chief of six tribes—"

"So this retaliation was *not* of your father," he said, relief tripping in his heart.

"Our father is full of sorrow," said George Seattle. "He could not stem the black thoughts of these men, just as you cannot stem the black thoughts of your men. I tell you this: many of our people have itched to do revenge. You have heard the rumors, the whispers. But always our father held them back. But when you lash our braves and you cut off their hair in your court . . . " The young Indian made a grim face. "Our young men remember only Masachie Jim—and that you do not punish Luther Collins. Their black hearts speak louder than Seattle's command."

It was a long speech for an Indian. David sat back unable to respond, relieved to hear that Seattle still stood by his word, but overwhelmed with his own guilt. All during court he had been bored. He'd signed his name carelessly, *D.T. Denny,* to the paper punishing the two errant Indian youths. He'd had no idea that the other Indians, clustered outside of the cookhouse during that brutal storm, had been angered, reminded of injustice. If only he had known, he could have . . .

"Retaliation has been done and now you must act quickly," said George Seattle. "So that the old laws may be put away forever, our father has sent us to tell you, David Denny, what to do. You must send your men to arrest the guilty ones. They must be punished, but you must tell your people to be easy. There must be no revenge. You must move quickly and with great strength. Our father tells you this: move swiftly or," George hesitated, "there will be no safety. For anyone."

"You must remember," Jim cautioned, "our laws have been with us since the beginning of time. Our father cannot stem the anger of every man."

"Will you come with us?" A foolish question. He withdrew it.

The two braves stood and drew the corners of their blankets about their shoulders, signaling the end of the conversation.

"Take our canoe," said George. "It sails the water with Seattle's spirit power."

•   •   •

A collection of canoes and silent men crept toward Holmes Harbor on the south end of Whidbey Island the next morning in heavy fog, a soft, white, ominous fog.

Trees became menacing shadows that drifted suddenly into sight and then seemingly vanished, and fog rendered the clear green sea into a misty gray void. David huddled with four others in Chief Seattle's war canoe as it slid silently over the shadows and into the tension, thick as the white, wet air. Alert to the owl calls that could signal the whereabouts of the Indians, he warily watched the advance and retreat of the forests in the mist. Somewhere just ahead was Holmes Harbor, the beach of crushed white shells where Jim and George Seattle had said the culprits were hiding. Suddenly he shivered. The suffocating fog seemed to reach even his mind, penetrating everything. His eyes, his mouth, his nose, his ears, his throat, his heart, his soul.

"David?"

Charles Terry called from the stern and David twisted to see his friend. A black beard and unruly hair framed two black eyes. A crack shot, Terry was the gunman for this boat. Tom Russell, sheriff from Alki, was in charge of the canoe directly ahead. Dobbins, sheriff of Seattle and another crack shot, was in the third, trailing somewhere behind.

"What is it, Charles?" David asked, voice low lest it carry across the water.

"I think we ought to pull back. This doesn't smell good. I'm scared, Dave. Real scared."

They all were. No one argued with Charles. Five to a boat, they drifted, paddles propped against the gunwales. Cold sweat dribbled down David's back, and he longed for guidance, assurance that they were doing the right thing. Something, someone, hung in the thick white air around them. *Stataltch. Stick siwash.* Indian legends warped his nerve and he shivered.

Thomas Russell motioned for backstroke and his canoe slid in next to David's. "You feel it too, Denny?" Alki's sheriff asked, looming large into view.

"They're waiting for us," whispered Tim Grow, paddling the bow.

"Maybe we should go back," suggested Hillory Butler.

"No." Dr. Cherry shook his head fiercely. "The Seattle boys both said it. We have to act quickly. Demand the culprits, and leave. Show who's got the strength. We're just letting this fog spook us."

Tom Russell shifted in the canoe bobbing two feet from David. "What do you think?" he asked.

"Cherry is right," said David, and the men, in accord, dropped their paddles back into the water. The splash and dip moved them forward, skimming through the gray water like the slice of a knife. A whispering wake opened out behind.

Before long the fog thinned. The trees along the left bank eventually stood still, no longer a taunting, dissolving retreat. The sun broke through, dropping yellow shafts of pale light, turning the gray seawater steel-blue. They rounded a point and all saw it at once—the beach of white crushed shells.

Flayed salmon, pierced at head and tail with wooden skewers, lined the shoreline in a clutter of crucifixes against oak crossbars, and the vulgar scent of the open fires and smoking fish assaulted their nostrils. Squaws and children looked up, but made no happy movement to come close as was the usual custom.

David waited for the scrape of rocks beneath him, then stood. He felt the tipping of his canoe as he jumped to the shore. Others followed, leaping from their boats with the sound of splashing water and the grinding of pebbles underfoot. The oarsmen remained behind, two per canoe, ready to make a quick exit.

David advanced. "Where are the men who killed William Young?" he asked in Duwamish. His hand tightened on his gun as a score of men emerged suddenly from the woods.

"You know why we've come," David called.

A short man with skinny and badly bowed legs nodded. He was naked, glistening with oil in the cold newness of the pale sunlight. Goosebumps stood visibly on his skin.

"Jim and George Seattle tell us you have the men who murdered William Young?" It came out a question and David cursed himself for the mistake.

But the two culprits were handed over without a word, as if they'd been expecting it and were resigned. David was enormously relieved as Tom Russell ordered one into his own canoe, the other into Dobbins'. Tim Grow and Hillory Butler, paddling the stern positions in both boats, were ordered to tie the prisoner's wrists to the center cross-boards.

David swung himself into his own canoe, grasping the gunwales. They were off. Young George Frye and Charles Terry backpaddled away from the beach. "Hey wait!" cried David. "What's the matter with Russell?"

"Looks like they're stuck. Prisoner weighing the canoe down."

Foreboding clutched at David's throat as he watched Tom Russell jump out, boots and all, into the shallow water, and begin working to tug the long boat loose, to free it from the shallows. Along the shoreline, the Indians watched too.

Tom's face turned red and veins popped out in his neck. "No good!" he hollered. "Cherry—get out on your end and let's give it a shove. Let's get out of here!"

Cherry leaped from the bow and bent his big back to the task, grasping the crude gunwales with both hands, pushing forward. Cherry grunted with the effort and then, suddenly, gunfire exploded and Cherry toppled forward, face first, into the canoe.

For a long sliver of a second, time seemingly stopped for Indian and white man alike. And then a single naked Indian raced for the water and Tim Grow, directly in front of Cherry, scrambled to his feet, took aim, and fired three shots so close together they sounded like one. David's own breath seemed to whoosh out of him as he watched the Indian take one of Grow's bullets in the chest; the man's heart exploded right before their eyes.

"Ah-hi-i-i-i!" cried David, leaping to his feet, beading down the Indian with his own rifle as Grow, seeing he was covered, dropped his gun and yanked Cherry's deadweight into the canoe. Russell leaped in on the other side and miraculously the canoe broke loose. Butler backstroked frantically.

"Move out!" David hollered, sweat pouring down his face and into his eyes. Five yards behind him, he could hear George Holt and the men in Dobbins' boat paddling fast, and it took only moments for George Frye and Charles Terry in his own boat to syncopate their strokes. David felt the blessed relief of escape as they slowly cleared the shore.

But no. Wait. The Russell canoe had bogged again and Grow was screaming for help. Lewis Wyckoff leaped from his own boat, stumbling through the water, and the splash and thrash of men and boats was suddenly drowned as Indian war cries curdled the air and sunlight caught the flash of their brandished knives as they tore down the beach, swarming like hornets into the water, loosing their bone-chilling banshee cries, their leader—the man with the skinny bowed legs—screaming to the front of the swarm.

David thought, *I'm going to die.* And then, without thinking, he brought his rifle up, aiming, jerking on the trigger. The leader went down, floundered, rose, ran again, knife flashing, triumph spewing from his lips.

The Indians reached Russell's boat first. One caught the bow, but fell back with a grunt when he took Lewis Wyckoff's boot in his chin. Another came up behind Wyckoff, knife drawn, and Wyckoff cried out when the knife struck home, tearing into his thigh.

BOOM! David fired, but missed. He fired again and this time Wyckoff's attacker whirled, spinning and jerking, and he fell into the water, bobbing up in a dead man's float.

"RETREAT!" screamed Butler, but the heavily weighted boats were scarcely a match for the advancing Indians, splashing through the water, giving chase. The prisoner between Butler and the wounded Wyckoff somehow managed to free himself from the crossbar and steel flashed above Butler's head.

David cried out Butler's name before fear turned his knees to wax and he watched, horrified, as the other prisoner freed himself and smashed a vicious blow against Dobbins who fell, head cracking against the crossbar. The canoe tipped, sending everyone in it into the Sound.

A scream, a war cry, a shriek from his own lips, and David was on his feet, the reflexive, mistaken motion toppling his own canoe. He went overboard and came up spewing sand and water, pulling to his feet in the icy shallows, backing, backing, conscious that he had somehow, by the grace of God, kept his rifle dry.

The canoe lay upside down. George Frye tried desperately to right it as David staggered, struggling for position. Gunfire and the cries of men rang everywhere around them. He had the rifle locked against his shoulder when, backing away, he bumped into something behind him: Charles Terry, face down, blood flowing from his head.

David moaned and reached for the back of Terry's neck, grabbing a fistful of shirt. Terry revived, staggered to his feet. David gave him a push, sending him toward Frye. "Get in! Lay low!"

"DAVID!" Dobbins' cry rang out.

David whirled and ducked just as the Indian's knife descended, slicing into the water. The Indian gave another blood-curdling cry as his arm rose up again. David was close enough to smell the oil and fear of the man; the knife poised just over David's heart. He pulled the trigger, firing point-blank. Blood sprayed everywhere, streaking the air and water.

From a canoe Dobbins called to him, "Get in!"

"DOBBINS! BEHIND YOU!" But the warning was too late: a flash, a streak of blood, and even as cold fury wrapped around David's heart, even as his hand pulled the trigger, even as the Indian fell backward, so Dobbins fell forward, folding over the gunwale, knife in his back.

Ed Hanford raced to the rocking boat, righted it, pushed Dobbins in, and leapt after him.

"Shove off!" screamed Wyckoff. George Holt bent to the oar and shot clear. Tim Grow churned the water from the bow. One canoe was free.

"David!" bellowed Wyckoff. "Duck! He's got a gun!"

David saw only the pistol, yards away, aimed at his face. He turned just as the huge, endless explosion erupted and lead sliced through his cheek, slamming into his jawbone. He watched lead and bone leap from his face—splinters of lead and bone. He listened to the snap of gristle tearing, bone shattering, blood spurting. Gristle and tendons in his face, ripped and torn bloody. And even in this he saw, too, an Indian carrying a gleaming knife, racing toward him. *You're going to die,* he told himself again. Would it hurt?

A shot rang out and suddenly, it was over. Only a vast, implacable silence reigned. Dazed, David looked around. Bodies floated on the scarlet water. Naked bodies, he noted. Indians. A roar began in his head and pounded out to his ears as he glanced up at the deserted beach. Smoke still curled lazily from the fire. The women and children were nowhere to be seen. He turned back to see George Frye, bleeding heavily from the nose, paddling the righted canoe toward him. David tried to clamber in, but couldn't. His legs would not obey. George reached over and pulled him in.

His mouth felt all wrong. He wanted to ask if they had left anyone behind, but the words, formed clearly in his head, would not gather on his tongue. He felt the wind against his wet hair and the freeze of rushing air around his trembling body. He tried again to speak. Something rattled loose, but not words. He spit. A bullet. He began to shiver and slumped forward over the crossbar. Darkness came for him, but by then they were out in the open water.

-17-

Monday, March 6

*There is a magic power about the waterfront—a
kind of strength I find hard to define. It gets in your
blood and stays there. I can't remember a day when
there wasn't the sound of laughter, or the silence of
sorrow.*

—a pioneer woman

To keep busy, and their minds off what was happening
across the Sound, Anna and Louisa took Gerty and Emily
for a walk early Monday morning, leaving the house long
before the fog burned off.

"Let's invite Ursula," Louisa suggested, shivering in the
dampness and wondering where David was, and if he was
all right.

No, I must not fret. He is in God's hands, she thought.

Resolved, she took hold of Gerty's wee hand, and with
Emily strapped to her back, she and Anna set off through
the woods to Seattle's clearing—and Ursula's cabin at the
edge of the forest.

"But it's wash day," said Ursula somberly, answering the
door and letting them in.

"Just a short walk, Ursula," said Louisa. "It would do you
some good to get out."

"All right." Ursula looked at Gerty strangely and picked up Eugenia to dress. "Georgie?" she called, standing at the foot of the ladder. "You want to come with us or stay here?"

"I don't want to go in the woods, Ma."

"Very well," said Ursula, looking to Anna and Louisa with despair in her eyes. "He won't leave the loft. I don't know what to do with him."

"He needs to feel safe," said Louisa. "He'll come down in time."

"I suppose you're right." Ursula put on her coat and hat, then tied the ribbons of her bonnet under her chin. "Come," she said, "let's go."

On their walk, taken slowly so that Eugenia could tumble along behind them on her short, unsteady legs, they found a fallen hemlock tree. Louisa picked up the soft, pink fibrous bark in her hands and squeezed it in her fingers. "This might make a nice dye," she said. "Anna? Don't you have some wool skeins that we could experiment with?"

"But it's wash day," said Anna.

"Please, let's do something different," Louisa pleaded. "I shall go mad if we have to scrub clothes today."

They returned with an armload of bark and stood talking quietly at Ursula's door, each hesitant to say goodbye. They needed each other today, in their own way. "We'll show you how the wool turns out," said Louisa at last.

Ursula paused on her stoop. "I'm sorry the day is so hard for you," she whispered, looking to both Louisa and Anna. "I'd go mad if I knew my husband was out after wild Indians. It's a relief to know George is only gone to Olympia. I will pray for you."

The wool came out a soft peach, and Louisa, taking a liking to it, dusted off Anna's spinning wheel to spin up the rest of the wool Anna had packed away in a box. She would dye all of it and make Gerty and Emily each a sweater. Her fingers felt all thumbs, and she laughed as the unevenly spun yarn came out the shuttlecock. Emily cooed on her lap.

"You're doing fine," Anna said. She sat on a three-legged stool skeining the yarn, hands a foot apart, twisting figure eights patiently. It was catharsis for their souls as the long day drew on, and by supper several peach skeins of wool hung from the rafters. Louisa pushed the spinning wheel into a corner, squeezing it between a barrel of sugar and a box of ammunition. *Goodness*, she thought, *the way we live.*

•   •   •

Louisa had gone out to put the chickens to bed. Peek-a-boo, the rooster Doc Maynard had given her the year before when she'd been married, had recognized her and had come running for feed from her hand, and she'd stopped to pat his proud neck and quivering feathers and felt a longing for spring when the cry rang out.

"Dr. Cherry's been shot! Dr. Cherry's been shot!" Mrs. Yesler hollered as she ran up the trail. "Everyone's been injured! Bring blankets! And soup! And bandages! And lots of water!"

Louisa threw the bolt on the coop. "Anna!" she gasped, running for the cabin and throwing open the door. "Take the children over to Mary's! We've got to go down to the cookhouse! David and Dobbins have been hurt!" And then she was gone, running down the trail in the gathering dark.

Canoes lay empty on the black beach, and Louisa followed the bloodied path to the cookhouse door, her eyes sweeping the bedlam and noise.

"He's over here!" Catherine Maynard called, "with Jim Seattle!"

Louisa flung herself over bodies and blankets, dropping to her knees. His face. What had happened to his face? Blood oozed from a gaping hole in his beard. He groaned, and Louisa stifled a scream, tears spilling down her face.

Jim Seattle knelt beside her. "He took bullet in jaw."

Boiling water. Sheets. Blankets. Warm soup. Brandy. Women ran back and forth, racing up and down the dark trails, popping in and out of the cookhouse door, carrying bundles and buckets. Louisa lost track of time and events, everything a mad scramble to strip the men of their wet, bloodied clothes and get them wrapped in warm, clean blankets.

Everyone was injured, all suffering from exposure and shock and numerous wounds. Dr. Cherry was the worst, unconscious and riddled through the back with bullets. Dobbins had a knife wound in the back. David had taken a bullet through the cheek where the bullet had flattened against his teeth and jaw, and he'd spit it out. Mr. Butler had a slash in his right shoulder, Lewis Wyckoff one in his upper thigh. George Frye swallowed blood from a broken nose. His forearms were slashed and bleeding, his knuckles raw. Charles Terry sat holding his head, complaining of light flashes across his eyes. Everyone prayed anxiously for the swift return of Doc Maynard. He'd gone down to see about Mrs. Holgate's bursitis, and Dr. Williamson and Henry Smith couldn't work fast enough. Unable to move from David's side, Louisa heard Dr. Cherry sucking for air on the table, gurgling in his own blood. She thought of little Ursula and was nauseated by the sounds and smells, and she grew sick with fear.

Henry Yesler built the fire to a roar, putting children to work collecting scraps from the incinerator. "Cedar!" he barked. "It burns hot!" And little Katy and Becky Horton, and Georgie McConaha, roused from his loft, scattered to find what they could. Mrs. Butler and Abbie Jane Holgate brought in another batch of blankets. "Like this!" ordered Yesler, showing them how to open the blankets to the hot flames, warming them quickly.

George Seattle put a warmed blanket into Louisa's hands. Together, she and the two Indian braves pulled off David's wet clothes and wrapped him in the warm wool blanket. "He's so cold," she wept, tucking the blanket under his bloody chin.

"What happened?" thundered Maynard from the doorway, Salmon Bay Curley right behind him.

"Over here! On the double!" shouted Dr. Williamson. "Cherry's taken a bucket of lead in his lungs!"

Maynard moved fast, discarding his jacket as he went. He stood beside Henry and looked down at the man who lay stretched out on the table, more dead than alive.

"Don't think he's going to make it," said Williamson across the table, scalpel in hand.

"He will." Maynard's voice was final.

"Better take a look at Dobbins, Sir." said Henry. "Catherine can't get a pulse on him."

Dobbins? Louisa thought wildly, looking up. Mary Ann knelt beside him, weeping softly while she worked, cutting away their brother's clothes with long shears, snipping away the jacket, his shirt, then the blood-soaked underwear. *Where was Anna?*

"Liza?"

"Oh, David!" she sobbed, dropping her head to his chest in anguished relief. He lay with his eyes closed, and she was frantic to do something, anything. He could not lay here like this, his face buried in blood. But then Ursula knelt beside her.

"I think we have to clean him best we can, and shave off his beard. That way the doctors can mend the wound. See? I've brought you George's razor."

"Oh, Ursula," Louisa sobbed, seeing the basin and cloth Ursula set between them, the sharp razor and tin of soap. "He's going to die ..."

"No, he's not," Ursula snapped. "Do you want to do it, or shall I?"

"You do it." Louisa looked down at her trembling fingers, and then took David's hand in her own, curling her fingers between his, grateful to feel a slight squeeze. Ursula began to wash his face, easing up when he moaned and pulled away. The shaving was the worst, razor against torn flesh, and Louisa fought back a retch when she saw the raw, gaping wound in his lower right jaw, the exposed bone.

"Now let me see what we have here," said Doc Maynard suddenly above her. "Oh, hello, Jim—George," he said, greeting the Indians, then, "Oh, my, my." His hands were gentle as he probed David's shorn, gaping cheek. "He's lucky," said Doc Maynard, pulling his finger out of David's mouth. "No teeth missing. A cracked jaw that'll mend. And as soon as we get Dobbins off the table, I'll sew him up for you, Liza. A few weeks with a poultice and he'll be as good as new. His worst problem right now is exposure and cold. Keep him warm."

"Dobbins is alive?" she asked.

"You come from a tough stock."

"Louisa Denny?"

"Yes?" she answered, twisting to see Henry where he called to her from the table. Dr. Cherry had been taken away; her brother lay in his place, stomach down, back bared.

"He's trying to say something—"

"But David," she stammered. "I can't leave David!"

"But Dobbins is calling for you."

She stumbled past Ursula, busy now with Lewis Wyckoff who sat in a chair, braced beneath a blanket, dressed in long johns cut away at the thigh. Sweat poured off his brow as Ursula cleaned the knife wound, a deep gash through his thick thigh muscle. He grimaced when he saw Dr. Williamson beside them, threading a needle.

"Excuse me," Louisa mumbled, bumping now into Mr. Yesler overseeing the arrival of yet more blankets and dry clothes. She gasped when she saw the deep puncture in Dobbins' back, throbbing, puckered purple and thick with blood. "Dobbins? Dobbins? Can you hear me?" she asked, kneeling by his head.

Kate Blaine was wiping the blood from his back and pink water ran down his ribs to puddle and stain the sheeting. It dripped onto Louisa's skirt and the floor beside her. The new blankets were brought, freshly hot, to wrap him. His eyes were shut, his face drawn in pain. But he was alive.

"Dobbins? It's Liza," she said, stroking his head the way they used to do for each other when they were children, in those long ago days.

"Tell Anna..." Blood caught in his throat. He tried to swallow, spit instead. "Tell her not to..."

"Not to what, Dobbins?"

"The baby... tell her not to hurt the baby..."

Rage pumped through Louisa's whole body. Little Ursula not two weeks dead and Anna was thinking of killing her own unborn baby?

"Liza..."

"Yes, Dobbins."

"Will you take Gerty?" Blood gurgled again in his throat and he coughed, spitting more blood. Tears leaked from his closed eyes. Blood oozed from his clenched lips. "Anna doesn't want her."

"I won't need to take Gerty," Louisa said firmly, stroking his hair. "You'll be fine. You will." With the hem of her skirt she cleaned his mouth. Impulsively she leaned to kiss him and felt him relax.

"Tell Mary Ann to take the baby..." More gurgling.

"Louisa." The voice belonged to Henry and she looked up to see his kind, green eyes. "Louisa, tell him we're going to put him to sleep, and that you'll be here when he wakes up."

"Dobbins, they—"

"I heard... Liza, tell Mary..."

He was asleep. Louisa looked up at Henry again, but he was busy.

• • •

All night long Louisa moved between her husband and her brother, holding them by turn, feeling them grow warmer, their hearts beating steadier, stronger. The hours passed slowly, torturously, as other women changed bandages, helped men with water when thirst woke them, bathing sweating brows, and Louisa, refusing to leave Dobbins and David and knowing that Mary Ann watched over Emily, listened to the hushed whispers, the low singing, the crackle of the fire, the rasping, struggling breath of Dr. Cherry. What would happen now? The Indians were in open rebellion. Her mind raced with a thousand questions, and no answers.

She fell asleep, but awoke almost instantly. Something was wrong. A lamp flickered low and she saw Doc Maynard kneeling over Dr. Cherry, head bowed. Dr. Cherry had died.

Dawn tinted the sky and sorrow settled over all of Seattle like a nightmare from which none could wake.

Part VI

THE MURDER OF McCORMICK
Mid-March

WANTED!

INFORMATION of WM. MONTGOMERY McCORMICK, who left Oregon City in 1851, with a company bound for Puget Sound, who designed forming a settlement there. Said McCormick is 30 years of age, light hair and fair complexion. Any information of an only brother will be gratefully received by his sister, if directed to Adams and Co., Express, Yankee Jim's, California, or his wife, Anne E. McCormick, Lock Haven, Penns.

—The Pioneer & Democrat

-18-

The whites were all wounded, one of them mortally; he died last night....Another received a bullet in his cheek, which flattened against his teeth and he spit it out....A company immediately volunteered to go this morning and attack the Indians, but upon more mature thought they decided to refer the case to the governor for his action upon it. The citizens... drew up a set of resolutions informing him of the affairs, and requesting him to take immediate action. They sent it off to Olympia in a sloop but unless the winds shall be fair, we cannot hope for aid from him before Saturday....

—Kate Blaine, the schoolteacher

The nightmare did not pass. Indeed, it deepened. The pioneers, after first making hasty plans to go after the Indians, calmed down and drew up a resolution for the governor requesting martial law and sent it off on a sloop for Olympia. Less than an hour after receiving the news, Governor Stevens himself, along with George Gibbs and Mike Simmons (Catherine Maynard's brother and territorial Indian agent), left for Fort Steilacoom. There they boarded a revenue cutter carrying the army, under Stevens' direct orders and command, and sailed toward Whidbey

Island to bring the Indians in. But a vicious storm came up en route and the ship capsized. Every man aboard but two drowned. Only Mike Simmons and the governor survived, and when news of this crippling loss reached Seattle, the pioneers were paralyzed, caught in the net of grief and fear—and wide-open vulnerability.

The Indians had vented their rage. With this taste of blood, would they seek more? Would they now seek retaliation for their own dead, killed in the fray on the white-pebbled beach of Holmes Harbor on Whidbey Island?

No one knew. They only knew that a smoldering hatred between the two races simmered, and that just a spark, a foolish word, a hasty move could ignite those smoking embers into open flame. The pioneers were but a handful amidst many, without protection and defense, while the Indians, well-armed, could, if they wished, descend without warning.

David and Louisa returned home, taking with them one of Moreover's pups, a little wobbly-legged mutt—and a new pistol. The days passed, tension mounting as they waited for word from Jim and George, dispatched immediately to bring Chief Seattle into town. During these days David tried in vain to connect the tragic chain of events. What had happened? he wondered with despair, sorting through the gloom of grief and fear so thick around them.

A killing, yes. A skirmish in which at least five or ten Indians had been killed, yes. The death of one of their own, yes, yes. But the worst by far was the death of an entire squadron of soldiers. Like everyone else on the Sound, only now could he begin to understand the magnitude of their loss. It was like coming out of a daze, perhaps much like a drunken man who finds himself waking up in a strange bed defenseless, vulnerable, caught without strength.

No, this was not true, David knew. They were not entirely without strength. They had Seattle and Pat Kanim. These two chiefs could be counted on to seek peace.

David took to walking the woods, short walks at first, and then as he regained a small measure of strength, longer and deeper ones into the darkness of the forest, chin tucked into his collar against the damp, slow drizzle of waking spring. He found solace in the ageless trees, the strength of creation and God's presence in the slip of wind, the song of a bird, the careful, watchful eye of a doe hidden in foliage waiting to give birth. Sometimes he and Louisa went together, holding hands, saying little, stopping to watch without word a squirrel forage his way up a tree.

"David," said Louisa one day. "I read a verse yesterday that seemed to me to be written for us."

"Tell me."

"Be merciful unto me, O God, for my soul trusteth in thee; yea, in the shadow of thy wings will I make my refuge, until *these* calamities be overpast."

"It is for us, Liza."

The middle of March, a Sunday morning, they woke to a clear sky and sunlight. David slid from the bed and opened the door. "Liza," he whispered, "can you smell the spring?"

She sat up, hair tumbling down around her shoulders and looking all sleepy and pretty. "Yes." She smiled, and it warmed his heart to see it. They'd been so serious lately. "I suppose you'll go for a walk today?" she asked. "After I poultice your face again?"

"Do you want to go with me?" He climbed back into bed, shivering beside her warm body. "Do you? I don't mean to leave you behind."

She smiled and touched her fingers along the raw wound in his jaw. "It's still festering," she said. "How does it feel?"

"Like I'm going to lose my teeth. Let's go together, Liza. It's Sunday."

"No, I think maybe I'll work on my garden today."

"But the ground is too wet."

"It won't hurt to do the spading."

She fell back asleep in his arms, and when they both

woke again the sun was streaming through the window. Emily was howling, but only reluctantly did David let his wife go. As she fixed breakfast, he dressed. He sat down at the table to suck the porridge through his teeth, and he took her hand in his and did not let it go.

• • •

Right after lunch he headed out, taking the trail that ran deep into the back of his claim. Maybe he could make it all the way out to the little lake today—*tenas chuck*, the Indians called it. He passed through the glen where he wanted to build Louisa a real house. An old abandoned Indian shack sat right around the twist in the trail. As he approached it his head throbbed, his jaw a dull ache, but he kept walking slowly forward.

Angry voices suddenly broke the forest calm. Cautious, he pressed forward, ears straining to catch the words.

"I didn't kill him! You did!"

He froze in his tracks, hand moving to his hip. But he was without a weapon.

"DOG! *You* were the one who crushed in his skull!"

"Not until after you shot him in the back of the head!"

"It was you! We said only to rob him! But you killed him! And then you killed Chodups because he was going to tell David Denny!"

David stood rigid in the trail, listening against his will as the argument in the abandoned shack escalated and the drift of ugly truth dawned. He caught sound of Curley's familiar voice and, without thinking, stormed forward. "What's this all about?" he demanded, ducking into the old shack where he found half a dozen young braves squatting around a bone game. The Indians fell back on their heels. One scrambled up, backed toward the wall, and edged for the door.

"Sit down!" David ordered, surprised to hear the strength and anger in his voice and to feel the pain in his jaw recede. He looked from one dusky face to the other and recognized the blunt haircuts of the Snoqualmie, cut square over their eyes in a bang and then across their shoulders in the back. Then he remembered Louisa's words: *A Snoqualmie killed Chodups, David. I know, because of the* yachit *prints in the snow.* His gaze fell to the Indians' feet. They wore moccasins made of dog hair and beads, and suddenly he realized the danger they all were in. This was the spark, the spark that would ignite the smoldering flame.

"Curley, you'd better tell me what you know," he said firmly, his back straight, his eyes steady. "Who killed Chodups John?" he demanded, and he felt his throat close with something like agony. "And who killed Montgomery McCormick?"

•   •   •

The story came out slowly, Curley oddly reluctant to speak. Four of the Snoqualmie youths, not long after the lynching of Masachie Jim, had come across a white man in a forest glen eating blackberries along the eastern shores of *tenas chuck.* He wore new clothes, carried both a rifle and a revolver, and when asked if he had money, had foolishly said yes, he had money. *Hiyu chicamum.*

So it wasn't retaliation! It was murder! Cold-blooded murder! There was a significant difference. Murder was not condoned by either race. The Indians themselves would be appalled to hear of it. Pat Kanim—once he heard of the news—would even help bring in the murderers. David was sure of that. The danger receded, the spark sizzling and going out. There'd be no hatred spawned for bringing murderers to justice—unlike the fury and rage that had erupted after the death of William Young. Revenge promised danger, but murder...David felt almost weak with relief.

"Kussass killed the white man," said Curley in Duwamish, thrusting a chin at the sinister-looking youth in the corner who was glaring at them all, brows knit together in a scowl. "The others wanted to rob him, but Kussass shot him in the back of the head with his Hudson Bay musket."

"But it was Stahowie!" Kussass hissed, "who took the man's axe and smashed in his skull!"

From another corner a brave bolted for the door. David let him go. Kussass saw and edged along the wall. David couldn't hold any of them; he had no gun. They made their escape, but only for the moment.

Curley and David, the only ones left in the damp shack, stepped outside. David found a mossy log and straddled it.

"They didn't mean to kill McCormick," said Curley, taking the other end of the log. "But when Kussass shot the musket, they panicked and Stahowie grabbed the axe—"

"And bashed in his head," David finished. So this was the ill-gotten fate of Montgomery McCormick, he thought, and now that the fear had passed, he felt sick. He watched a sunbeam spill through the trees. But better murdered than sacrificed for revenge. The danger, the smoldering hatred retreated further and further, and for the first time in a long while he felt as if he could breathe, relax.

The rest of the story tumbled out while he listened. The four braves—Kussass and Stahowie, along with Petawow and Klap-ke-latchi—had, after the wicked deed had been done, taken off the dead man's clothes—his jacket, shirt, and pantaloons—and gambled for the booty. Then with the man's body still warm, they'd rolled him into a ravine—dressed only in his underclothes. Two days later, Curley's *klootchman*, out picking blackberries had, by sheer chance, stumbled across the bloating body. Frightened by the grisly scene, she'd raced home for Curley. Curley went out immediately and buried the body.

"Why didn't you tell me?" exploded David suddenly, his fear turning back on him. Curley had known all along! *What else hadn't Curley told him? What other dangers lurked, ready to fan the flames of hatred?*

"David Denny, how could I tell you? The *tamanuse* ..." Terror laced Curley's voice and in his face was unspeakable misery. "... the evil spirits," he whispered.

They're like children, David thought with a measure of pity. Children afraid of ghosts. But his own fear was there too. "All this year *we've* been afraid!" he cried. "A white man disappears—we think it's because—" David could not bring himself to say the word "lynching." He tried to continue more calmly. "You knew it wasn't revenge. You knew that McCormick was murdered for his money. Why didn't you tell me? What other secrets—"

"No, no!" Curley begged with wild eyes to be believed. "I tell you everything but this! David Denny!" he pleaded. "The *tamanuse!* When there is murder, the *tamanuse*, the evil spirits, they rise, they follow forever!"

"But *you* didn't kill McCormick."

"I bury him. Maybe this *tamanuse* doesn't know the difference. The dead man is white. I am Indian."

"Still, you should have told me. Chodups wasn't afraid of the *tamanuse*. I heard them say he was going to tell me."

"Yes—and look how dead Chodups is."

"No *tamanuse* killed him. Someone wearing moccasins killed him."

"What does it matter how you die? You die."

"Then tell me, by whose hand did Chodups die?"

Curley rested his elbows on his knees, studying the forest floor. A blue jay landed nearby, squawking and scolding. "Kussass. He use McCormick's revolver."

David ran a heavy hand over his aching brow. "Kussass killed him because Chodups was going to tell me who murdered McCormick. How did Chodups know?"

Curley shook his head and snorted. "All the Indians know. Petawow won only a knife when they gambled for the booty, but he did not like the knife. He kept fighting with Kussass. He wanted some of the money. You can bury a body," said Curley, "but you can't hide loud words or bad scowls. All the Snoqualmie know of the wicked deed."

"The Duwamish too?"

"Some of us."

Sunlight and shadow played over the forest floor and David watched the dance, absorbing the news, testing it in his mind. "How do you know all this? You only found a body."

"One moon after the evil deed was done, Stemalyu—a Snoqualmie elder—came to *wah-wah* with me," said Curley, breaking momentarily from Duwamish into Chinook. "He too had a story."

David raised an eyebrow.

"He heard Kussass and Petawow fighting over the knife and money—and heard Petawow accuse Kussass of killing a white man. Stemalyu made Petawow tell the story. His heart grew too heavy with fear. He came to see me."

"And you, of course, knew just where and when the white man had been killed."

"It was not hard to put our stories side by side and discover the truth."

"But how do you know the name of this murdered white man?" The ugly thought crossed David's mind that this was not McCormick at all, but another man.

"Kussass won the purse. In it was $200 and marks on a paper. Stemalyu matched the marking with your newspaper."

"Montgomery McCormick," muttered David, too relieved to be sad. "Well, we're going to have to go tell Maynard in the morning. He'll know what to do." He stood to go, adjusting his jacket. But one look at Curley's face and he knew he couldn't leave his friend alone in the forest, not where, in Curley's mind, the *tamanuse* reigned supreme. "Come home with me for supper," he said.

He was rewarded by a flashing smile and the two men set off together back down the trail.

• • •

After David left, Louisa pulled the shovel off the back wall of the cabin and set to work, grateful to feel the warmth of the sun burn through her woolen jersey. She turned the earth, spading the soft, wet soil in upside-down clumps and dropping them in scalloped rows between the four corner posts marking the borders of her garden.

Emily, wrapped warmly and laying on a patchwork quilt nearby, cooed in the yellow rays of sunlight breaking through the forest leaves. She was on her back, and her feet, caught in the knit ends of her leggings, engrossed all her attention. She blew bubbles, happy to see the swing and kick of her own feet—and the bright red pon-poms sewed to the end of each bootie. Beside her the puppy, Watch, lay sound asleep, curled into a ball.

Louisa paused to view her work, resting her chin over her smudged knuckles as she leaned heavily upon the shovel's handle. In her mind's eye, she could see the carrot greens all lined up to wave in the breeze, beans curling up their trailing posts, peas flowering all white and sweet green. Spring *would* come, she thought to herself, smiling. No matter how long or how hard the winter, it always rolled around. She had to believe that. She heard something in the woods and glanced to the stump and her pistol, then over to Emily. Slowly she scanned the forest, circling. But the woods were quiet.

An Indian? Or was she just hearing things again? The crazy man? No, that was silly. He'd been taken down to Steilacoom. She'd seen him go.

She sank the shovel into the ground, kicking the blade when it snagged on yet another tree root. She bent to pull at it....Someone *was* watching her! She tugged, knowing that eyes were on her back. Yet if she turned around—she knew no one would be there. Just then Watch lifted his nose from his paws and growled, low in the throat. Pin pricks trickled down her arms. The root snapped loose and she nearly fell over backwards. She brushed off her hands, hung the shovel back on the wall, picked up the pistol, and went to get Emily. "Come on, Watch," she said, calling to the dog nonchalantly. "Time to go in."

But once inside she sat weakly on the bed, pistol in hand, staring at the closed door wondering, *How long can we go on like this?*

And that night, curled into David's arms, feeling the weakness that still lingered in his body and listening to him tell of the murder of the missing McCormick she asked herself again, *How long can we go on like this?*

-19-

Monday, March 13

Shortly after...D.T. Denny, Dr. Maynard, E.A. Clark and one or two others, with Curley as a guide, went out to the lake...

—Emily Inez Denny, Louisa's daughter

Tom Mercer drove David and Curley into town first thing in the morning, none of them talking much. But Dobbins, still bedridden when he heard their news, had plenty to say and insisted on going with Doc Maynard and the rest of them out to *tenas chuck*.

"But you were just stabbed in the back two weeks ago!" complained Doc Maynard, standing beside Dobbins' bed and leaning forward, both hands in his pants pockets.

"But I'm sheriff," said Dobbins, coughing.

"See here," said Maynard, "you've got to lay back and get your wits about you. We can do this ourselves—"

"I can go easy enough in Tom's wagon," said Dobbins stubbornly. "And as for my wits, I got more than a pumpernickel doctor any day."

The squabble was cut short when Tom and Guthrie Latimer came into the cabin announcing they'd made up a bed in the back of the wagon. "You're going to have to tie him to the bedposts, Doc," said Guthrie slowly, "if you leave him behind. Come on, Dobbins. I'll help you onto your feet. Lean on my arm. No, there you go, just like that."

"Anna? My badge?" Dobbins asked. Sullenly, she brought it out and handed it to him.

Six of them went with Curley. Doc Maynard and Tom rode up on the wagon seat. Eddie Clark, a new settler who made no bones about his hostile attitude toward the Indians, sat on the wagon tail with his camera and tripod packed carefully between himself and Curley. David sat with Dobbins and their Uncle Guthrie, feeling nauseous and weak, skin wet with sweat. Would he ever recover? he wondered, staring at his trembling hands. Yesterday he had almost believed he was on the mend. But today he could hardly keep on his feet, and his jaw yowled in his ears. But he couldn't complain. He was lucky to be alive. So was Dobbins. They all were. He thought of McCormick and shivered.

It wasn't so easy finding the body. A half dozen of Curley's friends were waiting with canoes at the south end of the lake where the road ended abruptly at Tom Mercer's barn. After much ado, they managed to get Dobbins boarded, Maynard fussing and swearing, Guthrie calming the ruffled feathers. The Indians themselves appeared frightened, watching for evil spirits over their shoulders. How Curley had managed to get them to come out, David didn't know.

"So where is it?"

But Curley couldn't exactly remember the spot. He debated as their boat nosed along the beach. Sometimes he jumped out to splash ashore in the icy water before shaking his head, changing his mind yet again.

"I think this is it," he said finally, signaling for them to all troop out.

"Somebody better stay with Dobbins." Doc Maynard put his foot down and Dobbins didn't argue, white-faced and wheezing, badge winking as his chest labored.

"I'll stay," said Guthrie Latimer. David found himself wishing he'd spoken up, but followed after Tom and Clark and Maynard—and the Indians. He hesitated before heading into the damp forest, feeling Curley's *tamanuse*.

They had planned to remove the body to Seattle for proper burial, but when they arrived at the mossy logs where the body had been concealed all these months, they changed their minds. The shallow grave had made it easy for scavengers. David's stomach lurched and he had to look away.

Doc Maynard stooped to inspect what was left of the head, smashed in by the blunt end of the axe. "We probably ought to take back the skull fragments anyway," he said, using a trowel to shovel away the dirt.

"Wait! Don't touch anything!" said Eddie Clark, setting up his camera. "We need to get a picture for the jury!"

"Jury?" said David, startled out of his nausea. He and Tom exchanged glances. Curley sat down on a nearby log.

"Who'd you say did it?" Maynard asked him.

"Kussass and Stahowie."

"What's this about Petawow and Klap-ke-latchi then?"

"They were with wrong friends, that's all."

"I'm done," said Clark. "Pocket what you want."

"Please," said Maynard, pulling out his handkerchief and shoveling the broken pieces of bone into it. "A better choice of words, Clark, might make things easier." He picked up two pairs of glasses, one steel-rimmed, the other gold-rimmed, booty the Indians had apparently not thought worthwhile to take. He put both pairs in his pocket.

• • •

The horses snorted gently when Tom pulled them to a stop with a low "whoa" beside the trail leading to David's house, and David slid gratefully off the back of the bouncing wagon.

"Maynard, you going to go out to the Snoqualmie camp with Curley today?" he asked, standing at the side of the road.

"Yup. You just keep your feet propped up and the home fires burning, and we'll bring those scoundrels in."

"We need Kanim in this," David said gravely. "It would show the Indians we're not without justification."

"It wouldn't hurt to have Chief Seattle show up, either," mumbled Maynard, rubbing his neck. "Where is he, anyway? What's taking him so long in getting back to us? I got the big powwow all arranged—if the governor can get the salt water out of his lungs long enough and quick enough to grace us with his presence."

"When is it?"

"Next week."

Dobbins let out a low groan from the back of the wagon and startled, they looked back to where he lay on his bed, stomach down, chin in his hands. But he was only thinking out loud. "What are we going to do with those fellows," he asked, "once you bring them in, Maynard? We got no jailhouse. And if Collins should get ahold of 'em—there'll be all hell to pay."

Suddenly David was tired of it. All the killing and fear. The secrecy and animosity. The inability of grown men to be just. He wanted to go home. He wanted to be with Louisa, to hold their baby, to watch the new puppy frolic over a bone. He wanted to split shingles, cut down trees, haul timber into town, chop wood. He waved and headed down the trail, light-headed and sick, and knowing he hadn't chopped wood in two-and-a-half weeks and that they were running out and that he really didn't know when he'd be strong enough to sling an axe again.

"Denny! You all right?" Maynard called after him, but he waved them on. By the time he got to his clearing he was breathing hard. He sat down on the chopping block out behind the cabin to rest. He'd wait just a minute and catch his breath. No sense in alarming Louisa. What was that, he wondered, leaning over to get a better look. Footprints ...all alongside Louisa's garden. He stretched his leg, matching heel to heel, and stared down at the three inches beyond his toes.

The crazy man was back.

-20-

Friday, March 17

Investigation followed and as a result four Indians were arrested. A trial before a Justice Court was held in the old Felker House, which was built by Captain Felker and was the first large frame house of sawed lumber erected on the site of Seattle.

—Emily Inez Denny, Louisa's daughter

A quick Justice Court was called into session a few days later, on David's twenty-second birthday, to determine if charges should be brought against the four Snoqualmie Indians Pat Kanim and Doc Maynard had brought in late the night before. Friday, March 17th, at ten o'clock in the morning, the hearing was held in the Felker House, Captain Felker's fancy hotel up on the Point. Collectively, they'd decided not to hold the session in the cookhouse, too recently the scene of Dr. Cherry's death.

Louisa sat with Mary Ann, Anna, and Ursula in the back row of a large, open room to watch the proceedings. This was her first visit to the hotel and at first she'd been distracted by the polished oak floors and gleaming brass banisters and wondering why in the world she'd never come to see it before. Then she saw Doc Maynard, Court Clerk and Justice of the Peace, take his place at the table in front and she remembered why she was here now. It was not a good feeling and she sought David's face. He spotted her and offered a gentle, unsure smile.

He sat with the other jurors—the same men who'd sat through District Court just a month earlier. Many of them, Louisa realized, were survivors of the Whidbey Island skirmish: Charles Terry, Lewis Wyckoff, Eddie Clark, Mr. Matthias, David. No wonder the stiffness in their backs, the suppressed emotion.

"I wish they'd hurry up and start," said Anna. "I'm not so sure Katy can manage Gerty."

"Katy will do a fine job with the children," Mary Ann replied.

Dobbins, Louisa saw, sat in the front row, next to three empty chairs, looking pale and weak, but alive and up and around, and she was suddenly filled with a sense of blessed assurance, a blissful, passing moment of peace. God was with them. She could never doubt that—not even today when fear etched the faces of everyone. The Chief of the Snoqualmies sat in the courtroom with them. He was an answer to prayer, Mary Ann had said. *But how did Pat Kanim feel*, Louisa wondered, *having to bring in his own men?*

He sat to the other side of Dobbins, dressed in corduroy jeans and a plaid shirt, complete with suspenders. Arthur had always said Pat Kanim was more white than most whites, and today Louisa gratefully believed him right.

The gavel came down three times and the meeting was brought to order by Doc Maynard. Three of the Indians, wrists tied, were led in by Henry Yesler, and Louisa was surprised at how young they looked. They couldn't be much more than 20. A fourth, Petawow, was carried in, strapped to a chair because his leg had been broken. The charges were read, the pleadings recorded.

Guilty. Not guilty. Not guilty. Guilty.

"You understand," said Doc Maynard, leaning across the table, looking over the top of his glasses and speaking directly to the four defendants, "that if found guilty you will be bound over to Judge Chenowith in Steilacoom?"

Where, Louisa guessed, listening to Pat Kanim translate, their fate would be sealed in a proper court of law.

They nodded.

Klap-ke-latchi, pleading not guilty, was the key witness, along with Salmon Bay Curley, who'd heard the story from Stemalyu.

"For the record, who is Stemalyu?" Maynard asked.

"An elder of the Snoqualmie tribe," Pat Kanim responded.

"For the record, is he here in this courtroom?"

"No, he is dead."

It was duly written.

Klap-ke-latchi began, sitting next to Dobbins, his hands folded and eyes frequently darting back and forth between David and Doc Maynard—and Pat Kanim. To these three men he spoke, no one else; yet the others listened as the atrocity came out in bits and pieces, at first denied and argued and ultimately agreed upon. Louisa, knowing most of the story from David already, still found herself growing sick with horror to hear the Indians tell the tale.

How could it be true? She stared at the backs of their heads. How could such cruelty exist in the heart of any man that they might smash in the head of another human being? And for what reason? Two hundred dollars? And a revolver? An axe?

The fear in the room gradually sharpened to anger, and she felt the change. Her own anger stirred, and her fear receded in the face of indignation and affront and the evidence. The axe and musket were produced. The revolver. The money? No one knew where it was. It had been stolen from under Kussass' bed. "No," said Klap-ke-latchi. "His *klootchman* was afraid of the *tamanuse*. She dropped it in *hyas chuck*."

"Kussass," said Doc Maynard, "it's been said by two witnesses that you not only killed Montgomery McCormick, a white man, but that you killed Chodups John, one of your own people."

"He wasn't one of my own people," Kussass sneered, drawing his black eyebrows together so that they met over his hawklike nose. "He was Duwamish."

"A pistol was dropped outside Chodups John's shack by the person who found him," Doc Maynard said.

Louisa went all numb and funny inside. No, please, the Indian must not know it was her. Please, Doc Maynard, don't tell him! She tensed, listening to the translation going on. Mary Ann reached over and put a hand on her knee.

"Did you pick the pistol up?"

"No."

"But it's missing."

"If I killed him," spit Kussass, "why would I go back another day just to look in on him?"

Doc Maynard sighed and slid a sheaf of papers over to Henry Yesler, court recorder, and Louisa let out her breath. How terrible to think the gun might have been in the hands of this young brave who looked like he might put a bullet into the back of anyone's head!

Examination. Cross-examination. No contradictory evidence offered.

"Why, trying them Injuns is as easy as wringing a chicken's neck!" declared Collins, burping loudly and patting his stomach. "Guilty right down the line."

"Silence!" thundered Maynard, stopping the nervous chuckles that sprinkled the room.

All of their fear had been sharpened into anger on the grindstone of testimony, and now even that was quickening into self-righteousness. People no longer looked afraid, Louisa realized, not even angry. Just smug. Led by Luther Collins who lolled back in this chair, cowboy boots thrown out into the aisle. She shivered, knowing her own guilt—her own fear and anger clambering for the self-righteous satisfaction of the white man's revenge. Yet if this were done, then it would be a game of power and fear, not justice.

Before noon Kussass and Stahowie were charged with murder and ordered to be held over for trial in Steilacoom.

Petawow was acquitted, Klap-ke-latchi held on suspicion. Without George McConaha to clarify the finer points of law, the jurymen couldn't decide whether there was sufficient evidence to render guilt. "Court dismissed!"

"Now wait just a minute!" shouted Collins, leaping to his feet and making his way down to the front. "You think we sat through this confession just to hear you announce *guilt*? Where's the hang-until-you-are-dead part?"

Charles Terry, his head still bandaged, came around from the jury chairs and stood before Luther. "Come on, Collins, what did you expect? You know the law doesn't work that way. They're entitled to a fair trial."

"Get your hand off my shoulder, you Injun-lovin'—"

"Clear out!" cried Maynard. "Go on! Court's over."

Collins stomped off and Louisa, stepping back to let him pass, pulled in her skirts. *But was she any worse than he?* she wondered with a start, *when she too wanted to see the murderers hanged?*

• • •

David and Louisa stayed with Ursula that night, David much, much too weary to go back on home—and wondering, too, if they should stay on for the big "pow wow" Maynard had planned. Already some of the Indians were arriving. Word had come, right after the hearing, that Stevens and Chief Seattle were both on their way—the governor finally back on his feet after his near drowning a week-and-a-half ago.

David, Louisa, and Ursula sat around the table talking, the night ticking away by the hands on Ursula's mantel clock. The children had been put to bed, George Jr. upstairs, Eugenia in the trundle bed, Emily in a box by the fire. Watch, one eye lifting open now and then, dozed beside her. Louisa sensed the missing child and avoided looking over to the bed where little Ursula had bled to death in front of their very eyes.

"You have enough wood?" David asked. "I can try in the morning—"

"No, no, that's all right," said Ursula. "The blacksmith has been wonderful. I haven't had to worry about a thing. No, he even comes and takes Georgie out of my hair after school. Has him running errands down at the smithy."

"His leg must be healing all right then," said Louisa.

"Oh, he limps still. I think that's why he's got Georgie helping out. You know, Liza, he really is a very nice man. Too bad there aren't any young ladies around these parts for bachelors like Lewis."

"What about Ellender—Henry Smith's sister?"

"I think Captain Plummer has an eye on *that* woman," said David.

Ursula, still only a shadow of her former self, did not rise to the bait, and Louisa, seeing a stack of newspapers in the corner, asked, "Any word on the suffrage bill?"

"No talk of suffrage yet." Ursula picked a paper up absently and looked through it. "They're too busy debating the Maine Liquor Law. Here—you see this, Louisa?" She pointed to a column on the front page.

" '*Honorable Victor Monroe will deliver an address at Olympia,*' " Louisa read, " '*in the Representatives' Hall, on Thursday evening, on the subject of, and advocating the propriety of, the adoption of the Maine Liquor Law by the people and legislature of the Territory. A general attendance is requested.*' They must have met last Thursday," she said, "Do you have the newest paper over there somewhere?"

Ursula handed it to her and Louisa glanced down the column for the report of Victor Monroe's address. "Look here, David," she said, holding the figures under the lamp. "He says that in ten years it costs the United States all this money because of liquor. Want me to read it to you?"

David nodded and Ursula picked up her knitting. "It's a little astounding," she told them.

" '*It's cost $600,000,000 in judicial fees,*' " Louisa read, " '*has sent 100,000 children to poor houses; has seen 300,000 lives lost; 15,000 murders; made 1,000 maniacs;*

sent 100,000 people to jail; cause 2,000 suicides; done $10,000,000 in fire damages; made 1,000,000 orphans; and last but not least, 100,000 widows!'"

"And it's not like we don't see the same results right here in Seattle," said Ursula. "But just read Chenowith's rebuttal—next column."

"It's awful long."

"Read it anyway, Liza," said David, relaxing. Louisa thought his smile looked tired—but happier. They'd been under an awful strain lately, but now Stevens and Chief Seattle were on their way. They just had to hold on a little longer.

"Wait a minute. Before you begin, let me check the children." Ursula slipped up the ladder, cocked her head and came back down. "David? Where have the prisoners been locked up?"

"I don't know. Somewhere on the Point, I think. Maybe the storeroom off Dr. Williamson's store. Why?"

"Nothing. I just get nervous is all," she said, biting her lip. "I could swear someone's been prowling around the cabin all this week. But then I've been as nervous as a she-goat lately."

"We all have," said David. "But it's over now. At least this crisis. Pat Kanim is as angry as the rest of us. And soon Chief Seattle will be here."

"I know, I know, it's just that . . ."

"It'll be all right," he said, then he grinned. "I'll sleep across the door if you want."

"Go on, read the paper, Liza," she chuckled. "Never mind me. I'm just a bundle of nerves. David, being a teetotaler, will be interested in Mr. Chenowith's response. But keep in mind, David, this is our territorial judge speaking!"

"The same man who will hear the case against Kussass and Stahowie?" Louisa asked.

"Yes, now read, Liza," Ursula urged.

Louisa began:

If there is any encouraging prospect of succeeding in removing every temptation out of man's reach, it might be some excuse for neglecting the culture of his moral nature. If you could crush and annihilate his will, his free, lofty, and commanding intellect, after all this is gone, you might compel him, or what is left of him to be temperate. But shall we be blind to all the lessons human nature has taught us on the subject of compulsion! Have we yet to learn that men *will not be coerced?* Men may choose to doom themselves to single blessedness, and by their choice decline all association with the fairer sex—

"It's a ridiculous analogy," interrupted Ursula, turning her needles and beginning a new row of her knitting. "As if—well, never mind, I'm just thinking out loud."

—but, sir, if you want to witness the terror of the storm, the outburst of volcanic fires, just pass a law to prohibit marriage, and all intercourse of the sexes, and you instantly clothe our peaceful land in terrible flame, and the very men that now from choice isolate themselves from the fair ones, would instantly spill their heart's blood for the privilege they choose to forgo. You pass a law that men shall neither buy or sell liquor, and you instantly arouse the lion's rage. Men who seldom buy, or even think of it, would instantly buy a year's supply, for fear that when they wanted it they could not get it.

"Now read George's response," said Ursula, a hint of pride in her weary voice.

As to the great evil sought to be removed there can be but one opinion,

read Louisa, smiling, almost hearing George's voice leap from the printed words.

The dreadful consequences of intemperance have been too often delineated by masterhands to leave any doubt that it is one of those dreadful blights upon the human race; the removal of which should engage the head and heart of every philanthropist!

"Did you see that a Mr. Foley in Olympia has begun a petition?" Ursula took the paper from Louisa's hand and set it back in the corner. "He's collecting signatures from citizens to prove to Chenowith and the legislature that the majority of us want temperance. I'm going to make up one of my own, I think, and take it around. Will you sign it, David?"

"I'll sign it twice. You keeping an eye on the Eastern Question?"

"No. I don't want to know anything about the war in Europe. We have—"

"Ursula?" Louisa asked, glancing to the window.

"It was the crazy man!" Ursula shouted, coming to life and jumping to her feet. David followed, both of them running out the door. But the man was gone and they came back in, hair damp from the rain.

"Well, if that doesn't beat all," said Ursula, standing at the window. "Didn't he get parceled off to Steilacoom, or am I just seeing things? Or am I losing my mind?"

"You're not losing your mind," said David quietly. "He is back."

•   •   •

"How come you didn't tell me?" Louisa asked him later. Ursula, after having David carry George Jr. downstairs half asleep, had given them the loft to themselves.

"I didn't want to worry you."

"So you just let me go out of my mind feeling like every time I turned around, someone was watching me?"

"I didn't know you thought anybody was hanging around! Why didn't *you* tell *me*?"

"Because I didn't want to worry you."

They both started to laugh, catching each other in their arms.

"David! What's that?" She sat up and whacked her head on the roof, forgetting they'd been put to bed in the loft.

"Just the mill whistle."

"But it's the middle of the night!"

"Liza." He flopped to his back. "It always blows at midnight. Change in shift, remember?"

She felt silly. Of course. He laughed and pulled her close, and she snuggled in, laying her head against his shoulder. "I forgot to tell you Happy Birthday," she whispered, and then started to sing in a low voice "For He's a Jolly Good Fellow." He reached up to jam the pillow next to his arm, to take some of the weight of her head, and she was about half way through the song when someone pummeled on the door downstairs. Both of them started up at once, Louisa hitting her head again.

"David, DAVID!" cried Ursula. "It's Dobbins. There's trouble. Get down here!"

Louisa handed David his shirt. He pulled on his pants and scrambled down the ladder, Louisa close behind. He buttoned the shirt, took his coat and rifle, and followed Dobbins out the door without a backward glance or another word.

Ursula, her long hair flying and wild, tried to quiet the wailing Eugenia and frightened Georgie. Emily, Louisa saw, had slept through everything. She lit a lamp and shadows leaped at once. Methodically and not knowing what else to do, she put on some water for tea while Ursula frantically comforted her children. Louisa then sat at the table, hands clenched, in prayer or anguish—weren't they the same thing now?

Neither could drink the tea. Silently the two women paced the room for nearly half an hour. A soft knock sounded and David let himself in. One look at his face and Louisa collapsed onto the bed.

David closed the door behind him, leaning against it heavily, breath coming hard. Ursula began to scream, but Louisa leaped from the bed to stay her. "Tell us, David," Louisa pleaded. "Now."

"Luther Collins lynched Stahowie and Kussass tonight. He and Eddie Clark, along with a couple of sailors, hoisted them up on a tripod of spars with a block and tackle out on the Point. No," he said, seeing the question in their eyes. "We didn't get there in time. They're both dead."

Part VII

CHIEF SEATTLE
Mid-March

The Bay swarmed with canoes and the shore was lined with a living, swaying, writhing, dusky humanity until Old Chief Seattle's trumpet-toned voice rolled over the immense multitude, like the startling reveille of a brass drum, when silence became as instantaneous and perfect as that which follows a clap of thunder from a clear sky.

—Dr. Henry Smith

-21-

Saturday, March 18

Not yet satisfied with the work of execution, a mob...determined to hang [Klap-ke-latchi] also. They therefore obtained the assistance of some sailors with a block and tackle from a ship in the harbor, set up a tripod of spars, cut for shipment, over which they put the rope.

—Emily Inez Denny, Louisa's daughter

Before daybreak David whispered in Louisa's ear. "I'm worried about your brother. He started coughing blood again last night. Think maybe I'll slip over and see how he's doing."

"Now?" she asked, rolling over in his arms. "But the sun's not even up!"

"I can't sleep."

"He and Anna won't be up."

"But something's wrong. I can feel it in my bones."

"Everything's wrong, David. Everything."

He sighed and began pulling on his clothes again. "Louisa, I didn't tell you, but Dobbins took Klap-ke-latchi over to his place last night after the lynching and locked him into the bedroom. I'm thinking now I should have gone back over there to help guard."

She half sat up, then fell backward into the covers and closed her eyes.

191

"Liza," he said more gently, leaning over to kiss her. She surprised him by throwing her arms around his neck and pulling him close. He could feel the trembling of her body.

"Oh, David!" she cried softly, "What's to become of us?"

"We're going to weather the storm," he whispered, looking into the shadows of her eyes, "and then we're going to grow old with a hundred grandchildren at our knees. I promise," he said gently, kissing her one more time.

The air was soft with fog and mist, the sun just beginning to stretch in the eastern sky behind the ridge of hill and trees, casting ghostlike shadows over the still-sleeping world. He cut through the cow pasture in back of Dobbins' cabin, catching the dew on the cuff of his pants, and breaking into a run when he heard a cry from the cabin.

He burst in, winded, and looked past the cluttered room to the empty bedroom. Anna sat in a heap on the floor, head over her knees, arms wrapped around the top of her head.

"Anna! Where are they? What's happened! *Where's Klap-ke-latchi?*

But she only sobbed. Furious with her for being so stupidly helpless, David yanked her up by the arm. "Tell me what happened before it's too late!"

"Someone came to get Dobbins, said it was urgent. I don't know. And then they broke in—"

"Who, Anna, who?" He shook her.

"I sent Gerty to Mary's. She kept crying." Anna wiped her nose with her shirt.

"WHO, ANNA? Who came? Tell me!"

"Luther Collins! And that new man, Eddie Clark!"

He was out the door, and took off at a run, down the darkened trail and into town, leaping stumps and tree roots, muscles in his legs still so clumsy, heart throbbing in his jaw. *Not again,* he kept thinking. *God in heaven, not again!*

Breaking the forest growth and racing past cookhouse and mill, boots clattering over the puncheon of Commercial Street, he tore full speed up the incline to the Point, not even sure what he would do once he got there. A sob of air caught in his throat when he saw the silhouette of the tripod of spars still set up from last night, outlined dimly against the pale, foggy horizon. Klap-ke-latchi stood beneath, pop-eyed, with a noose around his neck.

Then David heard, "Put down that rope, you rascals!" *Dobbins!*

Spurred, he sprinted the last few yards and stood dizzy, sucking into his lungs the stinging, cold air. Four seamen held the rope, waiting only for the word from Clark, acting as hangman.

"You have no right to hang that man!" Dobbins said, breathing noisily and advancing, fog swirling from his mouth.

Luther Collins stepped in his way. "It's the only way to stop these murdering Siwash!" he said, towering over the stooped sheriff. "If we're a bunch of yellow-bellied lizards afraid to call a spade a spade—"

"Stand aside, you fool! And drop that rope! Now!" Dobbins skirted around Collins, but Collins grabbed him by his coat sleeve. Dobbins slid neatly out of his jacket and left Collins holding an empty sleeve, and stumbled toward the spars, blue-faced and white-lipped. He whipped out his pocket knife and before Clark or Collins could give the order to yank, Dobbins set the blade and began sawing hemp just over Klap-ke-latchi's head.

David watched the rope go, end snaking to the sky, curling and snapping around the top of the spar, and then come twisting out of the fog and landing with a soft thump onto the ground. The noose fell loose over Klap-ke-latchi's shoulders and the men without another word slunk away, disappearing into the white breath of dawn.

Somewhere a rooster crowed and a dog yapped. Trembling, David closed the gap between himself and the makeshift gallows, hurrying now, for he saw that Dobbins' wound had come open, blood staining his shirt. He picked up the jacket and laid it over his brother-in-law's shoulders.

"Tricked," muttered Dobbins. "They tricked me. I should've seen it coming. Dragged me away on some pretext or another to do with those barrels I got stacked on the beach up by Arthur's."

"Come on," said David, alarmed at the wheezing in Dobbins' lungs, and his own scream of pain—20 separate toothaches in his jaw. Between the three of them—Klap-ke-latchi just as badly shaken and weak—they headed downhill arms entwined, propping each other up as they went.

They made it as far as Doc Maynard's store where Maynard, hearing the trio at his door, met them with a low whistle and angry curse for Collins. He barked orders for Catherine to throw new sheets on the bed and to get the water boiling. David, before sinking into a chair by the fire, saw the crazy man eating porridge at the table. What was to become of them all? he wondered with a sour laugh, and then let Catherine set a hot poultice against his cheek.

•   •   •

All that afternoon and into Sunday the Indians arrived, swelling the Indian camp down at the Point to more than 500. The white settlers, sobered by the lynching and feeling anxious, came out of their cabins to stand in clusters, watching the apparently peaceful invasion with cautious eyes, comparing apprehensions in nervous, low voices.

Canoes scattered along the beaches, pulled up past the high-tide rope of tangled seaweed and bark. Temporary huts of cedar bough went up. Fires burned, and all around was the sound of guttural shouts and the high-pitched laughter of half-naked children. David and Louisa spent the two days quietly, watching with the others and waiting.

In the middle of all this Mike Simmons, Indian agent and Catherine Maynard's brother, and Governor Stevens arrived by steamer. They came ashore pale and thin, coughing from the cold in their lungs, and were put up at once in Doc Maynard's store, cots brought and set up around the pot-bellied stove, syrups and chicken soup spooned into them—along with news of the "St. Patrick's Day" lynchings.

And then the shout went up! Chief Seattle was here! He and his sons arrived right after lunch on Sunday, their war canoe gliding over the water as nearly 40 warriors and slaves brought them grinding into the gravel just below the bank by Doc Maynard's store, swift oars flashing in unison. Whites and Indians alike surged to the beach, the whites gratefully mindful of the peace he'd brought last summer right after the first lynching.

David went out in front of the others to meet the tall, muscular Chief, and was reminded again of the intelligence that reflected from the man's large, expressive eyes. The Chief, David knew, saw beyond today into tomorrow—with wisdom few people possessed. There was a sadness in the Chief's eyes, too, he thought.

They spoke in Duwamish, exchanging greetings as Jim and George came to join them. News of the new lynchings had already reached their ears, and they spoke solemnly and gravely. Still, the Chief's very presence brought a welcomed sense of order into the chaos.

Doc Maynard came down the trail from the house and in genuine affection, hugged Seattle warmly. "Ahh," he said, speaking Duwamish, "it's good to see my old friend— although I am afraid we meet when the air is filled with bad tidings."

"Your tyee, is he here?" Seattle asked in his own tongue.

"In the house," said Maynard, taking Seattle by the elbow and leading him up the trail.

•　•　•

All Sunday afternoon the men met—Governor Stevens, Chief Seattle and his elders, Pat Kanim, and Mike Simmons, along with Doc Maynard, Henry Smith, and David Denny acting in turns as translators. Everyone in town went about their business in a mixed cloud of apprehension and hope, knowing, however, that the leaders of both races were at least meeting and were each, in their own way, dedicated to moving forward together in an effort to avoid any more bloodshed.

That night, in the cookhouse and throughout the cabins and up and down the beaches, the plans that had been drawn were told. The governor, they found out, had been given leave by the legislature to return immediately to Washington, D.C. following the Seattle agreement. Permission had been given primarily so that he could personally present to Jefferson Davis Lieutenant Tinkham's report of the Snoqualmie Pass, and to fight for the northern route of the transcontinental railroad. Rumor had reached the legislature's ears at the end of February that President Pierce was urging the present session of Congress to finish their considerations before adjournment, and—on Davis' recommendations—urging them to endorse the route through California. It seemed to the Washington legislature that if the northern route were to have a voice at all, it was imperative that their governor be in D.C. to speak for them. However, most of the pioneers shook their heads to realize that only a few months ago the railroad had been all they'd cared about. Now it almost seemed an affront to let their governor leave on railroad business when such serious immediate concerns plagued them.

But Stevens would also request of Jefferson Davis, Secretary of War, a special stand of arms to be deposited at Fort Steilacoom and a new squadron of soldiers in case of further trouble. And he would seek from Congress further appropriations and authorization—so that they could have enough land settlement monies to buy up Indian titles and move the Indians, en masse, onto reservations. This, the pioneers agreed, was the only solution for the rising tensions between the two races. Seattle and Pat Kanim both agreed as well, seeing—especially after the tragic series of events of the past three weeks—that hot heads lived on both sides of the fence. Peace, it seemed, could only be had at the cost of separation.

The Indians would withdraw to their separate reservations when Governor Stevens returned from the national capital later on in the year; the land would be divided and determined at that time. And in exchange for this peaceful withdrawal, the whites would furnish the Indians with medical care, schools, an Indian agent, and the purchase price of their old lands—the details to be worked out between Stevens and Congress.

There was one condition, and it stuck in the craw of many. Luther Collins, by direct order of the governor—and over protest of Doc Maynard—was to be tried for murder in the fall when the second session of District Court met. If Pat Kanim could set the example and bring in for trial his own men who were guilty of murder, the whites could do the same.

Those who felt outrage took comfort in Maynard's promise of top attorneys and hurried to sign Collins' subscription list to pay for the defense. Those who felt relief took comfort that there was at last law and order. And for those, the majority, who felt ambivalent, they took comfort in the fact that fall was still a long way off.

For David, before falling asleep that night, his only thought was, *The governor is finally waking up.*

-22-

Monday, March 20

When [the governor] sat down, Chief Seattle arose, with all the dignity of a senator who carries the responsibilities of the nation on his shoulders. Placing one hand on the governor's head, and slowly pointing heavenward with the index finger of the other, he commenced his memorable address in solemn and impressive tones....

—Emily Inez Denny, Louisa's daughter

Monday morning dawned with a slight breeze from the south, and down at the Indian camp, squaws and braves stirred. Soon the smell of their fires woke those who slept indoors, drawing them awake with the realization that today was the day Chief Seattle would make his long-awaited speech. After today they could forget all the ugly business that had descended out of dark skies. The old sense of manifest destiny, hardly conscious in their minds, rooted its way again into their hearts.

The meeting place was on the Point where the gallows had been. Ironically, Indians pressed with the whites, mingling and mixing, and Louisa, Emily strapped to her back, found Princess Angeline. They stood together under the canopy of a towering fir, allowing the throb of anticipation and festivity to seep into their guarded and still-wary minds. But it was hard to doubt the passing of bad will when Doc Maynard climbed up onto a high stump and started to joke greetings to whites and Indians alike, his raccoon-tail cap tipped back on his head, calling this and that out to friends.

Stevens sat beside him on a second stump, dressed in the usual blue flannel shirt and suspenders, brown corduroys, his hair all yellow and scratchy-looking. Chief Seattle stood behind them, wearing his blanket against the breeze, and Louisa was captured by the man's simple majesty. His integrity shone through and bestowed on him an authority beyond what any crown or royal coat could give.

Seagulls screeched off the wharf pilings to the north and, taken with their grace, Louisa watched them swirl and swoop beyond the Chief's head, thinking that such a picture was appropriate: the seagull, after all, was Seattle's spirit power.

"Fellow citizens!" began the governor, rising and addressing the throng, "we have bright omens to encourage us in our efforts to lay the solid foundations of the prosperity of this Territory! The intelligence and the virtue of our citizens, which are so strikingly exhibited in the kind, social relations which unite them, their deep interest in the prosperity of their social communities, and the labor which they freely render for the common good in opening roads, in establishing schools, in giving aid to the stranger, all these give us reason to believe that here the young blossoms of our youth will yield a horde of fruit. Here the dignity of our nation, the worth of liberty, the influence of a lofty intelligence will be shown in a truly noble theater. Be assured that my efforts shall be joined with yours to prepare us for the compilation of that sisterhood of states, which have made the name of America immortal!"

When the governor finally sat down, Chief Seattle stepped forward. A hush settled over the crowd. Even the children paused to see who this man was who stood silently before them. *He bears all the dignity of a senator,* Louisa thought, *who carries the responsibilities of a great nation on his shoulders.* David had found her, and was slipping his arm around her waist. She looked up and smiled, tugging on his hand to distract him long enough so he'd notice Angeline. But his eyes were fixed on Seattle.

Placing one hand on the top of the governor's head, and then slowly pointing heavenward with the index finger of his other hand, the tall, broad-shouldered Chief commenced his oration and Louisa, at first amused by the discomfiture on the governor's reddened face, quickly found herself caught on the drumming throb of Seattle's voice as it trumpeted and rolled over the multitude around her like a reveille. Although she couldn't understand his language, she recognized his strength—and, she thought, his sadness.

"Yonder sky has wept tears of compassion on our fathers for centuries untold, and which to us appears changeless and eternal, may change. Today it is fair. Tomorrow it may be overcast with clouds," the Chief began, Henry Smith translating, sentence by sentence. "My words are like the stars that never change. Whatever Seattle says the great chief at Washington can rely upon with as much certainty as he can upon the return of the sun." And then he spoke without letting his voice fall, pausing only briefly for Henry to translate before continuing on in his thunderous oration.

"The White Chief says that the Big Chief at Washington sends us greetings of friendship and goodwill. This is kind, for his people are many. They are like the grass that covers vast prairies. My people are few. They resemble the scattering trees of a storm-swept plain. There was a time when our people covered the land as the waves of a wind-ruffled sea covers its shell-paved floor, but that time long since passed away with the greatness of tribes that are now but a mournful memory. I will not dwell on, nor mourn over, our untimely decay, nor reproach my paleface brothers with hastening it as we too may have been somewhat to blame.

"Youth is impulsive. When our young men grow angry at come real or imaginary wrong, and disfigure their faces with black paint, it denotes that their hearts are black, and that they are often cruel and relentless. Thus it has ever been. Thus it was when the white men first began to push our forefathers further westward. But let us hope that the hostilities between us may never return. We would have everything to lose and nothing to gain. Revenge by young men is considered gain, even at the cost of their own lives, but old men who stay at home in times of war, and mothers who have sons to lose, know better.

"Our good father at Washington—for I presume he is now our father—sends us word that if we do as he desires he will buy our lands and he will protect us from our ancient enemies far to the northward. Then in reality will the White Chief be our father and we his children. We may be brothers after all. We will see. I think that my people will accept your proposition and retire to the reservation you offer them. Then we will dwell apart in peace."

The Chief sighed and profound sorrow filled his voice. "It matters little where we pass the remnant of our days. They will not be many. The Indians' night promises to be dark. Not a single star of hope hovers above his horizon. Sad-voiced winds moan in the distance. Grim fate seems to be on the Red Man's trail, and wherever he goes he will hear the approaching footsteps of his destroyer and prepare stolidly to meet his doom, as does the wounded doe that hears the approaching footsteps of the hunter.

"A few more moons. A few more winters— but should I mourn at the untimely fate of my people? Tribe follows tribe, and nation follows nation, like the waves of the sea. It is the order of nature." He looked out over the assembly of red and white. He glanced down at Governor Stevens. "Your time of decay may be distant, but it will surely come, for even the White Man whose God walked and talked with him as friend with friend, cannot be exempt from the common destiny.

"You may buy our land and dwell there, but you should know that every hillside, every valley, every plain and grove, has been hallowed by some sad or happy event in days long vanished. Even the rocks, which seem to be dumb and dead as they swelter in the sun along the silent shore, thrill with memories of stirring events connected with the lives of my people, and the very dust upon which you now stand responds more lovingly to their footsteps than to yours, because it is rich with the blood of our ancestors and our bare feet are conscious of the sympathetic touch.

"And when the last Red Man shall have perished, and the memory of my tribe shall have become a myth among the White Men, these shores will swarm with the invisible dead of my tribe, and when your children's children think themselves alone in the field, the store, the shop, upon the highway, or in the silence of the pathless woods, they will not be alone. The White Man will never be alone.

"Let him be just and deal kindly with my people, for the dead are not powerless. Dead, did I say? There is no death, only a change of worlds."

• • •

That same day Seattle left for Agate Pass, and Louisa felt the loss. With the Chief's departure, the other Indians scattered, and by nightfall only those who lived at the Indian camp south of the Point remained. The town felt empty to Louisa, the rest of them rattling around in the bottom of a bag that had once been full. So much tension and uncertainty, so much grief, and now everything seemed to be over. Was it?

Word circulated that Yesler had invited everyone down for free coffee, and so after supper, the children tucked into bed and older sisters and brothers put in charge, men and women alike headed for the cookhouse.

The crazy man was there. Eddie Moore sat in a corner like a huge, sulking child. Doc Maynard had scolded him for some reason and he took it like a three-year-old, pouting and muttering to himself over the injustice of it all. To make him feel better, Louisa took Emily over. He perked up at the sight of her and immediately nodded happily when she asked if he'd like to hold the baby. He folded Emily tenderly in his massive arms and gently touched her cheek with his own.

For the rest of the evening, he followed Louisa and Emily with his eyes. "Whatever are we going to do with him?" Louisa asked Mary Ann. "I don't think he's dangerous, but—"

"I suppose the men shall have to figure something out."

Louisa, beginning to get sleepy, slid onto the table bench beside David where he was playing checkers with Dr. Williamson.

"Want to go home?" he asked.

She nodded. "I'll ask Ursula if we can let ourselves in."

"No, I mean *home*. No reason to stay in town anymore." He grinned, and she felt as though summer sunshine warmed her.

Dr. Williamson, a small, shy man with a shock of black hair, cleared his throat. "Your turn, David."

"We can't go home, David," Louisa said. "Ursula and I, remember, are going to go around town in the morning to see if we can't get signatures for her temperance petition."

"You going to get Doc Maynard to head the list?" Dr. Williamson asked her, and she laughed.

"WHO STOLE MY CHEESE!"

"What cheese, Henry?" Maynard asked, downing a drink with the governor in a corner.

"Yesler let me put a slab of cheese on the grill!" said Henry Smith at the kitchen door. "And now that I've come back, it's gone!"

"I guess I did," said Luther Collins, hunkered by the fire.

"Did you *eat* that cheese?"

"Wal—yes. But I didn't think you'd care much!"

Henry hurried to Collins, tripping in his haste over at least three dogs and little Eugenia toddling around with an Indian ball in her hands.

"Care! Care? *Good thunder, I hope you didn't eat it!*"

Brazenly, Luther nodded.

"Gallstones! I just put a *double dose of arsenic* in it to kill the rats!"

Collins rose, wavered, gulped, and went green around the eyes. "Thought it tasted mighty queer. What can I do?"

"Quick! Come right along with me. There's only one thing that can save you," Henry said, grabbing him by the elbow and hauling him over to the table. Stunned, Louisa pulled back while Henry drew off a pint of rancid dogfish oil from the lamp and handed it in a cup to Collins and said, "Swallow it quick! Your life depends on it!"

Collins, too badly frightened to quarrel, took the cup, and gagged, swallowed, and gagged again till tears came to his eyes. Finally he handed back the empty cup, drained to the dregs.

"There now," said Henry, "go home and to bed, and if you are alive in the morning, come around and report yourself."

As soon as he was gone, Henry leaned on the door, grinning wickedly.

"You didn't," said Ursula to Henry as soon as Luther left.

"Oh, my lordie," wheezed Lewis Wyckoff, winking at Ursula and suddenly throwing back his head to laugh. "*He did!*"

The roar of laughter seemed to swell the very walls of the cookhouse. Louisa laughed till tears splashed from her eyes and she had to hold David's arm for fear of falling off the bench. But suddenly, she was buoyed by the thought that she had not heard rich communal laughter like this in— how long? Too long. Spring, she decided, was truly here.

Part VIII

THE AUCTION
Early May

This incident of the country's first pauper is of more than passing interest, illustrating as it does the embarrassment in the new Territory before provision was made for caring for public wards. An itemized bill of $621 for Moore's support had been presented by King County to the legislature...but the lawmakers, admitting it was "a case that should touch all the finer feelings of our nature," still felt they could not establish a precedent by paying the bill.

—Roberta Frye Watt, Katy's daughter

-23-

Sunday, April 30

Ordered that Edward Moore, the pauper, now in Seattle, be sold at public auction...for his maintenance to be paid out of the county treasury...

—County commissioners

Emily, now three months old and reaching for everything in sight and shoving it into her mouth, lay on a blanket in the sun sucking on a sock doll. Louisa came out of the house into the morning sunlight and shooed Peek-a-boo off the stoop and, with coffee in hand, sat down to read the very last of the legislative reports in the *Pioneer & Democrat*. Tomorrow the legislature would adjourn and the men would be heading home. She laughed out loud when Emily twisted and rolled over, surprised with herself. When the rooster strutted across to investigate, she chuckled happily. "Shoo!" she said. "Go on, git, leave her alone!" and she took the rolled up paper lightly to Peek-a-boo's beautiful blue-black tail plumage to push him on. The rooster ran squawking off, wings spread, to the four Rhode Island hens digging for bugs at the forest edge. *April showers bring May flowers.* The poem was all wrong, Louisa thought, going back to the steps. It should be more like *March winds mean April sings.*

All around, the world sang in her ears. The whole month had been a glorious spring song of days upon days of sunshine trumpeting the end of winter. From where she sat, sunshine on her face and reflecting off the logs behind her, she could hear the music everywhere: in the chirp and trill of robins, in the fuss and cluck of her chickens recently brought out from Dobbins' coop as they pecked and scratched in the forest mulch, in the yap of her puppy leaping amongst stumps and brush, nose into everything, and best of all in David at last strong again and out back whacking branches off a fallen tree. Crocuses along the cabin walls had opened silently, and the first green of leaf buds had formed on her sweetbriar bushes. All of spring sang, with crescendo and minuet.

But if April was a song, Louisa thought, newspaper in hand, there were a few discordant notes as well. All month the legislature had battled back and forth on the Maine Liquor Law and the suffrage bill, finally losing both to one vote. The women, with the exception of Mrs. Butler, had not danced over the news, and Ursula, who had worked so hard collecting signatures for the Liquor Law, had broken down and cried. The defeat of the Liquor Law was only a small disappointment in contrast to all that she endured—loneliness for George and the death of her daughter—but it seemed to break Ursula. Louisa herself had not been pleased with the news, and when no one was looking, she too had cried.

The sourest note was the legislature's refusal to create a pauper's fund for the care of Eddie Moore. Doc Maynard had submitted an itemized bill of $621. When that had been rejected, with the excuse that the territory couldn't set the precedent of paying a poor man's bills, Doc Maynard had lost all patience and gone to the county commissioners demanding that they do something. Quickly. He couldn't take care of this man all his life, nor could he keep paying for him.

The commissioners' answer? Auction Mr. Moore off. He was a big man, and could be made to stack wood and haul lumber and do any number of chores. The fact that it smacked of slavery didn't bother any of the men who, under other circumstances, preached abolition. To Louisa's disgust and disbelief, all of Seattle geared up for the Sunday afternoon event, as though a party would right their wrong.

A butterfly dropped down by her knee, and watching it bob and float, she was conscious of the ring of David's axe out behind the house. The song of spring again sang sweetly in her ears, and she whispered a prayer of thanksgiving for all that they had come through. David was right; they would live to a ripe old age with a hundred grandchildren at their knees. They just had to get through the auction this afternoon!

She ran her eyes down the April twenty-second issue of the *Pioneer & Democrat* in her hand, squinting against the small print.

> Council Bill No. 6, entitled an act to incorporate the County steamboat company, was taken up and read a second time. Mr. Crosbie said he should vote for the bill. He said he would vote for the right of way to Heaven if anyone should apply such a charter—he considered one about as practical as another.

No doubt about it, she thought, glancing up to see if Emily was happy. When the men weren't so busy being stupid, they were funny.

> Mr. Mosely said he should vote against the bill from principal—he was opposed to charters in any shape.
> Mr. Chenowith said he was in favor of the bill—the river was not navigable for steamboats now; nor could it ever be unless made so by a company, and he was in favor of all chartered companies which had in view the improvement of the territory.

Louisa grinned when next she read:

> Mr. Denny, rising, said he had little fear of being accused of being on the wrong side, for really he was

not certain of his position. He complained of not being able to discover the object of discussion—so far nothing had been said about the distance when the tide ebbs and flows, nor had it been said how far the company wanted a right to navigate the river.

He had noticed that several gentlemen who had voted against a previous charter, now contended strenuously for this, and if they were disposed to strain at a gnat and swallow a steamboat, it was their business, not his.

She laughed out loud. Why, she missed Arthur and his dry wit! But soon he would be back since the legislature was adjourning, and within just a few days, she would probably be arguing with him again. Such was life.

Goodness! But it was time to go to the auction! "David!" she called, hurrying around the side of the house. "Are you ready?"

He hadn't heard her and she stood watching him in secret. There was something beautiful about a man whose body and mind were combined in total concentration, working together to accomplish—especially when the man was someone you loved more than life itself. His shirt was off. Sweat glistened on his finely proportioned chest, rippled with muscles developed from hard work. Feet spread on either side of the tree, he bent to his task, striking rhythmically, whack, whack, the beat of spring in her ears, working his way down the tree, knocking off branches first to the right, then to the left with the steady slice of his axe.

"David? Tom should be hollering for us soon."

"How long have you been standing there?" he asked with a grin. His beard had grown in again, all sign of his wound concealed.

"Long enough," she said, teasing him.

He hung the axe up, hooking it over a spike on the back wall and then pulled her into his arms. "You sure you want to go?" he asked, kissing her softly and looking into her eyes with his own, searching her mind.

"I think it's shameful what they're doing, but we must go to see that he's all right."

"Liza, he doesn't even know what's going on."

They'd been through it many times, but she wouldn't, couldn't, change her mind. To put a man on an auction block, selling him off to the highest bidder, was perfectly barbaric.

"It's not as bad as you think," said David. "By keeping him busy, he won't be snooping around all the time, giving us the willies. It's the only reasonable solution."

"Let's not argue, David. It won't make any difference anyway. They're going to do it, and I can't stop them. But I can be there."

David washed up outside by the clothesline, whistling. Louisa went indoors to pack, putting into her grass bag enough clothes for a few days. David wanted to stick around town until Arthur and George got back. It would make for a nice holiday. Neither of them had been into town for six weeks, not since Chief Seattle had come and gone and everything had slipped back to normal. And despite the occasion for today's trip, she was happy enough to be going.

David came in, casting a shadow across the floor, buttoning his shirt. "Here, let me do that for you," she said, pulling his fingers away.

•   •   •

Frank Matthias had built a square wooden platform for the occasion. It sat down on the sawdust. Nearby a table had been set up and was heaped high with food of all kinds: pots of beans, venison roasts, hard-boiled eggs in a bowl, bread loaves, clam stew and chowder, lots of pies and cakes. Louisa added her rice pudding and Mary Jane Mercer added her contribution of sweet cinnamon rolls made with buttermilk. Tom and David disappeared. The three little

Mercer girls all went shrieking off, looking for friends. Mary Jane, Louisa noticed, stood near the mill where a group of sawyers played a hand of cards. Lonely Mary Jane, Louisa thought, watching the sunlight on the young girl's red hair. But it wouldn't be very long before one of those bachelors sat up to take notice.

Such a fuss this all was, Louisa thought, looking around. Her mind flashed to pictures she'd seen of slave auctions. At least they didn't celebrate their wicked deed like this, she thought grimly.

"Auntie, may I hold Emily?"

Louisa smiled to see her niece. "Why, yes, Katy, if you don't mind," and off Katy went, proudly carrying her cousin slung over one thrust-out hip. Neither Anna nor Mary Ann were anywhere in sight, and so Louisa joined Kate Blaine and some other ladies sitting along a couple of logs rolled up from the beach. "Now that it's about over, I guess our legislature has done some things creditable to themselves," Kate Blaine was saying, "but some disgraceful things to us as a territory. Hello, Sister Denny, and how is the baby?" Without waiting for an answer she was off again. "I just froth whenever I think of them giving half-breeds the right to vote, and then denying us the same favor! A question that immediately arises in my mind is whether we women ought to congratulate ourselves that we're not associated politically with such a set—or whether we ought to feel aggrieved that the highest privilege that can be conferred on citizens should be proffered to the most degraded and abandoned race imaginable and yet withheld from us." Then without taking a breath, Kate inquired sweetly, "Louisa, you haven't yet seen my new house?"

"Are you all moved in?"

"We are. You must come over and see the wallpaper."

"Wallpaper! In this town?"

"In my house," Kate assured her.

"LADIES AND GENTLEMEN," the cry rang out, "the auction is about to begin!"

Distasteful as the auction was, anything was better than listening to Kate Blaine. Louisa excused herself politely. Whatever the Methodist mission paid the preacher and his wife to preach their bigotry, she thought, it was too much. Wallpaper? Indeed! The rest of them made do with newspaper!

Louisa found David standing with Mary Ann and Ursula. She greeted her sister and Ursula and slid her hand into David's. He squeezed in secret greeting. She glanced about for Katy and found her with her friends, still holding the happy Emily. Up on the square wooden platform Eddie sat perched on a stool, looking hopelessly confused, biting his fingers and wiping his eyes.

Doc Maynard explained the system—they were selling Eddie Moore off for monthly lots, and any one could bid, providing they had the money and something for him to do. The money would go into a fund and then be used for his maintenance. Snickers broke out. Eddie's lower lip trembled. Louisa's heart ached for his humiliation, but she was powerless. She squirmed beside David as the bids rose and rose, the pioneers getting into a high good mood, joking about the worth of Eddie Moore. Was a big, simple, nine-toed man really worth—five dollars? Doc Maynard called out, "Five dollars. Do I hear six?" Beside him, Eddie seemed to slide right off the stool, his anguish painfully visible. Why didn't the others see it? Louisa wondered. Or didn't they care? There was one more comical reference to the crazy man, and suddenly Eddie jumped up behind Doc Manyard and from his pants pocket he pulled a pistol. It was *her* pistol!

"Five dollars. Going. Going..." Doc Maynard paused, alarmed by the gasp that had risen from the crowd. Slowly he turned to face Eddie—and the pistol pointing at his chest. Every eye in the crowd fixed on the round hole of the short barrel aimed right for Doc Maynard's black garbed shirtfront as the gun danced and trembled in Eddie's big, soft hand.

"Now see here, Eddie," said Doc Maynard, collecting himself.

"Give me that gun. It's just me, your old Uncle Maynard."

But Eddie shook his head, his face a kaleidoscope of pain, confusion, and fear. He stumbled backward, tripping on the stool. The gun fired into the air.

The panic was instantaneous, with loud cries and screams. Louisa drew a short, sharp breath. It was her gun! The pistol she'd dropped outside Chodups John's shack! She wasted no more time with reflection, but started for the platform, running, dodging elbows and shoulders. Behind her she could hear David calling her name, but she paid him no heed as she scrambled to the platform. Gathering her skirts in her hands, she sprinted up the crude steps and stood between Eddie and Doc Maynard. She faced Eddie, palms out. "What are you doing, Eddie?" she asked softly, so softly that only he could hear.

"They can't laugh at me," said Eddie, lip thrust out belligerently. "They can't. I won't let them."

"I'm not laughing at you, Eddie."

"They are," he contended.

"Why don't you give me the gun?"

Eddie shook his shaggy head and rubbed the back of his hand under his runny nose. Sun light glimmered off the gun.

"Please give me the gun, Eddie, or there'll be an accident. People will get hurt—one of the children might get hurt."

Eddie looked down at the gun, then up at Louisa's outstretched hand.

"What if one of the babies gets shot?" she asked.

The exchange between the two was visible to everyone in the crowd, as was the look of hard-won dignity on Eddie's face when he put the gun into Louisa's hand.

Dimly, she was aware of the buzz and noise, of Maynard leading Eddie away, soothing his tears with apologies and the promises one gives a child. She stumbled off the platform and into David's strong arms. He took the gun from her, and she rested her forehead against his broad chest, and breathed easier in the circle of his support.

-24-

Friday, May 5

There was considerable danger to the cabin homes
from falling trees, as one of many stories told of the
fortitude of Mrs. Holgate (John Holgate's mother)
illustrates. Her sons were hewing down a monster tree
which fell the wrong way...

—Roberta Frye Watt, Katy's daughter

Two days later, a Tuesday night in drizzling rain, Arthur
returned to Seattle, angry, disgusted—and alone. He kissed
Mary Ann and the children, wolfed down a quick supper, and
left for the cookhouse to give the pioneers a full, scathing
report of his struggles after leaving the legislature.

George McConaha was not with him because just as they
were about to push off from Olympia in separate canoes,
the "committee from Headquarters" gave chase. "Headquarters," Arthur said, blue eyes blazing, "is where the
boys were having a high old time. I was captured and taken
back, whereupon I was offered a glass of whiskey. But upon
declining, the shout of the crowd went up, 'Make him drink!
Make him drink!' They grabbed me by the collar, and I
settled back for what I supposed was going to be a nasty
fight, when Elwood Evans spoke up, giving the order to let
me go.

" 'Now boys, don't make him drink,' he said, 'I propose

216 • *Brenda Wilbee*

we drink to the health of the only member of the legislature who consistently lives up to the principles of the Maine Liquor Law.'

"This seemed to satisfy them. They drank up most heartily to my health, and I made my escape to the waiting canoe. But as I hastened along, I was stricken to see George, my good friend and president of the first council, running like a deer with another from the Headquarters committee at his heels. They caught him, and the last time I saw George, the committee was marching him back to headquarters."

"So where is he?" Ursula asked, white around her mouth.

Arthur threw up his hands. "We'd planned on reconnoitering with Ezra Meeker on McNeil Island, only he never came in. I expect he stayed on to party with the boys. It just makes me livid with rage," he said. "The man tries so hard to keep off the liquor!"

Ursula punched her fists into her lap.

"It's an outrage," Arthur said, his fury still unspent, "that a man can work so hard to pass a Liquor Law, and then when it falls to naught, to have the boys force the foul stuff down your throat. Why, it strikes at the heart of my righteous indignation. No, no, Ursula," he said kindly, "I'm sure he gave them a good fight—but he really didn't stand a chance. He'll sleep it off and come home."

"Well, I'm sure I don't care if he ever comes home."

"Oh, surely you don't mean that," said Louisa. "Of course you care."

"No," she said firmly. "He might come home now, but where is he?"

Days passed and no George McConaha. Anger gave way to fear and finally Captain Felker volunteered to go investigate, and Louisa looked around for ways to occupy her friend's mind until George came home. Once again, David and Louisa stayed on.

●   ●   ●

"Whew! Never counted on this bursitis to set in this time of year!" said Mrs. Holgate, grimacing painfully and rubbing her right shoulder. "Certainly do miss the Iowa dryness." She was standing on a footstool and reaching for the bundles of flax that were tied to the rafters of her roof.

"Here, I'll help you with that," said Ursula, moving Mrs. Holgate off the stool and then with arms over her head, teetering the stool back and forth under her feet until she got it steadied, Ursula worked the knotted strings that held the flax across the entire roof of the 12-by-18-foot cabin. "Who tied it up here anyway?" she asked.

"One of the boys. Don't know rightly which one."

That morning, a clear Friday dawn, just three days after Arthur's return, Louisa and Ursula had awakened to a knock on the door and found Princess Angeline standing in the May sunshine with her grandson and a bucket of clams. Thinking it would do Ursula good to get out, Louisa suggested they take the bucket to Mrs. Holgate who had a lot of men to cook for—her own three sons and the three Hanford brothers. They left Eugenia with Mrs. Butler. George Jr. ran off to the blacksmith. And the three of them, with Emily and Joey, headed down to Mrs. Holgate's.

And so here we are, Louisa thought, drinking tea out of a tin cup and looking curiously around the large cabin. It had been a long time since she'd come this far south along the bay, and she'd never been inside either Abbie Jane Hanford's cabin, or her mother's. Mrs. Holgate's place looked more like the inside of a barn than a house, thatched as it was with the flax from Iowa. Onions and salt pork and hams and garlic clusters hung from the rafters as well. Eventually Ursula managed to loosen a bundle of the flax and Louisa sneezed from the dust.

"You going to be able to scutch it all right?" Ursula asked.

"A body can only try."

"Let me do it. Tell me where your flax brake is, and you can wash up those clams. This should be fun," Ursula said, and Louisa heard the false chipper in her voice. So far no one had brought up the fact that late on Monday afternoon—there'd been a strong wind, and if George had been caught in it . . . No, there was no sense in borrowing trouble. Nonetheless, Louisa's heart went out Ursula. She remembered well her own empty pit of pain when she'd thought David was dying. And this was worse. Ursula didn't know whether to be bereft or angry.

"Thanks for these clams," said Mrs. Holgate. "The boys'll be glad for the grub. Felling trees is hard work. You see them on your way in, working that monster right out front?"

"We did," Louisa replied and, even as she spoke, the voices of the men echoed into the cabin. "That tree is so huge, it'll take them a month to fell it."

"Not my boys." The note of pride in Mrs. Holgate's voice was unmistakable. "They'll have it down this very afternoon. Mark my words."

•   •   •

"How's John, Mrs. Holgate?" Louisa asked. "Didn't he fall off his log boom last week?"

"Foolish boy. I'm afraid he's going to catch his death one of these days."

"Poor John, he does take his share of life's beatings, doesn't he?" said Louisa, thinking of the young man who had come West when he was only 19. He'd staked a claim along the Duwamish River, in the days before the clearinghouse had opened in Olympia. There was no place to record his claim and, by the time he'd returned from Iowa where he had collected his mother and brothers and his sister's family, Luther Collins had snatched the spot to farm. To make the loss all the more bitter, the 1850 Homestead Act had changed and John couldn't have 320 acres anymore, only 160—and even then he had had to wait until he was 21.

"Don't he though?" clucked Mrs. Holgate, fetching the flax brake from under the bed.

"Now you get right to work on those clams, Mrs. Holgate," said Ursula, laying the flax on the table. "We'll teach

Princess Angeline something new. You want to help me, Angeline?"

The Indian woman shook her head and helped herself to another sugar cube.

The flax brake was stuffed under the huge four-poster bed, shoved way into the corner of the south wall. The brake itself was small, maybe a foot and a half off the ground, two feet long. Four squatty legs supported the six-inch, grooved top board. The brake handle, set by hinges on one end, was designed to come down and meet the grooves like teeth. By laying the dried flax stalks across the grooved board, the down-swinging handle could then be used very gently to hammer the outer, twiggy bark loose. It was messy work, and took a smooth, patient arm and shoulder.

"Ha!" laughed Angeline, seeing how the hammer worked. "*Nanitch*," she teased ten-month-old Joey. In Duwamish she told him to put his pudgy fingers between the grooves and brake handle. "Like this," she said to the uncomprehending child, holding his baby fingers in place. She chortled furiously when he looked up, black eyes wide with wonder. His fingers were stuck! She laughed harder.

Louisa nursed Emily and when she had fallen asleep, sucking on her bottom lip, Louisa sighed and laid her on the four-poster bed in the far corner of the house, where it sat under an open loft. She was eager to be in her own home again, working in her own garden. For the life of her she couldn't remember if she'd brought the clothes in from the line when she and David had left last Sunday. But it was good to see Ursula chuckling now and then, laughing over her own clumsiness with the brake. Maybe, Louisa thought, George would be home when they got back to town and everything would be all right again—and she and David could go back out to the claim.

"Shoo!" Mrs. Holgate scolded. Joey had pulled himself up onto the coal scuttle. "Shoo!" She waved a wooden spoon dripping with stew at the fat little half-breed. Angeline stuck out a foot and the baby slapped it with two hands, smiling. They all laughed, and then suddenly from outside came the terrible sound of the earth uprooting, and then sudden cries and screams. She turned to look, but fir boughs crashing through the roof, dashed across her face and shoulders, and she felt the thundering echoes through her feet. The monster tree had fallen on the cabin, crushing it, vibrating the earth and everything on it. For a moment she sat stunned, bent over her lap, listening to the thundering echoes.

Then she heard Emily's cry.

"Emily!"

She leaped from her chair, but stood trapped. Between her and Emily lay the tree, boughs still trembling and settling just four feet away, slicing the cabin in half. Cold sunlight poured through the broken roof overhead and Louisa waited, confused, helpless, listening to Emily's piercing wail under the wreckage of the fallen roof. Then her mind cleared. Emily was buried beneath the tree!

"EMILY!" Blood washed through her limbs, pounding. "EMILY!" She dove after Princess Angeline who had already scrambled over the boughs and branches, squeezing between the shattered roof and crushed furniture and fallen fir needles and scratchy flax which had loosened and tumbled over everything.

"I can't see!" Louisa cried, peering into the jumbled chaos and cloud of flax dust. "Oh, help me someone! I can't find her!"

Princess Angeline, her feet sticking out from under a cabin log beam and a heavy, trembling bough, wriggled herself free, crying, "*Acha-da! Acha-da...memloose*"— the terrible death wail of the Duwamish.

"No!" cried Louisa. "Never! Never! EMILY!" She dropped to her knees and squeezed, pushing her way into the small space Angeline had just backed out of. "Emily, it's Mama! Mama's coming." She crawled into the tunnel where fir needles scratched and clawed at her face. But she could see her baby, screaming, fists punching and banging a cedar plank wedged just inches above her face. "Emily," Louisa whimpered. *If only I could move closer.* Oh, please God, let me move..."

"Louisa! No!"

She felt a tug on her skirt, then someone's hold on her foot.

"No! Please!" she pleaded. "Emily!"

"You can't! The whole thing is going to cave in!"

"Emily! EMILY!" she cried. Slivers from the floor raked her chin as she fought whoever was pulling her away. She came out clawing and scratching, attacking.

"Mrs. Denny! Mrs. Denny!" John Holgate begged, fastening her arms immobile against her sides. He stood winded, lungs bursting from his pell-mell sprint. "You *can't* go in! You *can't*! It'll fall for sure! And then..."

She crumpled to the floor, stumbling on a branch, and a jag of pain went up through her hip and into her back. Lemuel Holgate and the three Hanfords came racing up and peered over the dashed logs where the front door had been. Hats blown off, they stood winded, panting as heavily as John.

"Ma! It fell the wrong way!" cried Lemuel. "We're sorry, we thought—"

"Emily, Emily," Louisa whimpered, crying. "Please, we have to get Emily."

"The baby's under there," said John, looking at his brothers. Ed Hanford swung over the logs. Ebenezer Hanford ran around back.

John worked his way under the collapsed roof, crawling on all fours and then dropping down to his stomach. "Hey! I think we're in luck!" he hollered from under the pileup. "The tree's caught on the bedpost! Looks like the loft broke the fall, and everything's hung up on the bed."

"Can we pull away some of this?" Louisa asked, gesturing.

"No . . ." John inched out. "We're liable to send the whole thing toppling. Lem, see if you can't find out what's holding up the tree on the outside."

But Ebenezer had beat him to it. He came round the side of the house. "It's all resting on the loft joists! We're going to have to pull the tree up enough to—"

"But we can't do that!" yelled John, panicking.

My baby, Louisa thought. *My dear, sweet baby.*

"I'll go get help," said Ursula without expression. She handed Joey, crying in her arms, to Angeline, and then with a hasty, sympathetic look to Louisa, pulled up her skirts and scrambled over the logs, knocking something askew that sent a rumbling through the rubble. For a moment they all froze, then Louisa shrieked and started for the tunnel.

"Mrs. Denny! NO!"

John had her by the knee and wouldn't let go. "Don't thrash! It'll all come down! PLEASE! MRS. DENNY!"

His terror brought a check to her own. She held still, waiting for the dust to settle. Emily was still alive. Gratefully she listened to the baby's cries. Outside she heard the Holgate and Hanford men.

"If we could get a rope around the trunk, right here, and then swing the other end over the tree limb—no, no, the tree limb from the cedar out back. Right there! Over our heads! Get the rope up over that limb and then work some kind of pulley system."

Ebenezer Hanford swore. "We need a block and tackle, that's what we need."

"And Tom Mercer's horses."

Louisa heard one of them take off, and prayed that Tom was in town. And then, hunkered down in the jumbled mess of tree branches scratching her face, her arms, and clothes, she began to sing to still Emily's fright, and her own.

-25-

These gallant founders of the State of Washington were so few...the forest so deep and the waters so wide, no wonder each was solicitous of the other.

—Roberta Frye Watt, Katy's daughter

Yesler threw the switch and shut down the mill, saw whining to a stop. Indians and whites alike, after taking a moment to digest the news, grabbed rope and crowbars and raced for the Holgate homestead a mile south of Seattle, racing both trail and beach, moccasins and boots alike beating the ground. David, Doc Maynard, and Yoke-Yakeman threw a block and tackle, a two-in-one rig, into the bottom of a canoe— whose they didn't know—and paddled madly down the shoreline.

The sight of the cabin stopped David's heart and kicked pain into his abdomen. *Liza! Emily!* He felt the block and tackle slip from his fingers, and stooped quickly to pick the pulleys up. He glanced again at the destroyed cabin: a fir, with a girth of at least two feet, buried the south half of the log cabin. Even the north half had collapsed, the logs knocked out of line and dropping from the corners as easily as Paul Bunyan's toothpicks. *And Emily and Louisa were in there*, he thought, pain slicing into his chest so that he couldn't breathe.

"DAVID! OVER HERE!" Forest grew right up to the back of the cabin. A towering cedar tree stood just three feet behind the back wall, a heavy branch stretching across the wreckage, and Lemuel Hanford, David saw, had somehow climbed the tree and was straddling the stout bough. "DAVE!" he called again. "THROW ME UP THAT TACKLE!"

I can't just stand here, winding rope! David thought, lowering the block to his feet and coiling the tackle around it. Emily and Louisa are in there! His body fought to run, yet his mind told him to have some sense! There, the rope was ready to unfurl. He took the smaller block in hand and quickly checked the standing end to be sure the rope was spliced properly through the thimble. He tugged, testing it, then let the block swing from his fingers in longer and longer stretches. Lem in sight, he prayed, biting his lip, and then thinking of Emily and Louisa, let go. The pulley sailed through the air. Lemuel dove for it, caught the rope around his arm and the block fell over the bouncing bough. *Bull's-eye.*

"WE NEED A ROPE AROUND THAT TREE OVER THERE! SET UP THE OTHER PULLEY!" In an instant David saw what Lem had in mind: ropes and pulleys to lift the gigantic fir off the house, cedar branches overhead to take the weight. *Just like Collins' gallows*, he thought, frightened almost beyond reason, and he stood numb, stupid, unsure. And then slowly, in a whisper, came the words of Louisa's Psalm that day out in the woods: *Be merciful unto me, O God, be merciful unto me: for my soul trusteth in thee: yea, in the shadow of thy wings will I make my refuge, until these calamities be overpast.*

"Louisa!" he shouted, ducking under the fallen monarch where it had snagged on the front wall of the cabin. "Louisa!" And he peered inside, sick to see the smashed disarray of log beams and cedar shingles and tree limbs, even onions and ham ends—and broken glass. The stove and table were sitting on one end as if nothing at all had happened. "*Louisa!*"

"In here!"

"John? Is that you? Where's Liza?" *How could anybody be in there?* "John, where are you?"

"Never mind! Get your wife out of here!"

"David?"

"Louisa!" He ran around the corner and climbed through the window in the north wall, the only wall still standing, roof hanging precariously over it, and skirted the large stove.

"Careful, Dave!" hollered John from the middle somewhere. "It's all pretty loose in here!"

He found Louisa's feet sticking out of the rubble, and then when she felt his hand on her ankle, she started scooting backward. "Oh, David," she whispered, sliding sobbing into his arms. "You have to get Emily out." He helped her through the window, her skirt catching on the jagged glass. "You must."

"I will."

She stood on the other side, looking in, eyes drawn and tight, skin red, irritated from the fir needles. "David," she whispered, "I think she's dead."

"Lem!" John hollered behind him. "You got that pulley for me yet? Don't know how long I can hold up in here!"

"No, Liza," David said. "She's not dead. I promise."

But when she was gone he turned around, pulling back his hair. *O God in heaven, how could she not be?* he wondered, staring at the tree's girth and thinking he might cry. She was so tiny, so very tiny, and it was so big.

All around he heard the frantic shouts and the sound of feet running, friends rushing against hope. His heart ached for his daughter, for Louisa outside, and in a panic he dropped to his knees to peer up the tunnel, lidded by the loft floor, broken and jagged under the fir.

"Dave!" Ebenezer stood at the window. "Dave, do you see her in there?"

"Yes."

"Listen, we're going to ease the fir up a bit. It'll take some of the pressure off the attic floor—"

"But the minute the fir goes up, everything comes down!" David exclaimed, overwhelmed by the futility of it all.

"No! Listen, Dave! DAVID! LISTEN TO ME! I'm sending a few men in here to put their backs up under that floor so you can crawl in and get her!"

"John!" hollered Lem from the limb overhead and, twisting, David could see that Lemuel was lowering his end of the block and tackle, slowly dropping the pulley down to John, wormed somewhere into the middle of all the chaos. One more glance at Emily, tiny and still in the darkness— His eyes fastened on the thick cedar plank of the attic floor just over her head, and followed it up. A sudden whirl of wonder sent goosebumps across his back. In all this mess, Emily was trapped inside a little cave. Surely a guardian angel watched over her, and for some reason he thought of Eddie Moore.

"Got it, John?" Lem hollered.

"Yup!"

"Can you get it hooked onto the rope?"

Another rope had been tied around the girth of the giant tree, and John, working blind from underneath with his hands up over his buried head, fumbled to slip the pulley hook through. "Can you pull up a bit?" he called, voice muffled.

"Dave," said Ebenezer by the window, and David saw Maynard and Arthur behind him. And Butler. "We got to move fast. The whole thing is about to come down. Soon as they get the block and tackle set up—"

In David's mind he saw the hourglass turn, sand rushing through. "Why are we doing this from the inside?" he asked interrupting, thinking straight all of a sudden. "The tree must be hung up on something out back. Can't we wedge something under it and then raise it up that way? This—" he said, pointing with his chin, "makes me nervous. What if a rope breaks, or that limb snaps?"

"Can't figure how else to do it!"

"David," said Arthur, leaning in. "Come look for yourself. Maybe you can figure something different—we can't."

The tree lay across the back side of the crushed cabin about four-and-a-half feet off the ground, caught on the toppled attic floor joists. Just the other side of the wall, he knew, was Emily, a foot lower. If something broke and the tree came dropping back down, the weight would force the wall over and crush her. Time pressed in like fingers of panic.

"Hey!" hollered Lem from the cedar bough. "We're about ready out here!"

"Dave," said Arthur, putting his hand on David's shoulder. "The best we can do, given what we got, is to brace the inside. If the tree goes, at least we can scramble around in there. Might get an arm or leg pinched—it's a risk all right, I know. But out here, I just don't know."

"But as the tree goes up," said David, driven, dodging and ducking under the tremendous trunk, inspecting all angles and shivering in the dampness of the forest shadow falling over the entire back of the house, the time tick, tick, ticking in his mind, "isn't there a way we can wedge something between the top of the wall here and the tree? To catch it? To stop the drop?"

"What do you suggest?" Arthur, Maynard, Butler, and Ebenezer all looked at him, waiting for his answer. But there was none, and time was running out.

"We better get in there," said Ebenezer. Suddenly he shook his head, agitated. "Sure do wish we had Tom's horses. But it can't be helped. Everyone out here is just going to pull like crazy."

In the shadow of thy wings will I make my refuge until these calamities be overpast, David prayed, taking the lead and crawling back through the window. He crawled into the tunnel. Would this be the end of everything? How had he spent so much time worrying over the Indians, when it could all end like this? *In the shadow of thy wings I will make my refuge....* He inched closer in, elbows tucked close, toes scooting him up, blinking on needles slashing at his eyes as he pushed carefully through unbelievable chaos. "Emily," he whispered.

Lem, from his perch up over everything, backed up the bough toward the main trunk of the standing cedar. "We're all set out here! You ready in there?"

John Holgate hollered, "Ready!"

"I'll count to three," shouted Lem to the men outside, ready to play tug-of-war with a tree, "and then I'll holler pull! And by golly—PULL!" Lem looked down. "And let us know when you got her, Dave!"

Outside 20 some men, Indians and whites, heels dug in, hands spit and hanging onto the rope, waited for the word.

Inside, David listened to the shuffle of Maynard, Butler, John, and Ebenezer behind him, Arthur beside him, Ebenezer pointing out where the weak spots were, what was liable to go down, how to compensate. "Don't worry, Dave," Arthur whispered in the dusky gloom, "we'll get her out. You'll see."

"All right!" shouted Lem. "One! Two! Three! PULL!"

Outside eyes bulged, veins popped up. Faces turned red. Nothing.

Mrs. Holgate drew Louisa into a warm embrace. Princess Angeline, Ursula, and Abbie Jane Hanford, and some of the women from town who had heard the news and had come, stood beside her, watching, everyone praying.

Inside, the men wedged sweated backs against the fallen timbers and joists, ready for the jostling to come. David, in his tunnel, crouched, waiting, counting, eyes fastened to the shadowed bundle he could just barely pick out.

Outside, Luther Collins, taking the first position in the lineup, bellowed the lead, "One-two-three, PULL! One-two-three, PULL!"

Cedar bough bent. The fir didn't budge.

Again the bullfrog voice of Collins: "One-two-three, PULL!"

Inside, dust fell. A log rolled. Arthur caught it with his boot and David scooted what looked to be a broken flax brake across the floor. Arthur shoved it under the log and pulled his boot out.

"One-two-three, PULL!"

The tree lifted, sending a scramble of dislodged logs and timber. John let out a yelp.

"You hurt?" Arthur hollered.

"I got it! That's what counts!"

"One-two-three, PULL! One-two-three, PULL!"

Everyone chanted it now—even the women.

"One-two-three, PULL!" counted David with them, blood racing through his body, ready to make the dash.

The cedar bough bent even further and Lem scrambled off, climbing up the cedar for a higher branch. The fir cranked up two inches, and outside the men's faces turned red with pain, fingers burned on the hemp in their palms.

"One-two-three, PULL!"

"One-two-three, PULL!"

One by one men dropped the chant, saving their strength. Only Luther Collins yelled. "One-two-three, PULL!"

Inside, David inched ever closer, crawling along the splintered floor. "One more, come on, just one more!" he whispered, catching hold of the cedar plank that acted as the lid over Emily's tiny body. He felt a lump in his throat when he grasped at last the soft corner of her blanket.

"One-two-three, PULL!"

The blanket was stuck! Her feet were stuck!

"One-two-three, PULL!"

"One-two-three, PULL!"

Sweat poured down his face. He couldn't see. Everything swam before his eyes.

"One-two-three, PULL!"

His hand felt along the soft blanket. A nail!

"One-two-three, PULL!"

He pulled. A rip. Then he had her and was backing out!

"One-two-three, PULL!"

"Hold on! I got her! I got her!" he yelled as soon as he could expand his chest, backing, backing, backing, clutching all that mattered to his heart. "Shh," he whispered, not knowing he was the one crying. "It's all right. Father's got you, it's all right."

A crack and then a rush of wind. A howl went up from the other side of the cabin as men yelped in their plunge backward over each other, the rope whizzing fire through their hands. Inside, everything tumbled and bounced, falling over David's shoulders and back. He crouched over Emily, back arched. He could hear men scrambling to their feet, someone hollering orders, someone screaming.

"Dave?"

"Maynard? That you?" He felt the tug on his boots and started backing out again, then he was standing, Emily dead or alive in his arms, he didn't know.

"Out the window!" Arthur ordered.

Maynard crashed through. David handed out Emily and tumbled after them, ripping himself on the glass.

Then Ebenezer and Butler, and Arthur rubbing his shin. One by one they fell to the ground.

John hollered from inside. "Everybody out?"

"Everybody but you!"

Another crack. A pillow of dust inside.

"John!" David hesitated, then shot back through the window, blinded by the dust and flax and dark. He collided right smack into John. They both scrambled for the window. John took a flying leap, hurtling past David and out the square-cut hole in the logs. David, coughing and gagging, tripped over something round and went down. He grabbed for the window, caught the glass and felt the sharp jab of pain. His very soul seemed to leave his body as he slid lazily down the log wall. But someone had him by the shoulder and was hauling him up on his feet, and he felt the tumble and roar of the last standing wall give way, the rush of wind down his legs.

But he was on his feet outside, stunned and blinking. And then he had Louisa in his arms, Emily between them. "She's alive," Louisa sobbed. "She's alive. Oh, David, she's alive..."

He could hear the cheers, the hurrahs from men congratulating themselves, blowing on blistered hands and sucking fingers, and he hugged Louisa so close it hurt.

"A close call!"

"Rope slipped, but everyone's out!"

"Emily? She's all right?" he asked Louisa, unwilling to let go for even a moment to see for himself. He felt Louisa nod against his neck, and he felt the slow release of joy wash through his mind. The rope had slid from the men's grasp and the tree had come crashing down; only it hadn't smashed as hard as they'd expected, giving way only after everyone was out. "Oh, Liza," he whispered, holding her close.

But the cheering was short-lived. Doc Maynard, pushing his glasses up, signaled David to come round back. Whispers like a soft wind hushed the jubilation.

"What?" said David, seeing grave faces in the back shadow of the shattered cabin.

Maynard guided him to where the tree protruded off the collapsed roof and lifted a bough. "No," moaned David, catching himself on Maynard's arm.

Eddie Moore, the crazy man, was pinned between logs and fir trunk, both of his glassy blue eyes popped out by the weight of the tree on his crushed skull.

-26-

Col. McConaha [was] a backslidden Presbyterian,
who had, during the winter, torn the leaves from his
Bible to kindle fire. It seems dreadful. Yet this warn-
ing is unheeded, seems not to make any lasting
impression. I know not what judgment will yet be sent
upon us.

—Kate Blaine, the preacher's wife

Eddie Moore's giant body lay twisted under the weight of the crushing fir and in the roll of logs. David leaned wearily, shutting his eyes, against what was left of the walls.

"See here," said Maynard, "looks like he wedged himself between the loft joists and the tree as we eased it up. See his feet marks in the mud?"

"But why? Didn't he understand the danger?" someone asked.

"Why?" Maynard asked, voice strained. "Because if the rope broke and he didn't squeeze in here, the baby would be dead, that's why."

"He must have heard us talking about it," said David slowly. "Ebenezer and me. He must have followed us all, and hid in the woods, and then overheard the whole thing. But why? Why?" And then he knew.

Eddie Moore was a simple man, perhaps, without all his stuffing. But, as Louisa had said, he was God's guardian angel. He had given his life so that Emily might live. Humbled, David turned to go. He paused at the corner of the shambled house, knowing, too, that all his friends had done the same: risked their lives that Emily might live. He touched the wall, mind sore with grief and unspeakable gratefulness, and seeing now, too, the nasty gash in his palm.

"You expect the poor idiot knew what he was doing?" someone asked behind him.

"Yes, Collins," said David, turning around, lifting his hand to his chest and squeezing hard on his wrist to stem the bleeding. "Like everybody else today, he knew exactly what he was doing." He turned to go, but pivoted quickly. "Thank you," he whispered, and then, full of sweet sorrow, he hurried to find his baby and Louisa.

• • •

"You don't need to stay with me anymore," said Ursula as the three of them—David, Louisa, and Ursula—approached Ursula's cabin in the warmth of the Friday afternoon, the day still full. George Jr. trailed not far behind, chattering a mile a minute about his time at the smithy, oblivious to the strain and fatigue of the adults, or of the bittersweet tragedy and the high-priced victory that weighted their steps. Eugenia, picked up at the Butler's cabin as they had come into town, was in her mother's arms, sucking a thumb and playing with a button on her mother's dress. "After a day like today," said Ursula, "you need to go on home. I'll be just fine. And George, if he knows what's good for him, will come in today. It's still early."

Louisa, trudging right along behind Ursula, David at her side and still holding up his cut hand, wasn't sure what to say or do. She longed to go home. It had been five whole days, and she ached inside to be alone with David and the baby, her dear, sweet baby, and she hugged Emily, tears starting again. But Ursula...Could she leave Ursula yet? George still wasn't home and it seemed, as Louisa watched

Ursula, pretending anger, march ahead of them, braid swinging, that the very air whispered forebodingly. Or was it only her own sorrow over the death of the poor crazy man that squeezed inside her heart?

Or was Ursula needing them to be gone? she wondered suddenly. To see Emily could only remind Ursula of her own child that had not been spared.

"Who's that up in front of us?" Ursula asked, stopping in the trail so abruptly that David and Louisa nearly ran into her. "Why, Captain Felker! What are you doing at my house? And where did you get George's hat—oh, George!" she exclaimed, laughing and breaking into a run, Eugenia bouncing in her arms as she took off up the last of the trail and threw open the door. "George! Oh, George! You're home!" She stopped in the silence that greeted her cry and turned in the door. "Where's George?"

"I'm sorry, Ma'am," said Captain Felker slowly. "I was just bringing his trunk up and his hat."

"Well, why can't he do it himself?"

"Ma'am," the elderly captain said, his face twisted, turning the hat in his knobby hands, "there was a wind Monday—he must have. . . . What I'm trying to say is that the trunk and the hat, it's all we could find on the beach."

"But George?" Ursula asked, white-faced and rigid, throwing Eugenia to another hip and snatching the hat from Captain Felker.

"I'm sorry, Ma'am. We combed the beach two miles each direction. I expect his body's been washed out to sea."

Behind them George Jr. let out a sudden, piercing cry. "He's dead!" the boy wailed, throwing his arms up and crossing them in front of his eyes. "He's dead! God killed him! God killed my father! God killed my father for burning the Bible!" he cried, staggering backward.

"That's not true, son!" said David sternly, going to him. "God doesn't punish people like that."

But George Jr. backed away, peering out from under his

arms, tear-streaked face stricken, stumbling over his heels. "No, God killed him. I heard the preacher say—"

David caught the boy's arm and held him urgently. "If the Reverend Blaine said that, then he doesn't know anything of God," said David, squatting before the boy who pulled back. "Nothing! Do you hear me? There was never a finer man than your father, and we're all going to miss him, but I shall thrash you personally if I ever so much as hear you say God killed him! Is God a murderer?" he demanded, shaking the child and startling him out of his grief. "Is he?"

"No," blubbered the boy.

"I should think not, or we would all be dead."

Louisa watched her husband. There is no better man on earth, she thought, tears hot in her eyes as David gently took the boy's shirttail and wiped his face. He let the little boy go and Georgie went sobbing down the trail to the smithy, crying for Lewis as if his heart would break; and Ursula at the door was crying too, for she had no one anymore.

Part IX

THE JULY 4TH PICNIC
Wednesday, July 4

The picnic was held on the Mercer place at the south end of Lake Union.... When it came time for speeches, Mercer recommended that "Hyas Chuck" (big waters), or Lake Duwamish, should be named "Washington" for the Father of his Country, and that "Tenas Chuck" (little waters) should be called "Lake Union," for, as Mr. Mercer predicted, "This smaller body of water may sometime provide a connecting link uniting the larger lake with Puget Sound."

—Roberta Frye Watt, Katy's daughter

-27-

This year of '54 was not all calamity...
—Roberta Frye Wall, Katy's daughter

At ten in the morning of July the Fourth, Tom Mercer took his wagon down to Seattle to load up the women and their food. The Fourth of July picnic at his cabin was to be the biggest celebration the town had ever seen. For weeks he had been planning it, and now at last the day had come. All around Elliott Bay the pioneers prepared, spirits high, winter and hard times put behind. There were to be games, and races, and horseback riding—all the fun any of them had ever had in times past.

David and Louisa, dressing Emily in a white sunbonnet with pink ribbons, and a matching soft, pink cotton dress that Louisa has spent the last two weeks sewing, whistled to Watch and set off through the woods. David wore his cap, Louisa her sunbonnet, shielding their eyes from the brightness of the piercing sun. David carried Emily, six months old, bouncing in his arms. Louisa carried the basket, full of eggs and bread and Maloya raisin pudding, and a glass jar of fresh milk for her nieces and nephews. She slipped her hand into her husband's. "I can hardly wait to see Ursula! I still can't quite believe it's true!"

"Anybody with one eye could have seen it coming," he said, smiling down at her and jiggling her hand so that she laughed. Watch dashed ahead, tail wagging.

239

"I don't know! It seemed *logical*, yes. What else is a woman in the wilderness to do but marry? I'm just glad Ursula is wild with happiness. She always did think Lewis Wyckoff a fine man! And I'd hate to see her have to marry someone she didn't love—in order to make ends meet."

"He's a pretty fine man when he's willing to take on two children—as well as a wife."

"Well, he was father to that rascal of Ursula's long before George ever drowned. Lewis has been looking out for that boy for months now."

David readjusted Emily in his arms and pulled Louisa in close, slipping his arm around her. "Well, Ursula got herself a good man. They don't come any finer."

"Except for maybe my own husband," she said, looking up at him, pleased to see his embarrassed grin. "Curley coming to the picnic?" she asked him, her mind, however, still very much on Ursula and the wedding later on that night. What would Ursula wear for a wedding dress? she wondered, noticing how pretty the sunlight was in the trail up ahead, the way it fell in shafts of soft yellow through the green of the forest growth.

"Curley goes anywhere there's food," said David. "He'll be there. *And* Klap-ke-latchi."

The Snoqualmie Indian, Louisa knew, after escaping the near lynching, had been tried in Steilacoom and found innocent, and had, after coming back to Seattle, attached himself to Dobbins, grateful to him for having saved his life. Dobbins, his strength slow in coming, had been grateful for the extra help, putting Klap-ke-latchi to work milking the cows and cleaning out the chicken coop, and keeping the wood chopped and stacked. Even Anna, after a time, had gotten to where she liked having Klap-ke-latchi around; he did all of her more odious chores.

The trail led them out to the road and Louisa stood between the grassy, double ruts of the clearing, stretched each direction like wrinkled ribbons. Tom's wagon, creaking and groaning as it dropped and slammed over tree roots, pulled up alongside, Tib and Charley blowing softly through their noses. Louisa ran along behind as they passed, waving to her sister and Anna and all the other ladies packed into the wagon bed, dishes and plates and baskets of food on their laps.

"Where are the children!" she called.

"Coming along with all the men!" Mary Ann hollered back, waving and blowing a kiss to Emily.

"Oh, David!" Louisa exclaimed, taking up his hand again. "It's such fun, and we haven't even started yet!"

But when it did start, Louisa realized, helping herself to all the wonderful food set out on a table decorated with trillium and wild roses, it was all she could have hoped for. Tom's claim faced the lake, and all around was a wild meadow filled with the pungent scent of ripe grass and thick with the shrill and trill of hundreds of birds: robins and wrens, song-sparrows and snowbirds, thrushes and larks, all vying with each other in joyful song.

The cabin sat a short distance up from the mirrorlike surface of the water. After lunch, all across the front yard of a grassy slope, the children raced in potato bags, urged on by their parents, hopping like bunnies in the clumsy burlap sacks. Two of the Mercer girls stood up by the house, holding a rope stretched between them, and the children, amidst squeals and giggles, lunged and hopped and rolled to be the first to touch the finish line.

Louisa, stomach full and almost sick from eating too much, sat on the grass nearby with the other women, watching the antics and laughing at silly little Nora standing in the middle of it all, pouting. "Oh look, Mary!" Louisa shouted.

Arthur, seeing his daughter standing still, swooped her up and ran with her up the hill, bouncing her feet and carrying her through the rope with a whoop! "Nora won! Lookee here! Nora won!" he hollered and all the other children cried out in protest, but Arthur was pulling candies from his pockets for everyone and shushing all the clamoring with a tousling of their heads. "All right!" he shouted. "We're going to do it again, only this time Nora gets to hold the rope! Go on, everybody—line up again and we'll see who the winner is this time!"

"Now where did he get all that candy?" asked Anna, hands on her stomach swelling with child. "I should think Gerty would like a piece."

"Gerty," prompted Mary Ann, "go ask your Uncle Arthur for a lemon drop. Go on, there you go."

"Hey! Who's going for a horsey ride?" called Tom from the barn, and the children, halfway through the new race, dropped their burlap sacks to run pell-mell to meet him. George Jr. got there first and was up on Tib's snowy-white back in a flash, grinning from ear to ear.

"No, no, he'll be all right," said Lewis, reaching out to restrain Ursula from getting to her feet.

She sighed. "You're right, dear. It just makes me nervous is all."

"Ursula!" said Sally Bell, wearing her old lace hat with the blue "ribbon." "You simply *must* tell us what you're going to wear tonight!"

But Ursula only laughed and looked up at Lewis. He pulled her into his arms. "Now don't pester the poor woman another minute," he said. "A bride's wedding dress is not to be discussed until it's seen."

"Then I shall go twist Captain Plummer's arm," said Sally, smiling, "and make him tell me what you ordered— *from New York!*"

"He won't tell," said Ellender Smith, Henry's sister, adjusting her skirt and wrapping her arms around her drawn-up knees, a slight smile on her small face. "I've already tried to weasel it out of him."

"Ah, I don't like your smile," singsonged Ursula. "Do I hear other wedding bells?"

But Henry's sister said nothing, her smile answering well enough.

"I declare!" said Ursula. "Why, it must be catchy!" and she was off in a fit of laughter.

"Just don't tell Captain Plummer," said Ellender. "He doesn't know it yet." And then they were all laughing.

Several of the Indians in the area had come out to watch how white men did their "potlatches," and David and Dobbins were down at the lake with Klap-ke-latchi and Curley and some of the others. Henry Smith and Captain Charles Plummer sat with them and they all had their shoes and socks off, pants rolled up. Louisa watched from the ladies' blanket. Emily, on her father's knee, was laughing and reaching for a white butterfly. Curley's hand shot out. He caught it, held his fist, fingers up, in front of Emily. She slapped at his hands and the Indian opened his fingers and the butterfly darted up and away. Emily lurched backward, surprised.

Princess Angeline, sitting beside Sally Bell, chortled to herself. "It is good," she said. Then not knowing how to say it in English, finished with the Chinook *tillicum*—"friend."

A sudden clanging snatched everyone's attention and heads swiveled to where Doc Maynard rang an old, rusty circular saw hung from Tom's cabin eaves.

"Looks like it's time for the speeches," said Lewis, pulling Ursula to her feet. David brought Emily up.

"It's so hot," Louisa told him, taking the baby. "If you'll ask Doc Maynard to announce it, I don't mind sitting with the children down by the lake. They can swim while everyone makes their speeches. It'll keep them out of everyone's hair, too."

"But, Liza, you'll miss the best part!" he said, tipping back her bonnet brim to kiss her forehead.

"David! Stop that!" she scolded, flapping her hat back in place. "Really. We're out in public!"

"Oh, I don't know! Ursula and Lewis are doing their share of kissing."

"Kiss me again then!" she said, standing on tiptoe and

pulling her brim back herself. "Not on my forehead, David. Right on the mouth so they can all talk!"

Arthur was the first to make his speech. With George gone, he was the only legislative representative, and he stood on a high stump, sun bouncing off his sandy hair, to give a quick summary of everything the legislature had done. Louisa listened with one ear, her concentration mostly on the children. George Jr. had wanted to swim out further than she'd allow and she kept having to call him back.

"Olympia done, now the news from Washington, D.C.!" said Arthur, pulling a piece of paper from his back pocket. "I just got a letter from Governor Stevens!" A buzz rose up, and Louisa snapped her fingers, motioning for George to come in.

"What?" he asked, coming out of the water, shivering in his soaking-wet pants cut off at the knees.

"I want you to sit on that rock right there while I listen to what Mr. Denny has to say."

"But Mrs. Denny!"

"Don't argue. Now hush up and let me listen."

He slunk off to the rock and sat pouting.

Arthur began slowly. "I won't read you the whole thing," he said, "for it's hot and I hear tell Luther Collins has got a couple of watermelons cooling in the lake, and I'm afraid the news from Washington is not what we'd wanted to hear."

"So what's he say about the railroad?" shouted Henry Smith, propped against a tree, arms crossed, hat set low over his eyes. "Let's get on with it!"

"Shut up and let him talk," said Plummer, jabbing the young doctor in the ribs although, Louisa noticed, the captain's eyes had not left Ellender's face.

"There will be no railroad!" shouted Arthur. And taking up the letter from Stevens, he gravely read: " 'But Secretary Davis was in no kindly humor with evidence of our efficiency, or even with the demonstration that this northern route was not only practicable, but desirable. Jefferson Davis would give but scant attention to what I had to say, and finally, in laying his report before Congress, he *raised* our estimate of cost of construction, greatly *magnified* the physical difficulties, *depreciated* the agricultural resources of the country, and described that the country west of the Rocky Mountains was one of general *sterility*—' "

The simmering whispers of disgust, circulating from mouth to mouth, exploded into open howls of wild protest.

"Now just wait a minute!" shouted Henry, snapping to his feet and snatching off his hat. "Sterility west of the Rockies? So what's all this?" he demanded, waving his arm over the quiet lake, the ducks swimming along the edge and the green grass stretching from the shore, the deep forest beyond, the mountains far into the east. "Sterility?" he demanded.

"I'm only reading the report," Arthur replied.

"And what else does Stevens have to say about our lofty Jefferson Davis?" asked Doc Maynard, angry as the rest of them.

"Well," said Arthur, reading on. "Jefferson Davis ignored Tinkham's report of a reconnaissance he had made of Snoqualmie Pass, but he quoted McClellan's to Congress with approval."

"That does it!" shouted Henry, throwing down his hat and punching his fist into the tree, then shaking his hand out. "I can't believe it! So what route *did* Congress vote for? The one to California through *Mexico?*"

"They haven't voted yet."

"What about our request for the special stand of arms, and the formation of a militia?" Maynard asked.

Again Arthur shook his head.

"What?" Maynard crowed. "Davis has refused to send us arms or men? After what happened this winter?"

Louisa could hardly believe her ears and looked over to where David stood with Klap-ke-latchi and Curley. It was as if the sun had gone behind a cloud, marring the beautiful day. Why did Arthur have to go and ruin everything by bringing all this up at the picnic? Really, she thought, he had no tact, but then she realized she was only getting mad at him to numb the blow.

"It's not as bad as all that!" shouted Arthur, holding out his arms and quieting the crowd again. "We've been given money and authorization to extinguish the Indians' land title, and we've already had the pledge from Seattle and Pat Kanim toward the resolution of our difficult times. Perhaps what's needed here is a proper perspective. All of Europe is at war. The Russian ministers have been ordered out of Paris and London, instructions have been sent to the French and English ambassadors to withdraw from St. Petersburg. All hope of preserving peace has been abandoned in Europe. In light of such madness across the sea," he continued, "we would do well to remind ourselves that here in the isolated wilderness of Puget Sound the winds have indeed blown, but we, unlike our distant brothers, have weathered the bitter storm. We have survived without resorting to madness." Arthur took a deep breath. "Certainly, regret and tragedy haunt us, and not a day goes past that we don't remember with sadness all that we have lost, but if we succumb again to the despair Jefferson Davis would have us feel, then we might as well pack our bags and go slinking back to Oregon with our tails tucked between our legs, and leave this grand and glorious country to be tamed and shaped by men—and women—much better than ourselves!"

A roar went up and Louisa leaped to her feet, Emily over her arm, to clap and shout huzzah along with everyone else. Who was Jefferson Davis anyway? Did he hold their destiny in his hands?

There were more speeches. Tom Mercer, as host of the grand celebration, got up last of all to talk. He had a proposal, he said, and wanted a vote. "We live on the shores of the most beautiful, natural harbor in the world," he said softly and slowly, "where ships and trains will someday—maybe not as soon as we'd hoped, but surely someday—meet. We also live beside two beautiful lakes, lakes we still call by the Indian Chinook, *hyas chuck* and *tenas chuck*—big and little waters. I propose, in our resolution today to see that this country of ours realize its full potential, that we name the big lake to the east Lake Washington—in honor of the father of our nation. And not," he added with a slight smile that made everyone laugh, "after the city where lunatics sit in their asylum and discredit the word of good men."

"Furthermore," he said when the laughter subsided, "I propose that we name this little lake, which surely some-day will be the link between a channel between Lake Washington and Puget Sound, Lake Union." Suddenly embarrassed over his own enthusiasm, the quiet man dropped off the stump and stood against his house.

Maynard leaped up. "All in favor?"

A sudden cry for help caught everyone off guard, and Louisa whirled to see that Georgie was nowhere to be seen. "Katy! Take Emily, quick!" she shrieked and was plunging into the lake before she realized the cries came from the other direction.

"Ma! Ma! Help!" cried George as he came stumbling, crying and coughing, out of the high grass of the meadow behind the cabin.

Louisa could smell him a mile away. Well, she thought, taking Emily and waving her hand in front of her nose, now he's really gone and done it!

"Eek!" shrieked Ursula, squeezing her nose. "What have you done? Why you've fallen into a dogfish oil hole! Lewis!" she cried. "Do something with that boy!"

Lewis chuckled and sauntered off with Tom to meet the crying, smelly boy, all slimy with the rotting oil. "My, my," said Tom, holding a hanky over his nose. "So you've gotten into my fish pit, have you? Did you leave me anything?"

It was too funny, Louisa thought, laughing along with everyone else. They all had fish pits in the summer: it was the only way they were able to light the lamps during the winter. By digging a hole in the ground and putting a big bucket inside, they could lay a net over the top and set a dogfish over the hole. Then, as the sun rotted the fish, the precious oil would drip into the bucket.

"What are we going to do with him?" Lewis asked Tom, nose plugged.

"I'd say the best thing would be to get these britches right off and get them buried!"

"But Lewis!" cried George. "I'll be all bare!"

Beside Louisa, Katy giggled.

"Well, first thing to be done, son," said Lewis, prodding George Jr. in the back with the tip of his finger, "is to get you down to the lake and washed off. Then we'll see about what you're going to wear. Go on, git—before the rest of us keel over."

"*Georgie Peorgie, pudding and pie,*" taunted Katy, plugging her nose as he passed, head down and sniveling, "*fell in the oil and now he cries!*"

"Katy!" snapped Louisa, shocked at the child's impudence.

"I don't care, Auntie! He's such a smart aleck! *Georgie, Peorgie, pudding and pie!*" she hollered, and Louisa reached around and put her hand over the girl's mouth. Goodness—this would be Emily in nine years!

Lewis pulled off his shirt, rolled up his pants, and waded in after George, and they all stood watching while Lewis scrubbed the boy down, scooping soap out of a tin that Tom offered.

"Head under," Lewis ordered, and when George protested, he shoved it down.

"Now tell him to wade out and take off his pants!" called Ursula. "And he can just leave them at the bottom of the lake for all I care!"

"But what's he to wear?" Lewis asked, letting George surface, spewing and spitting and blubbering.

"He can wear your shirt!"

"But it'll get wet!"

"It's so hot, it'll dry!"

She was right. By the time the watermelons were broken open, Lewis' shirt was dry and George Jr. was running around in his "dress," stoically standing up to the little girls' taunts. And then the sun began to wane, leaning over the treetops behind Tom's house. The women began to gather up the empty dishes. Tom brought out the horses and hooked them up to the wagon. Excitement hurried their movements. At sundown, in Seattle, Lewis and Ursula would be married and everyone wanted to be there—even the men. Yesler was going to blow the mill whistle and Doc Maynard was going to let the fireworks blow.

-28-

*Mrs. Ursula McConaha, the plucky, hard-working
widow of George McConaha, was married to Lewis
Wyckoff.*

—Roberta Frye Watt, Katy's daughter

Louisa kissed her sister and the children goodbye, pinching Orrie's cheek. Mary Ann laughed and reached out the back of Tom's wagon to stroke Emily's cheek. "See you tonight!" Louisa yelled, standing on tiptoe as the wagon lurched and rolled forward. "Oh, and Ursula! Don't forget to wear something borrowed and something blue—"

"—and something old and something new!" laughed the other women as the wagon bumped onto the road and disappeared.

"Ah, David," Louisa sighed, falling back into his arms. "It's been such a fun, wonderful day." Watch whined at her fingers, and she bent to give the dog a scratch behind his ears.

"It's not over yet. We better hurry if we're going to get home and cleaned up, and down to Seattle in time for the wedding. Come on, Watch," he said, and whistled.

"So where are we going?"

"I'm taking you Curley's way—a shortcut through the front of Tom's claim, and then down the beach to our place."

250

In no time at all they were standing on the Sound, the sun a blinding yellow just over the mountains. The beach was lovely tonight, Louisa thought, with its wide strip of variegated shingle and bands of brown, ribbed sand. Holding hands, they took turns walking the logs, laughing when one or the other slid off, David carefully carrying Emily, the dog sniffing and searching and galloping down the sand.

"Careful!" he shouted, sliding once too many and having to let go of her hand to hold fast to Emily.

"Maybe we better walk along the edge," Louisa suggested, moving against him so that he was forced to walk closer and closer to the shallow water with each step.

"If you don't stop I'm going to get my feet wet, Liza. Hey!" he yelped, dancing out of the tiny waves.

"For shame—now look what you've done. You've gone and gotten your boots all wet," she teased, laughing. "Nincompoop!"

"Nincompoop!" he roared, then grinning, he shrugged quickly out of his shirt and spread it over the pebbles. He set Emily down, sitting her up, and before Louisa could catch her breath, he'd taken her bag and tossed it aside and scooped her up in his arms and was racing down the wave-washed beach. She tucked in her head and hung on tight, shrieking and kicking, her bonnet flapping in her face until she was dizzy. And then winded, he pulled to a stop and collapsed against the branch of a madrona tree poking out from the bank. He set her to her feet and pulled her up to his chest, arms wrapped tightly around so she couldn't escape. "Ah—" he said, his breath touching her face in the warmth of early evening, eyes laughing. "Nincompoop? You've never called me nincompoop before!"

"Emily!" she protested, kissing his bare chest, bumping her hat into him. "We can't leave Emily way back there!"

"Chin up."

"Why?"

"I want this bonnet off so I can kiss you properly, as befitting the very first bride in Seattle. Or have you forgotten that you were the first woman in these parts to be married?" he asked, tugging on her bonnet bows. "Liza. Chin up."

"I like keeping my chin down like this," she told him, refusing to comply. "I like the way your fingers feel on my throat."

"Why, you naughty woman!" he said so fiercely that it made her blood run swift, her cheeks burn hot. He chucked her chin and she gave in, helpless to resist, staring into his soft brown eyes, seeing the smile that was always there for her. She let him slide the bonnet back, heard it fall with a soft plop to the sand. Then his lips were on hers, soft and tender and very, very warm. "I love you, Louisa Boren Denny."

"And David Denny, I love you."

Emily flapped her arms when she saw them coming, smiling and happy, but then cried when they set her on the bed inside their cabin. They had to take turns holding her while the other washed and changed. Louisa, finally clean and feeling fresh, put on her new blue calico dress, made blue specially for the wedding. David asked her to turn around so he could see how pretty it was.

"Hey, where are you going?" he asked as she slipped outside.

Her sweetbriar was in full bloom, and she stuck her nose into the centers of the open pink roses to breathe in the sweet, heady scent. "Oh, David, the sweetbriar! It's so wonderful!" She picked several branches and stood before the wall mirror.

He came to stand behind her; she saw his reflection over her shoulder, Emily in his arms. She smiled, pleased. The pink roses in her black hair were perfect. "Louisa," he said, "it's beautiful. You're beautiful." And she slid into his embrace, happy and content—the promise of sweetbriar spring fulfilled.

"Are we going to need our hats?" he asked, opening the door to look outside.

She glanced at her sunbonnet hanging on the door between her husband's cap and her baby's hood. "No," she decided, "the bonnet will only ruin the sweetbriar in my hair. Oh David! I nearly forgot!"

"Liza! The sugar barrel?"

Very carefully she tore a long, skinny strip of paper from the barrel's lining. "Just in case Ursula doesn't have something blue. There!" she said, and triumphantly held up the blue "ribbon."

"Come on, we don't want to be late."

She tucked the "ribbon" into her pocket and took his hand as he closed the door to their cabin.

"Louisa?" he asked, kicking the door to make sure it was shut. "Why did you marry me?"

"Oh-h, I don't know!" She laughed and tossed back her head, hair spilling over her shoulders. The scent of sweetbriar hung in the air. "I had to marry you! There was no one else about!"

"You did not! You married me because you were wild with happiness—like Ursula."

"Wilder!" She squeezed his hand, he squeezed back, and together they headed for the wedding, walking in the brilliant glow of the western sunset, copper light spilling everywhere over the rocky beach. Behind them trotted Watch. Further back the chickens fussed and clucked, settling under the stoop for the night. And on the back of the door, still swinging from the jolt of David's boot, hung three hats: a baby hood, a sunbonnet, and a cap.

Epilogue

In the long ago we came to these shores, finding a goodly land. We have planted, builded, cultivated, nurtured all the beginnings of civilization. We have made homes and reared our children. Soon we shall go on to find that "better country." Press on, I say, for the great majority, our friends and companions of the long ago, are waiting for us over there.

—Louisa Boren Denny

Bibliography

1. *The Bible* (King James Version).
2. *Blazing the Way.* Seattle: Rainier Printing Company. © 1909. By Emily Inez Denny.
3. *The Curve of Time.* Sidney, B.C., Canada: Gray's Publishing Ltd. © 1968. By M. Wylie Blanchet.
4. *David's Diaries.* Seattle: Museum of History and Industry.
5. *Denny Family Pamphlet File.* University of Washington, Northwest Collection Room.
6. *Dubuar Scrapbook*, Vols. 77, 82, 86. University of Washington, Northwest Collection Room.
7. Fonda, W.C., *Scrapbook*, Vols. 5, 6. University of Washington, Northwest Collection Room.
8. *Four Wagons West.* Portland, Oregon: Binford & Mort, Publishers. © 1931. By Roberta Frye Watt. (Used by permission.)
9. *Frisbie Scrapbook*, Vol. 1. University of Washington, Northwest Collection Room.
10. *The Glorious Three.* New York: E.P. Dutton & Co., Inc. © 1951. By June Wetherell.
11. *Mighty Mountain.* Portland: Binford & Mort. © 1940. By Archie Binns.
12. *Nothing in Life Is Free.* Minneapolis: The Northwestern Press. © 1953. By Della Gould Emmons.
13. *Pioneer & Democrat.* Olympia, WA. Weekly newspaper from January 1854–July 1854.
14. Private manuscripts: Henry Smith, Henry Yesler, John Denny, Mrs. Carkeek, Sarah Latimer Denny, Louisa Denny, Emily Inez Denny.
15. *A Small World of Our Own.* Walla Walla, WA: Pioneer Press Books. © 1985. By Robert A. Bennett.

For Further Bibliography See *Sweetbriar Bride*.

A NOTE TO THE READER

This book was selected by the same editors who prepare *Guideposts*, a monthly magazine filled with true stories of people's adventures in faith.

If you have found inspiration in this book, we think you'll find monthly help and inspiration in the exciting stories that appear in our magazine.

Guideposts is not sold on the newsstand. It's available by subscription only. And subscribing is easy. All you have to do is write Guideposts Associates, Inc., 39 Seminary Hill Road, Carmel, New York 10512. For those with special reading needs, *Guideposts* is published in Big Print, Braille, and Talking Magazine.

When you subscribe, each month you can count on receiving exciting new evidence of God's presence and His abiding love for His people.